I0649757

The Zarnian Vodka Paradox

by

Robert A. Albert

Copyright © 2017 Robert Arthur Albert

All rights reserved, including the right of reproduction
In whole or in part in any form

Manufactured in the United States of America

ISBN-13:
978-0692855201 (RAAlbertArts)

ISBN-10:
0692855203

Decisions

I think back on the decisions of my life.
Some made quickly,
based on responsibilities perceived.
Where would I be,
if I thought through more carefully,
deciding differently?
Where would the others in my life be,
if I decided differently?
Where would the others in my life be,
if they decided differently?
Of course, I'll never know!
They'll never know!
And, what does it matter?
Perhaps my "heart" decided for me.
Perhaps their "hearts" decided for them.
Perhaps the currents of life gave no choice.
My decisions put me where I am.
And from here, I cannot say,
if this is the best place for me.
Certainly, free will has led me here.
Certainly, this is uniquely my place.

Robert A Albert

Contents

Foreword

I have placed some interesting information in the appendices. If you are technical, please read the appendices for details.

I have taken vast liberties with language and use English throughout this manuscript because it is hard enough to write a story in English. Trying to use various other languages would put my sanity in jeopardy! However, I have started learning the Zarnian language, and possibly my next book will be written in Zarnian instead of English.

All character names are fictional to protect the guilty. In most cases, names have been kept consistent when in real life they would have to be changed to keep the origin of a character hidden. There is at least one character with two names, and that is unavoidable.

Dedication

Dedicated to My Wife of Fifty-One Years
Elaine,
patiently waiting alone,
while I create the world with words.
Crafted from my imagination,
my dreams,
and my life's experiences,
as I dance upon this Earth,
together with all of you!

Chapter 1 – Traveling

Ray Berger awoke at 5:00 AM on 9/17/2016 Saturday morning to a cell phone alarm playing, "Crown on the Ground," by the Sleigh Bells. Disappointed, he realized his significant other, Lucy Lenora, had never made it to their shared bed last night, for the third night in a row. He would miss making love to her again this morning. As in the previous three nights, between naps, she continued to scan the heavens with her new telescope. Ray found Lucy asleep in her telescope chair and nudged her gently. Lucy woke quickly, sat up straight, and opened her eyes wide. She said, "There's something out there! I can see it, and it is headed this way! It keeps getting closer!"

Ray said, "What do you mean, something?"

She replied, "When I tried to find Mars two days ago, I didn't see any satellites except the moon. I've been scanning the sky for three days looking for anything of interest and testing this telescope. Four hours ago, I could see the details of the moon's features.

"Then at about 1:00 am this morning I saw it. It looks like a flying saucer! I followed it for an hour and then fell asleep. Am I turning into a UFO believer?"

Ray said, "Well, if you saw it, then all of the folks with bigger telescopes saw it. Have you checked the news?"

Lucy said, "There is nothing on the news. It might be too new, or someone is quiet to prevent a panic."

Ray said, "How will you track your saucer in Key West?"

Lucy said, "I don't know unless we have enough room to take the telescope with us. The curious thing is that I looked a couple of hours ago, and I can't find it. Damn! It's a good thing I took a picture of it. It was visible from 1:00 am to 2:00 am, and now it is nowhere. Well, I'm out of time. I want to get to Mona and Derick's place on time."

Ray said, "You took a picture?"

Lucy said, "Yes, this new telescope has an on-board camera." She showed the image, now on her cell phone, to Ray.

Ray said, "OK, we are taking the telescope with us! Lucy, on another subject, I miss our lovemaking, especially in the morning when we wake up. Is there something wrong? You don't come to bed and spend every hour you can on your telescope."

Lucy replied, "Nonsense. You are too sensitive! I promise to fix you up in Key West to the point of exhaustion. I've just gotten carried away using my new telescope! Remember how much time I spent on you when we first met?"

Ray said, "Yes, I do. That's what I miss!"

They showered and had a quick raisin bran breakfast.

Lucy put on jeans, sneakers, a tee shirt, and a baseball cap. Always, on her left hand, regardless of where she was going or what she might be doing, Lucy wore a prized possession, her Great Grandmother's engagement ring with the large blue diamond set with pink and white diamonds all around the platinum silver setting. On her left hand, Lucy wore a wedding ring even though she and Ray had not been married. Finally, she hung a gold crucifixion cross on a gold chain around her neck.

Ray wore shorts, a baggy shirt, no jewelry, sandals, a NY Mets baseball hat, and a concealed Smith and Wesson, M&P, .40 caliber pistol.

They loaded their bags into Ray's 2010 Ford Mini Van and put the telescope in its watertight container on the top of their car. Ray packed several liters of vodka. He fondly preached to everyone, "Before vodka became known simply as an alcoholic beverage, it was known as a healing tonic. People considered it a "holy drink" that could make you stronger and prepare you to fight. It could make you feel better, take the boring out of boring parties, heal wounds, reduce stress, reduce toothache pain, and countless other benefits."

Lucy and Ray did not have a very long history together. They met at a Sleigh Bells' Concert May 2nd, 2014, at the Big Guava Festival in Tampa, Florida. The Sleigh Bell's described as a "Noise Band" originated in Brooklyn, NY. Ray drove himself from Stuart, Florida to the concert. Lucy rode with friends. When they met, waiting in line at the concession stand for a beer, they both suffered from love at first sight. Lucy rode home in Ray's car, and they started living together in 2014, just months after they met.

Ray Berger, a six-foot tall,180-pound, muscled athlete caught Lucy's interest at once. He had thick blond wavy hair trimmed neatly around his ears, blue eyes, heavy eyebrows, a substantial nose, smiling lips, and tan colored skin. When Ray talked to you, he focused on your eyes as if he could read your brain activity. He dressed like a PGA golf pro.

Lucy, a five-feet-eight-inch tall, 130-pound, trim model caught Ray's interest at once. For the concert, she wore her long brown hair down to the middle of her back cascading over her shoulders. Her pale complexion seemed void of sun exposure. She trimmed her eyebrows and wore light pink lipstick on her thin lips under a tiny nose. When she talked to you, she looked to your left or right and not directly at your eyes giving the impression that she didn't want you to know the contents of her conscious mind.

Ray, 25 years old, had attended FSU for three years on a baseball scholarship majoring in computer science before the Mets drafted him. He had played a year with the St. Lucie Mets before going pro with the Mets in NYC. His record had been good until 2015 when an injury cooled his performance, and he began playing again for the St. Lucie Mets where his recovery to good form and performance had been proceeding well.

Lucy, also 25 years old, began a successful modeling career a year ago and now models all over the world. In the very competitive modeling industry, she has been quite successful at times. However, she now has long periods of inactivity.

They picked up Derick, and Mona Clark in Hobe Sound and the four of them looked forward to the five-hour ride seeing the Florida Keys up close on the way. They headed south to Fort Lauderdale, then south to Miami, and finally U.S. Route 1 to Key West.

Mona and Derick married on July 14th, 2014, claiming to be celebrating French Bastille Day. Both, sets of their parents came from France.

Mona, 27, taught history at the Stuart high school and Derick, 29, developed software for a local IT company called, "Programming Sciences

Corporation." The company slogan, "Reliable Software is Free," puts forth the idea that good software justifies itself by never breaking and saving you its cost in extra profits and savings.

Derick was very thin in a six-foot-three body weighing about 150 lbs. With his thin beard and homely looks, he could double for Abraham Lincoln. When you talk to Derick, he reads your face like a book with his eyes moving back and forth.

In contrast to Derick, Mona's body struck a rotund five foot three inches. Her bleach blond hair and pale white freckled face could be childlike. Mona's radiant smile and kind brown eyes, instantly, made you feel like an old friend.

Chapter 2 – Zarnia's Sun Chaser

From deep space, one light year away, at speeds up to that of light came an intergalactic starship. The ship carried hundreds of space travelers for over an Earth year to get to this point in the universe. Some of these passengers didn't know it yet, but they were about to change the lives of people on Earth especially four friends heading for a vacation in Key West, Florida, USA, Earth.

At 2:00 a.m. on 9/17/2016 Earth time, Saturday morning, Captain Damara announced to the crew and passengers of Zarnia's Intergalactic Star Ship, Sun Chaser, "I am addressing you in English, one of the languages you have all learned and must use while you are in the United States. We are about to enter Starlight's atmosphere bringing us close to the end of our one-earth-year journey. We'll dock the ship under water near a Florida island called Key West, one of the hottest vacation destinations for the people of Starlight. The inhabitants call Starlight, Earth. That is what we should call it from now on.

"Our ship, the Sun Chaser, and our excellent crew have made this a successful journey. Your skill and dedication in the use of the advanced technology on this ship, have made the trip as safe and as quick as possible.

"We will enter Key West as American tourists. Remember this always. All of you speak English and other Earth languages fluently without accents. Never use our Zarnian language. That way you will not slip while talking to each other, giving away your extraterrestrial origin. Make sure that you do not let anyone know you are from another planet. It is crucial for us to maintain ourselves as residents of Earth. That means that sometimes you must blend in by having some good old fun with the people of Earth. You have heard this before and will hear more in the future."

The crew and passengers had a good laugh about the good old fun. Gelzek, smiling at Zara said, "I'll bet the captain will have more fun than the rest of us put together."

Zara replied, "He is a party animal, isn't he? I think I'll do my share as well. The one-year trip to get here has me tight, restless, and ready to go wild!

"You should know that when the I refer to a, "one-year trip", I mean one of our light years, or the distance traveled by light during a Zarnian year. That is the amount of time it takes Zarnia to revolve around our sun, which is 730 days, or twice the amount of earth days. However, also realize, that the Zarnian day is12 earth hours. The planet rotates twice per earth day. So, since 730 times 12 earth hours is equal to 365 times 24 earth hours our Zarnian light year conveniently turns out to be equal to their earth light year! There is such symmetry in the universe!"

The auditorium erupts into laughter.

Then the captain, short and stout, with rosy cheeks, dark black hair and beard, and searching green eyes continued, "Thanks, Zara! This brings up another very serious matter. We are very similar biologically to the human beings on Earth. No one can reliably tell from outer appearances an Earthling from a Zarnian. Evolution on vastly different planets would not have made that possible if it did not have a great deal of help! We from Zarnia, know of our similarities to Earthlings because we have visited Earth many times over many centuries and documented our findings. So, we have investigated historical records to find answers.

"The people on Earth would not have even thought about this puzzle because they still think they are the only living beings in the universe.

"There is a famous theory stating that some third planet of enormous technological capabilities visited Earth and Zarnia in the past leaving their own people on both planets. It may have been an experiment, or this third planet may have been destroyed leaving their people stranded on Earth and Zarnia. Heck, since our planet may destruct, we are contemplating leaving Zarnians on distant planets all over the universe. So, someday, someone will realize that in spite of evolution there are many similarities among living things that exist on distant planets.

"I tell you this because we are similar but not identical. Your anatomy is different in many areas. For example, your knees are much stronger and resilient. An x-ray of your knee would cause a great deal of attention and questions about your origins. Do not submit to any medical treatment. Contact the ship for instructions if you need medical attention.

"Soren, as we discussed yesterday, we will put the ship down at Earth's GPS location, 24°36'26.33"N and 81°51'42.33"W. This puts us less than five miles from Key West. Please take over the piloting of the ship and make it happen.

"Zavier, turn on all of our cloaking systems. We are going in using radar countermeasures, and we will not be visible due to our cloaking and the darkness at 3:00 a.m. All our lights will be off or covered. Once we land and dive under water, we can resume normal lighting. Our cloaking will display dark sky and stars under the ship making it even harder to be seen.

"Londrina, set us up for a water-tight docking in the shallow trench at the GPS coordinates specified earlier.

"Zara, I need a meeting with your political committee in the auditorium fifteen minutes after we secure our position at the designated GPS coordinates."

The Sun Chaser approached from the northwest and waited until passing over the seaplane bases southeast of New Orleans before abruptly dropping straight down to an altitude of 1000 feet for the remaining distance to the GPS location outside of Key West.

A sailboat passenger near the underwater feature Lloyd Ridge[1] looked up just in time to see the Sun Chaser glide over them. "Hey Drake," she said, "Something weird is moving across the sky causing an area of distortion the size of several football fields. Or, maybe I've just had too many margaritas. No, it's there. See the strange distortion in the stars. The stars in the sky ripple like those on an American flag in the wind. What the heck can that be?"

Drake replied, "Rebecca, I don't see anything except stars. It must be the margaritas. I can't wait to get to Key West so I can drink Margaritas and join you in your alcohol-induced hallucinations!"

Sun Chaser reached the GPS coordinates designated by the captain and hovered just over

---

[1] Underwater ridge west of the Florida peninsula

the water in complete darkness. Very slowly, Soren guided the ship to approach the three-foot waves until they began slapping the ship's hull. Eventually, the sea water reached the window which completely circled the oval-shaped ship.

When the water passed over the top of the ship, Soren turned on the lights, and everyone on the bridge could see fish and other sea life swimming by as the crew of Sun Chaser invaded the realm of deep sea creatures.

More slowly the ship settled to the bottom and came to rest on the ocean floor. Sun Chaser had landed without incident in the water just northwest of Key West. The facility engineers adjusted the ships three legs onto the ocean floor, making the vessel level. During that process, they cloaked to match the ocean floor. Now, from above, they were not visually detectable.

At exactly fifteen minutes after the captain declared the ship docked, the political committee gathered in conference room A1. The captain and Zara sat on the auditorium stage as 200 members of Zara's political committee filled auditorium seats in front of the stage. Excited discussions, on the way in, raised the noise level in the small auditorium just short of deafening.

Once the seating was completed, Zara, about 5'8" tall, with the figure of a long-distance runner, striking red hair trimmed short over her ears, stood on stage to chair the meeting. She smiled at the audience with intense blue eyes, a petite nose, and a childlike face with no makeup. Zara wore light-blue jeans, a black and white checkered shirt untucked and loosely opened revealing only a nicely-filled T-shirt underneath. Sneakers and black and white socks completed her current wardrobe which she had obtained from the Starlight Clothing Closet on the ship.

When Zara talked to you one on one, she seemed to telepathically draw information from you.

"OK, quiet now," she said, "you all know why we are here, but I will tell you again."

Zara said, "We are here to determine the feasibility of merging some of our civilization and Earth's civilization. The determination will take place in six Earth months. You all have had training in multiple Earth languages, as well as all the political systems governing the 195 self-ruling countries on Earth. Each of you has a specific contact in one of those countries to meet and get close to. You're to discuss all the points on the list that I passed out on the way here. You must cover all points, if possible. In general, we need to determine if the people on Earth will cooperate with us while we move some of our population to Earth and possibly the moon or other planets in Earth's solar system. We bring incredible technology, and they bring a planet. Our planet will break apart around ten Earth years from now, due to the wobble problem which began shortly before we left. Cooperation between us is the only way our relocation can work, and the Zarnian civilization can continue.

"We have three other ships investigating three other planets in other solar systems on which to move our people. Certainly, we can't try to move everyone to the same planet. That would cause instant overpopulation, even using our advanced techniques for getting more people in the same space. When all our ships return to Zarnia in a year and a half earth time and compare combined experiences and knowledge, we will make final decisions and plans.

"You will all use public transportation to reach your assigned country. This way you can experience many people and cultures along the way. You are posing as American citizens considering moving to your target country. Use that country's language as it will indicate to everyone you meet how serious you are about joining their community.

"Once you get to know people, start talking about overpopulation that may occur in the future or is occurring now. Work on solutions. Find out how everyone feels about overpopulation. Ask about populating other planets. You've got the list of ideas and questions to work on. Use it. Learn the culture of the country you are visiting and find out what impediments might exist, like religious differences.

"Each of you has been issued a solar impulse phone. You can communicate with me or each other using these devices as standard Earth smartphones, or on impulse phones. On impulse, your conversations cannot be detected. When using these phones or any others, do not use the Zarnian language. Use English or your country's language. If you are overheard using the Zarnian language, who knows what conclusions will be reached by someone who overhears you? Even better, find a place to call for both parties where neither can be overheard.

"In six months, we will gather at this spot to travel back to Zarnia. On the way, we will document our recommendations.

Jack asked, "What if I determine my recommendations in less time? Should I return early and voice my decision?"

Zara replied, "No, make sure you use your laptop to document everything in a very detailed journal. All data on the laptops will be encrypted automatically. At all cost, you must keep an open mind until the half-year is over. Only then do you get to return to the ship and discuss your findings.

Coming back early is inexcusable and will be punished. There are no exceptions."

Sonora raised her hand, and Zara recognized her, "What if my assigned person is dead?"

Zara replied, "Again, there is no excuse to return early. Find someone else in the same family or as close as possible. That part is up to you. Return, only after a half-year with your decision, based on your original person or a suitable replacement, in case your original target is no longer accessible."

Zena asked, "What should we do if we become romantically involved with our assigned subject?"

Zara replied, "That is a good question. You must attempt to avoid that situation because it can cloud your judgment. However, we recognize that romantic involvement is possible since we are directing you to become as close as possible to your assigned person. If this happens, you must, after the half-year return to the ship to report your experiences and information. Then, if you want to return to your new loved one, you may. The ship will leave without you, and more than likely you will be called on in the future to help us out. If that is the case, you must cooperate or suffer consequences, which may be severe."

Tatham asked, "Why are we doing this? What is the motivation to merge with these backward people? Why don't we simply take over and make them slaves?"

Zara replied, "Okay, granted, if we want to take over today we can. We have the upper hand in technology. However, on the other hand, these people have covered ground that we may not have. They can contribute to our well-being. I cannot explain or know what their contribution can be. Until we investigate thoroughly, we will not know. Most people I talk with in our society have struggled with this question. The current plan is what was decided as the best possible strategy. Remember, our planet is due to destruct in ten years. We need help from people of other planets so we can find a place to live when our own planet destroys itself. Earth is one of those possibilities.

Lambert yelled, "Look, I don't care a bit about these people. We can take over right now and keep the survivors as slaves. Why should we care what happens to them? I know right now that we are superior and can just take over. In fact, I am upset that we have come here with no personal weapons. What idiot decided this strategy?"

Zara screamed back, "Me, that's who, I'm the idiot! This strategy will make sure that war does not start before we can complete our mission. We had to ensure that you could not, in a fit of anger, make war on these very intelligent and compassionate people on Earth. I will be watching you closely. If you step out of line, your life ends here, without any consideration beyond painless death! So, watch out. Do you understand?"

Lambert replied, "Yes, and I apologize. I get it."

The questions and answers went on and on. Eventually, the meeting ended. Zara established herself as the leader of the political committee and clearly asserted that her ideas and plan must be followed. Everyone left except the captain and Zara.

Zara said, "The meeting has been completed. Do you have anything else for me?"

The captain said, "As a matter of fact, I do. You recall that since you bear the key responsibility of the whole political committee and their findings, we did not assign you to a person on Earth to examine and help you decide whether or not settling here will be a good idea."

Zara said, "Yes, I do."

The captain said, "Well, we have changed our minds. Our reconnaissance has turned up a unique situation. We have found out that a man from Zarnia, whom we thought to be dead, in fact, has survived and is living on Earth with a woman whom he has taken for a wife, also from Zarnia.

They have a son named Ray. This man and his wife, in fact, have stayed on Earth from separate and previous missions made to Earth. Now, I know their son, Ray, has our genetics. I know he has special talents. So, you will get to know Ray Berger, now in his twenties. You will meet him in Key West the day after tomorrow. Do you understand?"

Zara replied, "Yes, I do. Please explain how I should meet him and what his great significance is."

The captain explained, "As I said, his name is Ray. You will meet him in Key West. His significant special talents put him at the top of our list of people on Earth to know and understand. We do not want you to know ahead of time what his talents are, as it may affect the outcome and/or your future relationship. For example, you may not think he has special talents. We could be wrong. You must meet him as planned and try to understand him. We have an idea that this one man may be significant in the Zarnian future. It is for you to understand and figure him out. So, meet him, know him, and after a half year, report to us like everyone else."

Zara pleaded, "What are you saying? What are you asking? Why are you picking me?"

The captain replied, "Just go to him and figure out what it is without me to cloud your judgment. Go now. Be wary because danger abounds in Malory Square tomorrow. Go. Just go, and let your instincts lead you to the truth of his significance. Once you learn it, help him."

Zara said, "I'd like easy access to the ship if possible. I don't think I should live in Key West, and I probably will need access to some of the ship's facilities. How should I do that?"

The captain replied, "Your Personal Amphibious Street Submarine Airplane awaits you. We have an acronym for it, PASSA. It has a gravity-focusing engine with an atomic core and battery that will last forever. This vehicle looks and feels like a standard jet ski when in amphibious mode. Everybody has jet skis here. Your PASSA will get you back and forth when you need to. Please, only use the submarine or airplane capability if you have an emergency. We don't want anyone investigating its technology and discovering you are from another planet with advanced technological capabilities. As you told everyone else, we must all keep a low profile."

Zara said, "But, won't it look different enough to attract attention?"

The captain replied, "No, it will either look like a jet ski, a motorcycle, a submarine, or an ultra-light plane. The transition from one to the other is automatic and quick. Why don't you take it out for a try?"

Zara replied, "That's a great idea, captain. I'm going to do just that, so I can more knowledgeably address everyone tomorrow about Key West attractions. See you later."

Zara walked to her private room, a benefit she had earned from her work organizing a big part of this mission. At 27, she had accomplished a great deal and had a very promising career. She grabbed the door knob of her room's unlocked door and walked in.

The Zarnian version of pizza from a couple of nights ago littered the coffee table. Her desk supported a computer and piles of books all stuffed with bookmarks. The bed with sheets and blanket in complete disarray held piles of wrinkled clothing. She saw none of this as she made her way hastily to the closet. She grabbed shorts and a T-Shirt, stripped off her clothing starting a new pile on her bed and floor. Now, naked, she put on just three items of clothing, a tee shirt, a pair of very short shorts, and a pair of deck shoes.

Amidst a great deal of male and some female observation, Zara made her way to the ship's garage deck. She found her new PASSA, mounted it, and started the nuclear-powered gravity-focusing engine. The PASSA, currently configured as a motorcycle, made very little sound compared to the Harley-Davidson motorcycles now on the streets of Key West. Zara simultaneously punched the ship's transition door opener, and the PASSA's accelerator as she raced toward a solid white wall in the ship. The transition room door opened, Zara flashed in, slammed on the brakes, and came to a rubber-burning halt. She pushed the green knob shutting the door she had just come through. Sea water flooded into the room, from a port on the bottom of the room, submerging the PASSA which automatically configured into submarine mode as a water-tight globe equipped with an oxygen supply deployed over her head. When the room completely filled with water, the outer door opened.

Down Zara went to the ocean floor breathing the pressure-controlled supply of oxygen provided by the crystal globe helmet. In the clear water, she rejoiced at the view as she passed sharks, dolphins, mahi-mahi, to name just a few.

Zara pulled back on the handlebars heading for the surface at high speed with the engine seamlessly changing gravity targets to go in the direction that she wanted to go while keeping Earth's gravity as a major influence. Thus, the PASSA seemed to perform like a standard Earth vehicle. Zara leaped from the water to about fifteen feet above the ocean. The PASSA came down hard with Zara's now wet T-Shirt revealing the beautiful and firm upper body of a young woman in prime physical condition. During one of the dives under water, her shirt almost lifted off over her head as the motion-produced water pressure pushed up on it.

She stayed on the surface allowing the crystal globe to retract and began riding three-foot waves like jumping ramps sending her into the air and then back down. She began to get the hang of jumping from one wave's incline to land on another's decline and surfing a bit before the next takeoff.

Zara, disappointed that she couldn't try the airplane function when she ran out of time, aimed for a boat ramp near Malory Square. The PASSA anticipated the dry landing and became a motorcycle. Zara rode all around town, visiting the Key West attractions that she would present to the others tomorrow.

She, an attraction herself, rode around the streets of Key West, stopping for a drink and food whenever she felt like it. Some of her attention from onlookers came from the fact that a woman in good shape driving a motorcycle and alone seemed to be a rare sight. She paid for everything with a credit card that the financial people had worked out on the ship. All funds came out of a bank account on Earth in New York City. This completed her objective of testing the Zarnian-issued credit cards that everyone would be using. She had no problems with them and assumed that no one else would either.

When she stopped, she flirted a bit, and realized she could have started a short-term relationship if she desired. Zara, however, drew the line on her escapade there. She would have to wait on that. She said to herself, "Stay out of trouble like you've told everyone else on board the ship." Besides, she had Ray Berger to think about and concentrate on.

Instead, Zara hunted the T-Shirt vendors near Malory Square for a new wardrobe of sorts. To Zara, good T-Shirts became half of her expanding wardrobe. She found shirts that said, "I'm from a different planet. What's your excuse?" "Follow me close enough, and we'll morph a bit." "Girl on a bike, both with warm engines."

While shopping from store to store, she found a bathing suit she couldn't pass up. She bought the pink-and-black-striped bikini and stuffed it into the bag full of T-Shirts.

The sun, close to setting, presented a beautiful view as Zara, with her shopping packed safely in the seat compartment, soared her PASSA in motorcycle mode down the boat ramp near Malory Square. She stopped, briefly, as she observed two men carefully watching her. Then she plunged directly down the ramp as the PASSA converted into jet ski mode. After a quarter of a mile, she put the PASSA into submarine mode disappearing under water. She headed back toward the Sun Chaser.

Two friends, who evidently had spent a good deal of time at "Two Friends Bar" witnessed Zara's plunge into the water and noticed that she did not come back up. They started screaming, "Hep, Hep; she's drawning. She's boot'tiful, but shez drawning. Call 911."

They both bravely jumped in swimming in staggering circles looking for her, while they choked and gasped for air. People gathered on the edge of the water watching with intent amusement as these two well-meaning gentlemen searched for Zara. Eventually, they gave up and talked to a reporter about what they had seen. The reporter, realizing how impaired they had become, put the following article in the "Keysnews.com."

> *Yesterday at sunset two patrons of a local bar witnessed a mermaid ride a motorcycle down the Simonton Street boat ramp and plunge into the salty water. The two friends searched exhaustively for the*

mermaid or her motorcycle. They found neither.

"Shesh bootiful! I doughnut timk a merymaid cooed ride a muttercycle," they said.

It is this reporter's opinion that the mermaid in question had highly technical skills. When on dry land, she had legs and, in fact, could ride a motorcycle. When she hit the water, her motorcycle became her tail making her much more of a classic mermaid.

The two gentlemen at the scene that tried so hard went back to the bar to spread their version of the story and begin preparing for their next diversion from reality!

When Zara returned to the ship and walked down the hall toward her room, she wore one of her new T-shirts.

Thankfully, no one on the ship that saw the article tied it back to Zara. Even if they did think about that possibility, Zara could explain the incident as two good friends who really had many great times together, but couldn't be relied upon as witnesses of anything.

The very next morning a young boy swimming from the beach near the Simonton Street boat ramp found a T-Shirt with the inscription, "Take me to your leader." He gave it to his Mom who wears it at the beach every time she takes her son.

Zara videoed the whole Sun Chaser arrival for future use. In fact, Zara videoed everything she could to file into the permanent records of, "Zarnia's Project Starlight."

Chapter 3 - Hog Heaven

Ray, Lucy, Derick, and Mona passed through Key Largo, Plantation Key, Wilson Key, and stopped for lunch at Hog Heaven Sports Bar and Grill in Islamorada, FL. Hog Heaven, situated on a beach overlooking the ocean, had excellent food for the price. A giant swordfish, a big knotted rope, and other ocean-oriented items marked the front of Hog Heaven. The tail of a small airplane that supposedly crashed nose first rose at a forty-five-degree angle behind the building

This stop, a Mona and Derick suggestion, had a parking lot half-full of motorcycles, mostly Harley-Davidsons.

Derick said, "Hey, Ray, do you still have your Harley?"

Ray replied, "No, it only took one narrow escape to encourage me to sell it and use the money as a down payment on this new-to-me minivan. I don't have a death wish like you or Mona."

Derick said with a grin, "Do you know that our first week in Key West, we'll be sharing the island with thousands of bikers from all over the country? Next time, we should take Mona and my cycles and ride double to Key West."

Lucy chimed in, "I'm not sitting on one of those death rockets with either one of you, especially since I'm sure some drinking will be going on."

Derick said, "That's what I figured. You have no spirit of adventure!"

Lucy said, "To be more accurate, I have no death wish!"

Mona added, "The bikes are as safe as cars."

Lucy said, "Changing the subject, did you see anything about a UFO near Earth? Look, this is a picture of it." Lucy showed Mona and Derick the image on her phone.

Mona replied, "I saw some references on Facebook this morning, but nothing on network news."

Ray and Lucy walked first toward the restaurant, and Derick and Mona followed behind out of hearing range.

Mona turned toward Derick and said, "Take a look at Ray's walking stride. I can't explain it, but it looks a bit mechanical and not smooth. There is just something different about his motion. Can you see what I'm describing?"

Derick replied, "Yes, I can see it, but everyone looks a bit different in the way they move and walk. I do know that in his baseball career he has slid into bases and twisted his knee into horrible positions. Never has he suffered permanent damage. Sports writers have commented on that fact many times."

Once inside they could see that most of the bikers looked to be fifty-years-old, if not older. The four newcomers took a table near a window overlooking the ocean, a dock loaded with boats, and a beach.

Inside, patrons played pool on four pool tables. A long green railing with tables for four lined up alongside. Lots of green neon adorned the ceiling. In the center of the establishment, sat a blue-topped bar circled by wooden bar stools of various colors and sizes. On the periphery sat a 1950s Cadillac.

Before looking at the menu, Ray said, "The road makes tourism possible so that more people can enjoy the wonder of the keys. Just look out the window! Unfortunately, the beauty suffers from traffic and overuse. It's as if the thing of beauty ensures its own demise!"

Derick said, "Lighten up, Ray. You are much too serious!"

They ordered seafood and drinks. Ray and Derick both drank two vodkas with lunch. Ray felt great. The vodka made him feel strong and adventurous, and they all knew that it would not affect his driving if he stayed under three or four shots. Curiously, Ray's reflexes became quicker when he drank vodka straight or on the rocks. He didn't know why other alcoholic beverages could have the opposite effect. Derick, on the other hand, slurred his words by the time he finished his second vodka.

They exited the building's rear entrance where Ray said, "First, let's stroll out to the dock and then to the man-made beach out there close to the ocean. I want to get a good view and smell the ocean."

The four of them walked to the beach area which had a table with a thatched roof over it and seating for six to ten people. Ray and Derick stopped to look at a small statue of dolphins, while Mona and Lucy continued a bit separating them about twenty yards from the men.

Derick asked Ray, "Didsh ou bring da ring? Rff ou go'n ta ask hrrr ta morry ya?"

Ray replied, "Yes, I have it, and will ask her to marry me sometime within the next week. The less you talk, the better! And no more beverages for you!"

Not far from the ladies, a group of young men with long braided hair wearing dew rags, strings of beads, and vests, congregated around the table. A couple of them with tattoos of the pirate skull and crossbones turned to look at Lucy and Mona. One of the young men yelled out and moved in their direction, "Hey, ya wanna ride with a real man, honey? I've got one hot engine on my bike, especially when I'm sitting on it!"

Mona asked Lucy, "Are they talking to us? How do you attract these nut cases? Our jeans and shirts reveal nothing. These guys must be hard up!"

Lucy, replied, "I thought he meant you! Maybe he meant Derick or Ray!"

By then the two tough guys had gotten close enough to hear that last comment and were not happy. The second guy pointing to Ray and Derick said, "Look, honey, please don't hurt my feelings. I meant both of you beautiful and sexy little ladies. If you want a real ride, ditch these losers and come with us!"

Lucy said, "Ah, does this approach ever work for you?"

The first guy replied, "Well, sometimes it does. Sometimes, it turns out that the ladies are not with anyone and they tell us they would love to try out our hot engine and go for a real hard ride. So, if we don't ask, how are we going to know. Right?"

Mona said, "I understand. Well, you lucked out this time. I'm married to the man with the neatly-trimmed beard back there, and Lucy here is living with the other. We are very much together with those two."

Waves of sea water crashed violently against the rock retaining wall sending sprays of water into the air with a great deal of crashing and splashing sounds. The four redirected their attention briefly to look at the spectacle on the rocks. When they focused back to each other Derick and Ray had joined them.

Derick said to the bikers, "Lawk. Baak off. We dunt want an'trable! Dere's a boonch d'action gong inside. Try yer line in dere! I tink u'll find mare than u can hendle."

Testosterone drifted in the air like clouds of a lightning storm. The first guy said, "Look, don't be so rude. How would you know how much action we can take, old man? You should drink and talk less!" While saying that, he quickly moved around the ladies and pulled a knife from a sheath attached to his belt, placing the point gently but firmly on Derick's throat. "Now, why don't you just apologize?"

Derick instantly felt like a big-mouthed idiot. In a reflexive action, Derick backed up a few feet, but the guy, with a menacing smile, followed him flawlessly with the knife on Derick's neck causing a small dimple at the knife point.

Derick pleaded and sobered up a bit, "Lawk, man, dese our women. U must know wat kind of responsibility that is. It takes time; it takes money. You guys have it made if you're single. Why change that? Trust me; you dunt want to. Neither one of these ladies wants to be with you, hot rod motor, or not."

Then Ray, who had stealthily moved to just the right location without attracting attention, held a Smith & Wesson, gun to the knife holder's temple. He said, "OK, son. You have come to a gunfight with a knife." Ray pointed up against the temple to ensure that a bullet did not hit someone else after exiting the skull. "Are you always that stupid? Back off instantly, or I will have no choice but to fire in self-defense." The guy with the knife held it in position for seconds. Ray applied more pressure to the knife-holder's temple. Finally, the knife holder slowly retracted it and backed away.

The two failing pirates instantly began apologizing, attempting to defuse the situation. "We're sorry. We were only fooling around. We meant it as a compliment. I apologize to the little ladies, but I must say, they are beautiful. We'll be over here if you change your minds."

As the bikers walked away, Ray said to Lucy and Mona with a broad smile, "It's up to you two. Make a choice! Them or US!" No one laughed at that comment.

Adrenalin pumped through Derick's body, sobering him up a bit more. He said, "That's not funny! Ray, how did you do that so fast? Does the vodka loosen you up? You told us many times that it helps you prepare for battle, but I've always assumed that meant baseball-diamond wars! And good grief, I didn't know you were carrying a concealed weapon. What the hell!"

Ray said, "We probably should get out of here before they come back with more soldiers and their complete arsenal."

Derick dropped the subject as Ray drove the rest of the way to Key West and their destination for the day, the "La Te Da." hotel.

The rest of the way, Lucy could not put down her cell phone as she searched for news about the UFO she thought she had spotted. NASA finally admitted that they were tracking something small headed toward Earth at incredible speeds.

Chapter 4 –Escape

Albrecht Stiefvater crouched in fear. Rubble, rubble, rubble everywhere around him. Explosions, explosions, explosions everywhere around him. What went wrong? How could this happen to the master race? He knew now how it felt when all your assumptions about life, and how you fit into that life, are suddenly proved completely wrong.

He took a deep breath filling his lungs with acrid dust and fine particles of masonry and evaporated flesh. He coughed as the irritation in his lungs reached the painful peak of possibilities. A faint whistle quickly pierced his ears becoming louder and louder. Now he could see it as it headed right at him. He hurriedly crawled into a hole in the rubble as deeply as he could, scraping his body through torn clothing. Then a sound so loud his ears went silent as rubble and dust flew high into the air all around him. He felt, more than he heard. The thumping as pieces collided and came to rest at the insistence of gravity.

The explosions stopped as bombers turned around to return to their bases in France and England. Now came the tanks from the East and the West. His imminent capture caused him to shudder. However, it beat the crushing and smashing death that men, women, and children suffered all around him.

He knew he could trade his knowledge for a new life helping the approaching conquerors develop weapons of the future. He knew a great deal about future weapons. The rocket program had caused its share of death. The nuclear program promised to provide explosive power greater than mankind could imagine. All the destruction around him, from months of bombing, could be the result of one bomb. The biological agent of grotesque death proceeded on schedule. Even now the use of Hydrogen cyanide gas helped eliminate the undesirables in his country. Yet, these techniques could all be replaced by his creative methods of destruction that only a few of his closest friends shared. He had participated, as an expert, in all of these killing techniques. His close associates respectfully called him Doctor Death.

Hunkering down, no longer ruled his actions when the bombs stopped. So, he grabbed a cigarette and climbed to the top of the rubble hill near him. Looking around him at the devastation, he lit the cigarette drawing smoke into his already painful lungs. He needed the calming drug that cigarettes provided. His torn and filthy uniform barely covered his body as he looked out to the horizon observing the destruction around him.

Interrupting the monotonous gray lumpy landscape, just ten yards away a woman, now face down and still in death, held a bundle she had tried to shield from the debris that had fallen all over them. Her tiny baby, wrapped in a torn and filthy blanket, lay still with eyes wide open and staring at the sky that had rained death down upon them.

He blew out a puff of smoke while thinking deeply. He looked at the insignias on his uniform that identified him as a high-ranking officer in that army of his destroyed nation. If they had only listened to him, none of this would have happened.

He blew smoke rings as the tanks and soldiers approached from miles away. Then he saw it. In the distance, a huge sphere broke the view of rubble. He carefully walked and climbed toward this curiosity that had survived the bombs and destruction around it. When he got close enough, he realized that this Volkswagen-sized globe showed all the countries on Earth the way it might be seen from space. The globe rested in a display stand with a drawer. Inside the drawer, he found a box labeled, "Escape Kit." Inside the escape kit, he found a harness similar to a parachute harness.

He thought about all the possibilities for his future when the invading armies reached him, and he decided to make a bold move by following the escape kit instructions. He had no idea what kind of an escape this would be. He felt, however, that he had little to lose. If he didn't take this chance, the rest of his life might be worthless. He had one of those gut feelings you get sometimes. So, he decided to take a chance on this mysterious possibility of escape.

First, he put the harness on and attached it to a port on the top of the globe. Second, he pushed the escape button on the side of the display case. A click sounded, and two more balloons inflated automatically to the size of the globe. The globes rose into the air until the harness attachment line became taut. Then he rose with the globe now a set of three hydrogen balloons. The display case stayed on the ground.

He witnessed the scene below as the conquering army advanced on the crippled city with him now rising above it all. Once again, his expectations of his future changed. Now, he saw himself drifting somewhere to a remote wilderness town and starting life over again. He knew he had the intelligence to become a successful businessman and earn his way to fame and fortune. After all, he rationalized, the nation he left had failed because of the mistakes of others, not his. And, if it had been left up to him, he would be ruling the world now.

The breeze blew his balloon and him across the landscape. An image of a black-and-pink-bikini-clad woman appeared on a broken piece of metal as he floated by. He recognized it and smiled. Then, as he rose higher, the scene below became an expanse of miniature moving pieces that could no longer be identified. Only continents and oceans could be discerned from his advancing altitude. Of course, he hadn't thought through the means of escape. This escape began to seem foolhardy as the air became thin and extremely cold. He shivered uncontrollably as the cold sank deeply into his body lowering his body temperature. He passed out into a sleepy haze of dreaminess slumping over into his harness as the balloon, and he rose higher and higher.

In the distance, at his altitude, a small vehicle the size of a WWII jet slowly advanced on him. When almost touching him, it began to hover, and a hatch door opened. Mechanical arms reached out to grab his harness and release the balloons. The arms slowly pulled him into the vehicle as the hatch door closed behind him. The craft, shaped like two dinner plates one upside down attached to the bottom one right side up, sped away at a high enough speed to disappear after one deep breath.

Dr. Death awoke half an Earth year later on planet Zoleron. His rescuers escorted him to a beautiful home in the suburbs near the city of Bunia. Once inside, a man in a military uniform sat down across a table from him. "My name is Dergano. Sir, we the people of Zoleron, have rescued you from either death or life in prison for your part in the atrocities, or what you would call, 'ethnic cleansing,' that you and your country performed on the rest of your sorry planet Earth. We have followed that conflict for a few years and know that you have the expertise we need to build an invincible fleet of ships and men. We need you for our weapons systems. You are the expert in our area of the universe."

Death said, "So, I get freedom, free room, and free board. You get my background knowledge in weapons systems. I like the deal and accept. Would you throw in one more little thing for me? I need an endless supply of women to keep me truly happy. You know what I mean."

Dergano said, "Yes, I do!"

Chapter 5 - La Te Da

La Te Da, on Duval Street, has semicircular brick steps at its front door with a blue-striped awning overhead. At the sidewalk behind a white fence are tables and chairs sheltered by dark blue umbrellas. To the right of the main building, still behind the white fence, a separate building contains an outside full sit- down bar.

Behind the bar is a pool surrounded by a building containing more rooms. Colors flourish, red, light blue, dark blue, light green, dark green, yellow, and more. La Te Da serves full dinners that compete fabulously with any restaurant in town. The efficient and entertaining bartenders both in and out set the mood at La Te Da.

In the evening, their live entertainment attracts an audience from all over Key West. Downstairs in the main building a singing piano player keeps everyone singing and dancing. The full bar in the back of the room helps. Upstairs, several nights a week, a cross-dresser entertains to a normally-full audience.

During the light tourist season, their cheapest room is $215 per night. During heavy tourist season, their most expensive rooms are $400 per night. On New Year's Eve, their rooms are over $400 per night. The prices are well worth it. La Te Da is where Ray, Lucy, and the Clarks would stay while in Key West.

Ray and Lucy had been trying unsuccessfully to conceive a child for a couple of years. They didn't know why they could not conceive, but had just started the process of finding out why and what they could do.

Ray did not feel that marriage was a requirement for raising a child. So, Ray had not proposed marriage to Lucy. From Ray's perspective, a child did not automatically require marriage for the parents. He would say, "Think of all the divorced parents who have children from previous marriages, and all of the single parents. We would be no different than them, right? Maybe better, actually."

Lucy, on the other hand, perceived that Ray wanted to marry her only if a child resulted from their union. Lucy felt like a commitment to her should be made first, and then a couple's commitment to a child.

Ray began to see her point and figured that this trip would bring them closer together and he would propose marriage during the trip, pregnant or not.

After checking in and unpacking, they all met downstairs at the outdoor bar. Ray had sobered up a bit since his Hog Heaven vodkas. He ordered another vodka martini and sipped on it frequently, while they discussed the narrow escape they had at Hog Heaven. Ray could feel the warm numbing sensation as the vodka once again invaded his body. He began perceiving everything moving in slow motion. He could easily sense all the action around him as if he had eyes all over his body. Compared to everyone else his moves had blazing speed. Why had he not tried this in a ball game? If he had, he would probably see the baseball's seams moving and know where that ball would break. He had thought of this before, but feared to try it because drinking had so much of a negative reputation. Only lately had he begun to understand that he performed better physically under the influence of vodka. The amount of vodka became the big question.

He played back the altercation at Hog Heaven, seeing the thug pull his knife in seemingly slow motion. As the man's knife headed toward Derick, Ray had plenty of time to think. Like in a slow-motion movie, he saw himself pulling his gun from his concealed belt holster, flipping the safety off, and putting it against the thug's temple. All of this had been completed while the thug's knife hand moved less than an inch. Ray put the gun on the thug's temple before his knife came close to Derick. The only problem seemed to be that Ray didn't know the correct dosage of vodka. If he took too little or too much the consequences could be dire.

He put these thoughts aside and suggested, since it was so early, they could walk up to the Conch Republic Seafood Company Restaurant on 631 Greene Street adjacent to the Wharf. It was 6:00 p.m. when they arrived.

Ray ordered another vodka martini while he waited for his Ahi Tuna appetizer. He began drinking another when the appetizer arrived.

The band played rock music that forced them to move to the beat in their seats and eventually stand up and dance in the space between their table and the band. People began to watch Ray carefully as he moved in ways that no one had witnessed before. He could bend to the beat in ways that would send most people to the floor. But Ray had the ability to defy gravity and to recover instantly without falling down. He seemed to be a circus act on steroids!

Then, while waiting for dinner, he drank another. Ray's condition went from unparalleled good performance to unparalleled bad! At some time during his fourth vodka martini, Ray's conscious mind stopped recording events.

Both couples continued dancing to the live rock band, until Ray, indicating that he must visit the restroom disappeared around a corner.

While Ray attended the men's room, Mona noticed a woman dancing nearby. She said to Derick, "Look at the way she moves. It's just like Ray! Do you see that, Derick?"

Derick replied, "Yes, I agree. She moves like Ray."

Ray never came back, and no attempts at reaching him worked. The three walked around the area in separate directions returning to the Conch Republic to compare notes. No one had seen him, so they decided to walk over to Malory Square to find Ray. When they got there, Key West police and State Police were everywhere. They talked to several people and found out that a terrorist had threatened to shoot all the, in the terrorist's word's, "Filthy American Capitalist Pigs." Based on witness testimony, he never got a chance. A man nearby had shot him in the head between the nose and eyes. The terrorist had died instantly dropping his AK-47 at his feet and falling on top of it.

Derick said, "Do you suppose that was the work of Ray? I hope not."

"Ditto that," said Mona.

Lucy said, "I'm not ready to call the police. We should probably keep texting and calling while we follow separate routes back to La Te Da, to see if he made it back there. He has his gun.

That could be good, or that could be very bad! I'm really worried!"

Eventually, they all met back at the La Te Da bar around 10:00 p.m. Ray had not returned. Lucy called the police who promised to let them know if Ray showed up at the police station.

Chapter 6 – Arrival

Waking from a deep sleep, he became aware of falling. *Something is wrong. My head is not on a pillow, and there is no sheet or blanket. Why?* he thought. *From where?* He abruptly opened his eyes just in time to witness the surface of the ocean devouring his shoes, then his pants, then his chest, and then his eyes as he tumbled underwater in a very deep salty place. He could taste the salt water as he breathlessly and instinctively used his legs to propel himself upward toward the surface. Reaching the air above the six-foot waves, he took a deep breath and looked around without seeing any land. What he did see turned out to be an unmanned sea kayak filled with water. *How strange,* he asked himself, *How could you be so fortunate after being dumped into the ocean, to have a mode of transportation to use, within twenty feet?*

He knew a bit about kayaking, one of his favorite pastimes. He mentally thanked whoever tipped over and fell out of this kayak for having the presence of mind to tether the paddling system to the kayak. Then nearby, face down in the water, he found the lifeless body of a woman wearing a pink-and-black-striped bikini. He couldn't help but wonder what had happened to this poor young woman in the prime of her life.

Likely, her demise would ensure that he would survive. *Although,* he thought, *it would have been nice to encounter her alive.* He thanked her and apologized for having to leave her body to save himself. From somewhere the muffled sound of, "You are welcome," reached his ears!

He reached into the cockpit to the left of the seat and found a water pump exactly where he would have placed it. He looked topside aft seeing a paddle float. This kayak could save his life. He saw no land in any direction. That probably meant that the closest land might be at least twenty miles away, much too far to swim. Besides, he wore a backpack which might carry something he needed. He would investigate that possibility later. He didn't know why or how he got dropped in the ocean, but did know what to do next.

He pulled the paddle-float from under the bungee cords on the rear deck of the kayak. He pulled his backpack off and placed it under some bungee cords on the front of the kayak. He unfolded the paddle float and inflated it. He grabbed the paddle and put one end of his paddle system in the bungee near the rear of the cockpit and put the paddle float under the other end of the paddle. In this way, he had a temporary outrigger on this kayak and could easily climb in by putting his hands in the middle of the paddle outrigger and hooking his left leg into the cockpit and then twisting himself into the cockpit. Once in, he began using the bailing pump to get the water out of the cockpit and the large sponge he found behind the seat to finish the job. Inside a coffee-can-sized container built into the kayak, he found a handheld GPS device. He read the latitude and longitude, GPS location, 24°36'26.33" N and 81°51'42.33" W, not far from Key West, Florida, according to the GPS device's map. He removed and deflated the paddle float, put everything away, and paddled toward Key West almost six miles away. He felt a presence near him which he could not understand. *There could be no one out here without a boat or a submarine*, he thought. After he had paddled about a half hour, he felt that presence weaken.

He suffered confusion about who he was and where he had come from. His name. His NAME. He couldn't remember his name, or anything else about his life before paddling this kayak. His memory had been erased.

He couldn't believe what he saw next in front of him, headed in roughly the same direction. A woman swimming, clad only in a pink-and-black-striped bikini. He pulled up alongside her and said, "Hey, you're a bit far from land to be swimming alone without an escort, aren't you? I thought I saw your lifeless body back there where I splashed down?"

"Oh," she said as she turned over to him and began treading water." We are not that far out. Look behind you. He did and saw the edge of a swimming pool, at first hazy but clearing and becoming sharply visible behind him. It moved with him, staying only a couple of feet behind. When he turned around, he was amazed that suddenly he was in a pool and not recognizing anything, or any of the bikini-clad women looking down at him. The bikini woman he followed into the pool climbed out and slowly became invisible.

The thought hit him, in a comical way, that he had died, and this might be an atheist's version of heaven. It didn't seem too far from the suicide bombers' wish that radical jihadists employed. That's when he witnessed the man with a gun pointed at him.

Thoughts of heaven vaporized as the gun holder said, "What the hell are you doing? Get out of my pool immediately. You have scared all my wives so that they might have nightmares for the rest of the year! What kind of trick did you pull to simply materialize out of the side of my pool without warning? Ladies, relax. It's just a foolish prank. You wouldn't get all worked up over a magician's trick, would you?"

"Well," said Susan, "That all depends on whose being tricked and the perceived consequences if the trick goes bad, doesn't it? If

the magician put one of us in a box full of
monkeys and told us to teach them to dance the
hokey pokey or he'd make us disappear forever
like we have never existed at all, I'd be scared to
diapers, wouldn't you girls?"

The man holding the gun said, "That is a
ridiculous analogy, Susan. Get serious!"

Susan replied, "Jake, you are too serious.
Why don't you drop your gun before you hurt
someone? Let's find out how he managed this
very entertaining trick. Okay?"

The jumper thought to himself and
unfortunately subliminally uttered, *Where the hell
am I. Maybe it's a retreat for the insane. What
man would possibly want these many wives? What
woman would want to share her husband with one
other woman let alone this many other women?
And this idiot, I guess Jake, pulled a gun on me
just because I splashed down into his pool! And
then this business about nightmares. I ....*

All the women in bikinis nodded yes to
something not shared with him.

The jumper looked again at the man with the
gun and proceeded to swim to the steps of the
pool and climbed out onto the concrete deck.
Several women yelled, "What do you want to do
with him, Jake?"

Jake, the man holding the gun, replied with a
question to everyone, "We should teach him a

lesson in manners, shouldn't we? Did anyone see where he came from?"

"I did," replied one of the women. "He came from that thing that cleans stuff off the surface of the pool."

Another woman volunteered, "Anita, you mean the skimmer, Darling."

Anita replied, "Yes, the skimmer. I happened to be staring right at the skimmer, imagining that if I crawled into it where would I end up. Under the influence of the contents of my vodka flask I thought, I might end up in some exotic paradise? I could see the paradise full of young people in bikinis. I would have been so happy to join all of them. So, I did and frolicked amidst such merriment until I had enough and started to return here. As I watched myself in this scene, that man squeezed out of the skimmer with me. We became a morphed version of the two of us. The closer we got to the center of the pool, the more his image took over until I was gone and it was just him in the pool and me here. I thought it to be quite a lovely trick. As he rose out of the water, Jake, you grabbed your gun and yelled at him to get out of the pool." She took another big gulp from a flask she held tightly in her hand.

Jake said, "Susan, you just saw him appear out of you in your daydream. Did anyone else see anything? And what is in that flask?"

The murmur from the crowd continued for minutes as the crowd discussed what they had seen. Ultimately, no one saw anything different than a man, suddenly, in the pool where there had been none seconds before. Most just looked in that direction as Jake yelled at him.

While the discussions went on, the jumper looked carefully at Jake's pistol, noticing that the safety was in the on position and that Jake did not have his finger on the trigger. As if he had done this sort of thing his whole life, the jumper acted quickly with unnatural speed and accuracy using unmatched hand-eye coordination. He reached out and grabbed the gun with his right hand raising it into the air with incredible speed. It was like a frog using his tongue to snap a fly out of the air. Within a microsecond, the jumper had the gun pointed at Jake with the safety off and his index finger set against the side of the gun over the top of the trigger guard.

The jumper said, "OK, Jake, you seem to be leading this crowd of women since you spoke first and with authority and they all seem to listen to you. It is beyond my comprehension how any man can control any team of women with verbal commands. You and I are going for a ride. Make sure everyone lets us pass as we make our way to your car. I have no idea how I got here, but just want you to bring me to the police where I can get a fair shake."

Jake replied, "Look, you startled us. Well, you startled me to be precise. We mean you no harm. I don't get along with the police very well, so I'd like to keep them out of this. Why don't I just take you to one of my guest rooms where you can shower and put on some dry clothes. We are about the same size so that I can give you an outfit."

The jumper hesitated but with incredible speed put the safety back into the on position, ejected the magazine, and cleared the cartridge in the breach of the gun. He handed it back to Jake and said, "OK, let's go." The crowd parted as he and Jake began walking toward the house.

Jake said, "What's your name?"

The jumper replied, "I don't know. I seem to have amnesia."

"Well," replied Jake, "you certainly relieved me of my Glock swiftly. Do you remember anything about yourself?"

"No, I do not remember anything." At that, the man pulled out his wallet and looked at a stack of cards. He found a license. "It says here that I'm Ray Berger, born October 22, 1991."

Jake replied, "OK, Ray, that's a start."

Jake led Ray to a restroom adjacent to the pool where Ray could shower and dry off. Jake passed dry clothing to Ray so Ray could be drip free before entering the house. The backpack that Ray had lost track of suddenly appeared near his pile of wet clothing. He put it aside until he showered, dried off, and dressed.

After that process, he looked at himself in the mirror and squinted a bit and wrinkled his face in a questioning gesture. "Who is that?" Next, he picked up the backpack and towel dried it. The seams were tight and covered with a sealant to make it waterproof. The zipper also seemed to be tight and water proof. Before Ray could look much further, Jake knocked on the door and said, "Ray Berger, are you finished?"

"Yes, I am and will be right out."

Ray emerged clean, dressed in Jake's clothing and carrying a towel full of wet clothes and a waterproof backpack.

"Well," said Jake, "You look better in those Walmart specials than I did."

"Jake, this backpack is waterproof, indicating someone with intelligence dropped me off here. That leads me to believe that you were picked as a person I could trust to help me figure out how to reenter my life after, who knows what has happened to me. I know nothing about me and, in fact, my image in the mirror struck no tremors of recognition before I walked out. But, tell me about yourself, so maybe we can make some sense of why I am here under mysterious circumstances?"

Jake said, "OK, I'm an Internet entrepreneur with one success, so far. I developed a website that helps people find relatives from the past. My system can be used to discover your ancestors or lost family members. That must be why you stand in front of me now! Maybe my website can help you find yourself!"

Ray said, "What's with the gun? I posed no threat to you in your pool. You were nowhere near shooting me before I relieved your weapon from you. And I, in contrast, seemed to have the swiftness of a gunfighter from the old wild west or what we imagine to be a gunfighter! So, maybe I have questions that your website can help me with. Do you have a computer I can use? I'm sure I have experience with computers but don't know for sure since I cannot remember anything before today."

Jake replied, "I'll bring you to your room and pick up a computer on the way. I have a bunch of computers for guests to use. As far as the gun goes, I have a permit to carry a concealed weapon. It's my second amendment right. I'll never use it unless I or someone close to me faces deadly force. I have a shooting range out back so I can practice a great deal. However, I've never practiced confronting a real person, especially one with your reflexes. I don't know how you reacted so quickly, but I wish I could have countered the move. It just doesn't make sense. I barely felt the gun leave my hands and you were already pointing it at me. What secrets are you keeping beneath your amnesia fog?"

Ray replied, "I have no idea where that came from and look forward to finding out."

Jake led Ray to a guest bedroom. On the way, they passed a workout room with free weights and aerobic machines, a professional kitchen, and entertainment center with a 70-inch television, a huge living room with overstuffed leather furniture that rivaled, "Rooms to Go." They proceeded up a semi-circle staircase to the second floor, down a hallway, and to a door labeled, "GUEST-1."

Jake said, "Ok, this is yours for now. I've got a meeting to attend for a couple of hours. Please, make yourself comfortable, dig into that backpack for clues and check out my website which may be useful. The password to the laptop is, 'GUEST-1' and my website is the home page for Google Chrome."

Jake brought him into the room, gave him a key, and said, "No tipping allowed."

Ray smiled as the door closed behind Jake.

Chapter 7 – The Backpack

Ray placed the backpack on the room's coffee table and sat down on the leather couch. Around him, he could see a couple of leather chairs, kitchenette, door to the restroom, and door to the bedroom. On the other side of the room from the hallway door, sunlight shone through a curtained window. Ray got up, walked over to the window, parted the curtains, and looked out. Below him, he could see the pool he had just been in, still loaded with beautiful young women. Beyond the pool lay a large field, perhaps five acres of heavily treed forest, and then a huge body of water that may have been an ocean.

Talking to himself, Ray said, *This guy claims he developed a website that helps people find lost relatives. He claims all the young women in the pool are wives. Where is that legal? Maybe he's running an Internet brothel. He can't possibly have a harem this large. These women would tear him to pieces. I just don't get it. Why am I here? Where have I been? How did I relieve him of his gun so quickly and efficiently?*

Ray sat down again on the couch and opened the backpack. Inside he found a Smith & Wesson, M&P, .40 caliber, handgun. Next, he found several boxes of defensive ammunition that contain bullets that are hollowed out. These bullets cause more damage and tend to stay in the body that has been shot. This way the target tends to be more affected and the bullet doesn't tend to travel on to accidentally strike another and potentially innocent person. He started talking to himself again, *Am I on a mission? Am I an assassin? Have I been trained?*

He had no answers. So, he pulled out another item, a cell phone. Of course, it had been password protected. He had no way of remembering what the password was. However, when he pressed the iPhone 6s home button the phone menu opened. He concluded that the phone recognized his thumbprint and must be his phone, or someone went to a lot of work to make it look like his phone. So, he pressed the home button for a long time activating SIRI. The SIRI reply proved nonstandard, "My name is Jean. I'm an upgrade to SIRI, with the ability to hear and remember all your questions, even if they are self-directed. I also have the power to anticipate questions. I have access to all of the Internet."

He checked the text messages. One was from Lucy Lenora! Lucy had texted him a week ago, "Ray, where are you? Please let me know. You had too much vodka to drink and were very drunk. I tried to get you to eat something, but you were so bad off that when you tried to eat it, it just fell out of your mouth and dripped down your chin and onto your shirt and then the table and finally the floor. We started using less and less vodka in the martinis, but by that time it was much too late. You drooled like an adult-sized infant. Suddenly, claiming that you were going to the restroom, you left and didn't return. I've been trying to call you and text you since then. It's been hours! Everyone is looking for you."

Then Ray read his reply from an hour after her question. "I'm okay and headed back to our room. See you later." However, he could not have been okay, because the only evidence that the texting occurred was the iPhone message log. He had no memory whatsoever of sending it himself.

He didn't remember drinking too much, leaving, or anything. Texting on his phone had to be his texting, right? "Drank too much" "Drank too much" He repeated that over and over in his head until he did remember something. He could see vodkas in his past as a very pretty woman looked on with a concerned look on her face. "Ray," she said, "Haven't you had enough?"

"No" he had replied. "I'm fine. When I have too much, I'll know it. Leave me alone. I know what I'm doing and don't need any help from you!" Something in his reply began to stimulate memory cells in his brain. They were not dead. Just sort of dormant or injured. Then, the rest of the days of his life began to fill in. They were in

Key West with friends at a restaurant drinking and eating. The vodkas were going down easier and easier. The vodka made him feel indestructible, and he did become quicker in fights or battles. Evidently, the positive effects diminished after a certain amount, and he obviously didn't know the optimum amount yet. The evidence of his diminished capacity came from Lucy's description of his condition the day he walked out. Apparently, he gained back his skills as the vodka gradually cleared from his body.

The name on his license is accurate. His girlfriend's name is Lucy. He cannot remember what happened after he left her. He can't remember the texting. Where had he gone after leaving her? What kind of trouble must he have encountered?

Ray texted back again, "Hey, I'm okay now at a rich polygamist guy's house." The message showed up as undelivered! Apparently, his cell phone carrier did not reach his current location. He punched the little-cogged gear wheel to gain access to the phone's configuration. He picked the Wi-Fi option and found one very strong Wi–Fi signal called, "DREAMER." But, what could the password be? He looked around the room and all over the laptop for a clue. *Where would you hide your Wi-Fi password? "DREAMER," what the hell did that have to do with anything*? Well, honestly, he didn't know the answer. Then he thought a bit harder about all the beautiful young women in bikinis just one floor down at the pool. *I'll bet the password is, "plethora." He typed in, "plethora" and that didn't work.*

Ray said to himself, *What the hell can it be? Look on the laptop.* That's where he found it, "Chibouk," scribbled on the back of the laptop. That worked! His cell phone, now connected to Wi-Fi, still showed his text messages as, "Not Delivered."

Ray decided that the local Wi-Fi he connected to did not have Internet access. That made sense since if he was a prisoner, the SOB that put him in here did not want his messages to make it to a destination that might be able to help him.

He tried calling the number, but there was no service.

In frustration, Ray flopped back on the couch's comfortable leather back and fell asleep. He woke up at the end of a dream that didn't make sense.

On a table against a black background a colorful red, white, and blue toy top spun in perfect balance until friction on the table top slowed its spin down, and the top wobbled and fell. Around a groove on the circumference of the top, "Zarnia" had been carefully carved twice. The two carvings balanced each other out. A child picked up the toy top, spun it by wrapping a string around the middle groove, and throwing the top away holding onto the string. When the top came to the end of the string, the top spun rapidly onto a pitch-black plane with a pitch-black background. The top spun on the bottom spire for a minute before it lost enough momentum to topple over. Before the first child could pick up the top, another child picked it up. He waved his hand over it and put it back on the table top. The first child then picked it up, wrapped the string around it, and threw it out and away from him. The toy top spun in a wobble this time and would not balance at all.

Ray had no idea what this toy-top dream had to do with him. So, he made some coffee in the kitchenette and logged into the laptop using, "GUEST-1" for an ID and Password. Then he connected with Wi-Fi so he could access the Internet using the same network and password as with his phone. Ultimately, he had the same Wi-Fi Internet access limitation. He yelled, "What the hell?" He walked to the hallway door to exit and found it locked on the outside. Now he had, in fact, become a prisoner! He picked up the phone on the table near the sofa and got no dial tone.

He pounded on the door. He screamed at it. "Let me out of here. Right now," no one answered. "Oh crap," he said. "Get the damn pictures, and we'll measure every step."

But, what did that mean? His brain was misfiring, and he couldn't control it.

Ray screamed, "What the burning brain cells does that mean?"

Siri, AKA Jean, answered, "I've been following your line of questions, and although I cover the entire Internet, I cannot find anything related to your questions. You are a very confused young man. You should seek professional help. I'm going to sleep now." His phone began to snore!

Chapter 8 – The Web Site

Gradually his phone's snoring began to fade, and it occurred to Ray that he had two options. One, he could start shooting his way out. But, there was no indication that he had encountered lethal force. Blasting away with a .40 caliber semi-automatic weapon could not be justified. He believed, wholeheartedly, that justification of lethal force in the form of a Smith & Wesson M&P only took place against something truly dangerous like a knife, another gun, a karate black belt, a sledgehammer, an ice pick, or some other irrefutable instrument of death. But, why not just blast the lock on this door. But, what waited for him on the other side?

Another option was to try the website that Jake called his website supposedly the home page set for Google Chrome on the guest laptops. It apparently could help him find relatives from the past. But, what good would that do him? Well, if he had access to that website and the rest of the Internet had access to the same website, then the Internet might well be available from the relative's website. It might be possible to set up a route on the website to pass traffic from his laptop or phone out to the rest of the world. Ray decided he should be able to accomplish this and worked on the idea for a couple of hours. Of course, he couldn't know if he knew how to do this or not!

He tried everything he knew or could remember but did not get outside of the local Wi-Fi network. There was only one website available to him, www.FamilyTreeFound.com. He followed the instructions by filling out almost nothing except, the data that existed on his driver's license. That's all he had.

This process took five minutes, and he pressed the "Report" button. The website started to churn away devouring data from his license. The facility saved the completed report and displayed it for Ray to read.

He read the entire report but didn't feel that he read about himself. He felt like he read about a stranger he must get to know again. Nothing in the report made any sense because he had no memories to verify that the report accurately represented him.

Only one thing struck him. He knew from his phone text messages that he had a significant relationship with Lucy Lenora. That is the only relationship he could verify. Oddly, Lucy Lenora showed up with an alias of, Karen Anne Potter! Maybe he knew that before his amnesia or maybe he didn't. It just seemed strange.

So, while he pondered this fact, he turned his attention to his phone. He looked at all the text messages. Of course, the one from Lucy was there, but there were several posted after that one.

One was from someone called, Jungle Rat, who asked, "Who da hell da yar tink y are blasting yar way in her like dat. We's a peasful people, and dunt deserves dat tretmunt. Yar gonna be fixed far wat yar dun."

Ray had replied, "I don't care what you think. I must get back to where ever I came from. If you know anything that might help me, tell me now, or I'll come in and start messing you up!"

Rat replied, "Na weigh. We's peaceful. Dunt know shit bout ya. Yar crazy. We dunt wnt no tubble. Da ya here me, ya nut case?"

Ray asked, "Why did you abduct me then?"

Rat replied, "We dudn't yar fool. Yar just be like a bad dream. Go bak whure yar com frm. Leve us alone."

Ray asked, "So, I can just walk out? You don't care?"

Rat replied, "We dnt wnt ya. Get out. Now!"

That ended the text message conversation. What the hell did it mean? And who the hell uses a slang dialect in their text messages?"

More text message conversations existed just as confusing and unexplained. How could Ray text these people anyhow? They weren't in his contact list, were they?

He looked and, in fact, they were. There, as plain as the moon on a clear day, he found Jungle Rat! Extensive contacts with text messaging to match littered his phone. None of them made more sense than the one with Jungle Rat!

Then Ray saw the photo app icon. He wondered if he had taken any pictures that might clear up his old and forgotten several days and most of the rest of his long-term memory. Just as text messages that he didn't remember might lead him back to his identity, pictures taken during his 'after too much vodka' experience might also help him find himself.

So, he opened the photo app and witnessed about a hundred photos taken in the last week or so. The first one showed a Key West bar with a table for four seating one young lady, a couple, and an empty seat. The empty place had a drained vodka martini glass and scattered remains of beans and rice. He guessed he took the picture and the others smiled because he could barely hold his phone to take any pictures. He had blurred and tilted all the images.

Ray knew the pictures carried GPS information that could be used to pinpoint the location of where each picture had been taken. Ray found Key West GPS data in all the pictures taken in Key West. Strangely, he could remember or figure out how to do many things, but couldn't remember any names.

He looked out the window and took a picture of the pool and all the bikinied ladies. When he looked at the GPS data embedded in the picture file, it indicated something quite remarkable. The GPS data, in the picture, contained a non-standard GPS latitude and longitude. He said to himself aloud, "What the heck does that GPS indicate? It makes no sense at all! What can I do with that information? Could we be on another planet? How do I process this information?"

"Well," said a voice from somewhere. "I've been listening to you talk to yourself for almost a day. I might be able to help you with some of your questions if you just ask the right way."

Ray looked around and realized that the voice probably came from his backpack. He opened it up and unloaded the gun and cartridges. He pulled out toiletries. His phone was already out. Out came a change of underwear and he began to feel like Jack Creature, the private investigator that didn't have a place to live or a place to keep things. So, he had no clothing except what he had on. When his clothing became dirty, he just bought new clothes. He simply didn't keep anything.

He dug in deeper into the backpack and found a vial of brown liquid. He opened the bottle and smelled it. He tasted it. "This is a bottle of Jameson Irish Whisky!"

The voice in the backpack said, "You are correct. Can you pour a shot for me please?"

Ray said whimsically, "Do you have a shot glass?"

The voice said, "Pick up the bottle and pour it into the palm of your hand."

Ray replied, "You can't be serious!"

The voice said, "Just do it!"

So, Ray poured the bottle slowly into the palm of his hand. To his surprise, he saw the brown liquid pile up in his hand formed like a small glass. He stopped pouring when he imagined a shot-sized glass would be topped off.

Ray said, "OK, that was weird. You are invisible, and everything you touch is also, right?"

The voice replied, "I am invisible. There is a small whiskey salad ... Well, it is a surprise. Did you ever hear of whiskey salad?"

"Uh, no," confided Ray. "I can't wait to try it. So, how do I try this salad?"

The voice said, "Just hold the palm of your hand out again, and I will serve the salad for you."

That's what Ray did, and he found a fork in the kitchen and dug into where he thought the salad would be and then put it into his mouth.

"This salad is amazing!" he said. "Okay, Mr. Invisible! How long have you been here? How can I help you? How can you help me?"

Mr. Invisible responded, "My real name is Boris Bodoni, and I can't help you. Only you can help you. I can talk to you and explain what I can see, but you must figure out what will make your situation better. Frankly, you are in a world of trouble, and I don't think you have a chance of surviving. For one thing, you became aware of yourself and your pitiful life at the age of, what, when you kayaked into that pool?"

Ray said, "Well, based on my license, I'm 25 years old."

Boris said, "Yes, doesn't it strike you as a bit odd that you have no memory of anything before?"

Ray said, "I do, though. I know my girlfriend is Lucy Lenora and I do remember having too many vodkas."

"Right," Boris replied. "But, most of your memory is gone. What would explain a loss of memory?"

Ray said, "Some injury to the head would do it. But, I don't have a head injury, do I?"

"Well if the injury is bad enough you might not even know you have the injury. In fact, if a head injury is bad enough what might be the case?"

That's about the time when Ray heard a commotion outside of the one window in the room overlooking the pool. He jumped up, walked quickly to the window and peered out at the crowd of bikini-clad women. They had formed a line that circled the pool in a long spiral with the pool at the center and the end of the line being out of site in the distance. One by one they were walking down the pool steps into the pool.

The pool had become a raging spiral of moving water. Women caught in this spiral circled the pool repeatedly as they moved closer and closer to the middle of the pool. Once in the middle and vortex of this water tornado, they got sucked in and disappeared.

Ray dove at the backpack and grabbed the gun and magazine. He put a handful of cartridges into his pocket and used more to load the gun's clip. Once done, he pushed the magazine into the handle of the gun and racked the slide, effectively loading one cartridge into the chamber. Now he was ready to do combat. He jumped up and virtually flew to the door.

Boris said, "Ray, what are you doing?"

"I've got to save the rest of those women."

"What women?"

"The ones in the pool being sucked out of a drain in the center of the pool?"

Boris replied, "No! When I look out the window, I see a peaceful Intracoastal. Can't brain injuries cause hallucinations?"

Ray said, "No, this is not a hallucination. I'm going to blast myself out of this room, run downstairs into the pool area and stop the line of women being devoured by that thing, that drain from hell!"

At that, Ray held the gun with both hands and pointed it at the latch. His arms were outstretched and stiff with both hands gripping the gun steadily. He had unlocked the safety and was ready. He pulled the trigger. The pistol erupted in smoke as the firing pin engaged the center of the cartridge causing a great explosion inside of the metal tube of the cartridge. The pressure became intense but the walls of the cartridge backed up by the gun barrel would not let the explosive forces travel back or out the sides. The only option was for the pressure to push the bullet down the gun barrel and out of the gun. This happened as the gun's recoil pushed back on Ray's hands. The gun raised into the air lifting Ray's hands and arms. Ray re-aimed for the next trigger pull.

The bullet hit the door latch, blowing pieces of the latch and door all over the room. Ray fired again and again until the latch and part of the door exploded out. Ray swung the door in.

Of course, by the time he got through the door, everyone would know he had blown the door and was armed. Ray instinctively knew that, and did one head over heels roll to a spot behind a desk that provided good cover. He peaked through the under part of the desk and saw Jake unarmed. Jake pleaded with him to cease his aggressive actions, "Ray, you don't know what you are doing. I just wanted to keep you safe until I could neutralize the threat you apparently witnessed. I'll explain the whole thing if you put your gun down and come with me."

Ray replied, "There is no way I'm coming with you. Just let me get back to the pool where I can help those innocent women draining out of the pool."

Jake replied, "OK, have it your way. Come on out, and I'll walk with you to the pool. But, you don't stand a chance against, 'Barney the Atomic Pool Drain.' He'll just pull you in with the women."

Ray gave him a blank stare.

Jake said, "That is a joke. Settle down."

Ray said, "I have to try something, and he came out from his cover to confront Jake. He took no more than five steps when Jake pulled his concealed weapon and fired a shot in Ray's direction. Ray was ready and ducked and fired a shot at Jake, who went down hit in the abdomen. He grabbed himself in the midsection."

Knowing that every second of delay meant more and more people went down the drain, Ray ran as fast as he could down the hallway, down the staircase, past the gym and kitchen, and to the pool. When he got there, the crowd consisted of middle-aged men and women in conservative bathing suits. People swam in the pool, smiled at him, waved at him, and just looked like they were having a great time.

He yelled at the top of his voice, "What just happened here?"

From somewhere came Boris's calm and soft voice, "Ray, what are you doing? Explain to me what all the commotion means. I've never seen anyone move around so crazily as you are today. What are you doing?"

Ray explained everything to Boris, the voice behind the invisible man. It took an hour or so. To his dismay, Boris said, "I cannot understand a word you are saying. Tina, would you come here for a minute or two. Listen to him mumbling. I think he is coming out of his coma."

Ray heard this as clear as a beer salesman at a baseball game. "Coming out of his coma." He repeated to himself over and over. No wonder nothing made any sense at all. Was his brain going through some healing process by pulling things randomly from his memory and putting them together randomly? He thought that maybe he was suffering from a nightmare gone bad. He said aloud, "A nightmare that went bad! Only a sick mind could utter that reverse oxymoron!" Maybe when he came from nowhere into the pool, he was sinking into this coma. But, how could he trust what the invisible man's voice had said to him? What, in fact, made what he said any more factual than anything else he was experiencing. Did he own a gun? Did he have reflexes like a James Bond? What about all the bikini-clad women? Were the text messages his? Was he Lucy Lenora's significant other? What about the pool drain? What about this? What about that?

He felt like he couldn't trust his memory. He felt like he couldn't trust his vision or his perceptions of reality. He lay down on the pool deck and broke down tossing and turning like a baby having a tantrum. Suddenly, the pool began to dim as a hospital room began to materialize. Through squinting eyes, he saw an intravenous bottle hung high on a rack with its tube connected to his arm. The pool and that other world faded to nothing. He viewed the television on the wall. He saw people passing through the hallway door. Another bed in the room sat unoccupied.

To his eyes, the hospital room became clearer. The pool was becoming less clear to his injured mind, and that troubled him. Finally, he found himself in a hospital room with no memory of who he ever was. He was back to square one with no identity. He closed his eyes and fell to sleep thinking that he might never find himself, his identity, or his anything. Blackness crept in, and he rested suspended between dreams, premonitions, and reality.

But then. even the hospital room began to falter into transparency.

Chapter 9 – He Doesn't Suspect

Feeling guilty, she thought back into her past, daydreaming about her once-a-month wonderful special activity which always started at the same strip mall that contained Toys"R"Us, Total Wine, Best Buy, Gander Mountain, Bed Bath and Beyond, and Sears and Roebuck. She had used them all for her transitions into Karen Potter a name that had been generated randomly from an Internet website. This time she had rolled a 5 on her pink die which meant Bed Bath and Beyond.

At 9:00 a.m. Friday morning, she parked her car at Bed Bath and Beyond, put her backpack on, and walked inside the store. She wore denim shorts, a sleeveless red checkered top, and blue sneakers. Once inside the store, she entered the restroom, went into one of the handicapped toilette stalls, and opened her backpack putting its contents on the sink counter top. She turned the reversible backpack inside out turning it into a tote bag of a different material, texture, and color. She took off her blue sneakers, red checkered top, panties, bra, and shorts, placing everything neatly into the tote bag. She took off her ring with the large blue diamond set with pink and white diamonds all around a platinum silver setting and placed it into a special pocket in her tote bag.

She put on frilly and delicate panties and bra. Then she put on pantyhose, high heel shoes, and a very short casual dress with spaghetti straps, and a blue print full of hearts and cupids. Next, she spent five minutes changing her lipstick, eye shadow, hair wig, and walking style. She turned off location services on her phone and placed it into the tote bag. A careful examination of security videos, as she entered and exited the restroom, would not have identified her as the same person. A process of elimination might have found her out. But no one really looked if a significant crime hadn't happened. Yet, she looked both ways as if expecting someone to pop out at her and say, "Hey, I recognize you!" But, of course, no one did, and she continued.

She used her other phone, a burner phone, to text him, "OK, I'm on location. Where would you like to meet me? Love Karen."

He texted back, "Pamela's Chicken and Fix'ns, and I can't wait. Love Steve." Pamela's had been picked by a roll of a die also. So, there were 36 combinations of where her transition to Karen Parker took place and where they would meet for lunch.

Karen bought a hair dryer and added it to her tote bag. She always bought something at her transition store to avoid suspicion by store employees. Also, when she returned home she could say, "I went shopping, but this is all I could find that I needed." Then she called a cab to take her twenty miles away to Pamela's. The meeting places were in six different directions from the strip mall. All the directions were around a 60-degree heading from each other. She walked into Pamela's wearing sunglasses.

Steve, another randomly-generated name, joined her at Pamela's after a half hour. He wore casual business attire. They ordered a bottle of Merlot and an order of fried chicken with all the fixings to go. Karen insisted on, "to go," because she felt that the longer they spent in public, the more likely, she would be recognized.

She had imagined what it would be like, "Hey, I know you. What are you doing way over here for chicken? I don't think I ever saw you dressed like that. Oh," pointing to Steve, "who's this?" But, of course, this didn't happen.

They called another taxi to take them to the Inn by The Sea and checked in as Mr. and Mrs. Potter for one night. Again, the motel had been generated by a role of the die so that the combination of transition place, lunch spot, and motel became six raised to the third power or 216.

Once in the room, they were alone, just the two of them. There were no witnesses. There were no judges. Just them, doing what they do when they get together. They worked hard to protect their secret, and no one would ever know, so they thought.

They consumed the chicken, fixings, and Merlot; and trashed the packaging, the empty wine bottle, and chicken bones, not so carefully. The love making ended several hours and naps later. Both took showers and sat down together on the bed just thinking without talking or holding hands.

Steve broke the silence, "Karen, does anyone suspect anything? I know my wife doesn't. Owning my own business gives me a good excuse for long days away from the office and sometimes overnighters. When you worked for me, we could get together more easily, that's for sure. I wish you had never left, but understand your reasons. An affair with a married man seldom has a happy ending."

Karen replied, "No, he has no idea. We have been together long enough that neither one of us thinks one could have a secret from the other. It helps that I knew you before I met him when I worked as your secretary. I had left for my new work before I met him, so he never knew you, and he had no reason to suspect anything. We are committed to each other. That is the way it must be, for now. I just can't give either of you up! I've thought about it, but I just can't. What is wrong with me?"

Steve said, "I don't know, but I will wait and honor whatever decision you make. What if I told you I'm thinking of divorcing my wife? I can give her up, but not you! If you decide to go with him, I'll accept your decision, but never get over losing you. So, what's wrong with me? What's wrong with both of us?"

Karen said, "I thought you two got along fine with each other. She doesn't suspect anything, does she? You have been careful, right? You and I must continue. From my point of view, that is the way it must be. I would never leave either of you unless one of you left me first."

Steve said, "I have been careful and remain true to the procedures that you and I developed when we started this. Do not worry about that. I just feel bad continually tricking my wife. I'm so hung up on you; I can barely return to her."

"We can never be together the way we want to be until we both break our other relationships. These meetings must be enough, at least for now. Do you understand?"

"Yes, I do, unfortunately! Divorcing my wife does not change my relationship with you."

They checked out of the motel and took taxis to their respective transition points. Karen walked into the Toys"R"Us restroom and changed back into her plain underwear, denim shorts, sleeveless red checkered top, and blue sneakers. She put on her distinctive diamond ring with the large sapphire diamond set with pink and white diamonds all around the platinum silver setting. She turned her tote bag into a backpack. Her other clothing, she donated, anonymously, to a local charity on the way home, by placing the clothing into an outdoor bin. Then she went grocery shopping and arrived home just after her significant other returned from his thirty-six-hole golf extravaganza. He had played well. So, he was in such a good mood; he made love to her for a long time.

Chapter 10 – He is Back

First one eye, then the other. He looked around without remembering anything that took place for at least the last twelve hours. Ray Berger woke up in his room at La-Te-Da, where he guessed he had been sleeping for a day. Next to him was his girlfriend, Lucy, sound asleep. He had a slight headache but no other symptoms of anything irrational. He just felt like he had had a bad dream that he couldn't remember.

As he had planned to do this whole vacation, Ray got up at 5:40 am so he could walk a few miles, before Lucy, Derick, and Mona arose. Ray put on light weight shorts, a T-Shirt, socks, walking shoes, and a belt. On his belt, he clipped his holster and gun covering it all with his shirt. He took his wallet with credit cards, ID, cash, and especially his, "Florida State Concealed Weapon or Firearm License." He connected his earphones to his cell phone, so he could listen to an audiobook while walking.

Next, he put on a wide-brimmed hat to block out the sun or rain if either of those happened before he finished his walk. He set his phone on the Audible App and started the next segment of Stephen King's, "The Shining." He hung a key to the room around his neck and under his shirt.

If he was lucky, he would meet the same young man near Malory Square selling marijuana. He liked to walk while smoking a bit. But, he couldn't often. The illegal status of marijuana presented a significant deterrent. He didn't consume a great deal, but it sure helped, to make his sore feet feel a bit better. Besides, Stephen King's writing made more sense with a bit of cannabis.

Ray knew that marijuana remained illegal only because it would be incredible competition for the drug industry and the alcohol industry. Some claimed that marijuana did damage to your brain or caused a dependency on it or other drugs. If that was true then smoking tobacco would be illegal by now, for causing cancer and creating a major dependency and health issue. Right? As he pondered this and the fact that lobbyists were the reason that the American government couldn't make an intelligent, informed decision about these issues, he saw the Key West police approaching him and instantly thanked his luck that he had not seen the marijuana salesman yet.

The police approached him and waved him over to them. "Sir," one of them said, "we apologize for interrupting your walk, but we are looking for a young lady dressed only in a pink-and-black-striped bikini. She has been reported missing by her husband. They are celebrating their honeymoon at the Key West Bungalow Suites. Have you seen anyone like that this morning? Her husband told us that he last saw her at the Key West Bungalow Suites two nights ago, about 9:00 p.m. She left him to go to the bar and order a vodka martini and never returned. She had on that pink-and-black striped bikini. Strange story, don't you think?"

Ray replied, "I do have a vague recollection of a woman in a pink-and-black striped bikini somewhere, but, no, I haven't seen anyone matching that description this morning. I'll keep my eyes opened. If I saw her this morning, I'm sure I would have remembered. If I do see her what should I do?"

The female officer said, "Just call 911. You have a phone with you, right?"

"Yes!" As they walked away, he had this feeling that he had seen her, but couldn't remember where or when. Maybe she had been part of his adventures over the twelve-hour period he couldn't remember clearly.

Then, when he looked around again, he could see the young weed salesman being led away in cuffs by the Key West police. What a shame. The corner grocery store and local package stores could exercise their form of capitalism without risk. Legal drugs were prescribed way too quickly by doctors, and alcohol and tobacco were major health issues. Ray realized that he certainly had controversial ideas about life in the USA. Skepticism infiltrated all aspects of his thought processes. Why, then, did he allow vodka to be such a big part of his life? He rationalized that for him, vodka seemed to be a healthy drug. For others, it could be poison. He wondered why! All he knew for sure was that a sip of vodka in the morning helped his walking. Did it make sense? No. Did it work for him? Yes.

Now, with his mind wandering all over the place, he had to rewind "The Shining" and try to concentrate.

He knew that this day would be different than other walking days for him. His mind wandered from the novel again as he kept thinking back to the night before. He remembered drinking many vodkas at a bar with Lucy, Derick, and Mona where they listened to incredible live music. It had been a fabulous time. From 6:00 p.m., his memory slowly faded to nothing until he woke up this morning. For example, he couldn't remember walking back to the room with anyone. In fact, he couldn't remember walking back to La-Te-Da at all. The last thing he could remember, dancing with Lucy, seemed vague. He knew that he could barely keep his balance. He moved this way and that, rocked his hips, swayed this way and that, coming close to the ground many times before catching his balance. It seemed to be like he had fallen asleep in the middle of his dance with Lucy. Maybe he had fallen and knocked himself unconscious. He felt no pain anywhere. He found no bumps on his head.

He remembered something else. A woman had been dancing near them. She had been plain but beautiful with her red hair tied in a bun. She kept looking at him with an alluring smile. He guessed that she had never seen anyone this inebriated who could almost hit the floor and recover as he danced under the influence. But then, as if challenging him, she negotiated a dance move that seemed to tangle her legs and knees into a pretzel and untangle it with a great deal of ease. The woman kept watching him until his memory of the situation ended.

Well, he thought, I must slow down on the drinking, especially when carrying this gun. Ray felt that it was his duty and responsibility to defend Lucy and himself. If someone threatened their lives or others close to them, he could use his concealed firearm to fight back as he had on the way to Key West. Surviving a gun battle, although not guaranteed, would be more likely if he could shoot back. Carrying concealed is a huge responsibility, and he knew that he could make a mistake more easily if inebriated. He thought that he would quit drinking alcohol completely. That would solve one problem.

But, he thought, what about the positive effects of vodka? Where is the balance point?

Feeling better, he went back to the words of Stephen King and got lost in the story. Ray would love to be able to write like Stephen King, his favorite author. But then who wouldn't want to be able to write like Stephen King?

He finished his walk after a few miles and reached for the key tied around his neck. Quietly as possible he inserted the key into the lock and turned it, opening the latch. A loud clack sound seemed to boom as loud as a clap of thunder. He winced because he did not want to wake Lucy if she hadn't already been awake. Upon slowly opening the door, he saw them all looking at him. Lucy, Derick, and Mona watched him as he passed through the door.

Lucy spoke first. "Where have you been?"

Ray replied, "I walked all of Duval and White Head taking pictures and getting some healthy exercise. My Fitbit tells me that I already have covered over 10,000 steps."

"You've been gone for a day," said Derick. We were worried into hysterics. We called the police, and they asked us to let them know if you hadn't returned by this morning. Then they would start looking. Lucy couldn't sleep all night."

Ray said, "Wait, you mean I didn't sleep here last night? I thought I had. In fact, I used this very key to lock the door this morning. I woke up around 5 am in bed next to Lucy. Then I dressed for my walk and locked the door on the way out." He showed them the key in his hand.

Mona said, "That is impossible. We've been up all night and would have noticed you coming back or leaving. To keep Lucy company, we all sat here last night waiting for your return."

Lucy said, "You know, of course, that you left us at the Conch Republic. When you went to the restroom, after leaving me on the dance floor, you apparently just walked out. Derick, Mona, and I tried to find you but couldn't. I tried texting you, but you didn't reply."

Ray said, "I don't remember anything past my dance with Lucy. I could barely stand up. After that, I remember waking up and leaving the room this morning to go for my standard walk this AM. I'd better call the police and let them know that I've returned."

"Yes, I guess that would be a good idea. But, Derick will call since he talked to Sargent Barry Brown last night."

Derick called Officer Barry Brown and said, "Barry, I talked to you last night to report my friend missing. He just walked in claiming he didn't know where he had been." They waited as

Barry asked a question but couldn't hear what he asked. Derick replied, "He has no explanations. Whatever he says, I'll email to you so you can close the case."

There was a long pause as Derick listened to Officer Brown for minutes and then hung up. "Well, he just gave me the police department standard prose about people who go missing on their own and cause loved ones to involve the police department which has precious few minutes to look for the voluntary gone missing crowd! Do you have any idea how dangerous it was that you became a vodka imbecile, especially while carrying that gun"?

"Yes, I do," Ray said.

Lucy said, "Look at your phone, and you should see that we texted you, over and over. You never replied because you either passed out somewhere or maybe you just didn't want to answer."

Ray said, "Maybe I had shut the sound off on the phone, so I probably just didn't hear it. I do that a lot. In my state, I probably just had no idea what was happening. I drank too much and became an idiot. It's not the first time, as all of you know. I don't think I'm an alcoholic, but I do like to get blasted from time to time. The frequency is going up, I think!" He looked at his phone and found a dozen text messages from

Lucy asking him where he was and if he was okay. The last one he had answered coherently. He read it aloud, "I'm fine and back to the room. I apologize for frightening you."

"So," Lucy said, "you did respond once but don't remember. That's crazy! You shouldn't have consumed so much vodka. How often have I warned you? You might be destroying brain cells that you can little afford losing. Remember, your grandfather died of dementia and maybe it's because he drank too much. I don't want you to go through that. Everybody will suffer if you cannot take care of yourself. You always tell me that you couldn't take care of someone like that. You would disappear one day. Be careful. Besides, there are a lot of other horrible things that could happen to you should you run into the wrong person."

Ray said, "I know, I turned into an idiot. However, the interesting and frightening part of all this is that I was not here. I was somewhere that looks the same and uses the same key and with a strange woman in the bed where I slept. Holy crap, I'll never touch another drop of vodka!"

Lucy said, "How do you know you were in a strange place. Maybe you just didn't make it back here until now, and you are already on the downhill path in which you remember less and less of our lives together. You always say you learn from your mistakes. Eventually, you'll forget more and more of your mistakes and in a sense, start unlearning the lessons of a lifetime. Ultimately, you'll make more and more of the same mistakes you learned not to make, and I'll have to shoot you with your damn gun before you use me for target practice. Quit the vodka or quit the gun or quit me! Well, now that I think about it, that will not work. Just about anything can become a lethal weapon. Just, quit the vodka or quit me!"

Mona said, "The three of us were fine. None of us saw you anywhere. We looked here and around the neighborhood all night and continued texting. Did you get the texts on your, smarter than you, smartphone?"

Ray said, as he got up and looked out the window, "As a matter of fact, I didn't." Just as he said that two things happened that further spooked the situation. First, a red-haired woman walking down the street looked up through the window at him. She smiled seductively and continued. She looked familiar to him. Second, the ring on his phone that he receives when a text message comes in sounded at least ten times. Ray looked at the phone and said, "There are the rest of the messages. Of course, I replied to none of them because I just got them. Why were they delayed, and where was I?"

Ray considered this dilemma. After becoming a vodka-induced non-memory tourist in Key West, when he left his girlfriend and friends, where did he go and what did he do? Almost knowing and dreading, he looked at his gun and found that someone had fired it. One magazine contained no cartridges. Now that added a very serious dimension to his period of lost memory.

He had taken a lot of pictures during that time frame also. Some were of beautiful motorcycles. Several pictures of a church appeared on his phone. He had taken pictures of St. Paul's Episcopal Church on Duval Street. One picture showed the street view of the white façade with multiple steeples and beautiful stained-glass windows on multiple levels all over the architecturally-complicated structure. He had even taken a picture of the interior, a close-up of the altar with five separate stained-glass windows high over the altar. All of them were colorful beyond anything he had seen elsewhere. A dark wooden-slatted ceiling above the stained-glass windows contrasted against the altar of pure white and the white interior walls. Behind the altar, covering part of the white interior walls had been built a dark-blond complex-paneled section. Ray couldn't figure out why he had taken these pictures, and especially why he entered the church. He considered himself an atheist. This church would not have any significance to him other than the power that religions have over people, and how all religions have abused that power over world history.

Other pictures were of people. Some were of signs and store windows. These image files had one thing in common. Technically, they were excellent, not those of a person in a complete state of inebriation. And most disturbing, many were poses of the woman he saw just a while ago walking past this room while looking up at him with an air of recognition. He had to think of a way to investigate his memory loss about his whereabouts and his activities without letting the others know, for fear that he had done some inappropriate things!

He wondered to himself. *Where had he gone? What had he done? Who was the beautiful woman in many of the pictures?*

Chapter 11 – Going Fishing?

He decided to tell Lucy, Mona, and Derick that he was signed up for an all-day deep-sea fishing trip. He knew the others would refuse to go deep-sea fishing. This meant he could justify walking the streets of Key West alone trying to remember the previous half-day or so. He decided that he would start at the bar, where he began his undoing and proceed toward the room looking for signs or faces that matched his pictures. This was like Hansel and Gretel's directional bread crumbs.

The others, in unison, said, "You're going deep sea fishing!? What, are you crazy?" Lucy wanted to know what she could do while he went deep-sea fishing.

Ray replied, "You'll just have to sacrifice and go shopping until I'm back. Or, you can come with me. I think the shopping will be your choice."

Lucy decided that shopping would be a lot more satisfying than deep-sea fishing, especially if she could make another special arrangement for part of the day. She said, "I'll go shopping. I can get fresh fish at the fish market, where it is less costly in time and money. Everyone knows my favorite fishing hole is Publix."

The real choice was up to Ray, however. His fishing would be wherever his legs, piecemeal memory, interrogations, and sheer instinct would lead him in his attempt to find out what he had done during those twelve hours of memory loss.

There, however, would be a problem. Key West is not like New York City. If two people go shopping in New York City, starting at two undisclosed locations, they would probably not run into each other. In Key West, the same experiment would end with the two parties seeing each other within an hour or so. He decided a clothing store followed by a costume store, would prepare him for his so called, "deep-sea fishing trip."

He told everyone that he would be gone Wednesday before they woke up and vaguely described the fishing boat.

It was Tuesday, and he told Lucy that he would have to go shopping for the right clothes to use for deep sea fishing. After buying a backpack that he could use to carry his regular clothing when he transformed himself into another, he proceeded to a clothing store that catered to fashion-conscious people.

He met a young woman eager to help him with the latest fashion choices. Her enthusiasm poured out as she explained to Ray all his options. Her recommendation guaranteed that no one would ever recognize him. He purchased a yellow short-sleeved striped crew-neck tee, a brown Aiden Cord Pant, a pair of workman boots, and a belt to match. He picked out a pair of blue socks with tightly packed little yellow text messaging faces in various moods and forms. Next, he completed the outfit with an MJ Panama Straw Outback Hat. All this fit nicely into his backpack. The hat had to be filled with the shirt and pants to keep from crushing it in the backpack.

At the costume store, he obtained a good quality hairpiece to cover his hair and a beard to hide his smile. This set him back $500, but he just couldn't risk being recognized.

When he arrived back at the room, Lucy asked about the loaded backpack. "Oh," Ray said, "I am responsible for various fishing items. They must be contained in a backpack to keep everyone's gear organized." He had some line and hooks on top just in case he had to show some of his, so called, fishing gear. No one must know that the fishing trip he would be on the next day had nothing to do with creatures of the deep, but everything to do with creatures of the night!

Ray told Lucy that evening, "Lucy, I'm going to stay here tonight to get plenty of rest before the rigors of boating and fishing tomorrow. Is that all right?"

Lucy said, "Sure. I think I would also. I don't want the rigors of shopping to be too much for me tomorrow, right?"

They both laughed and started reading the evening paper which had mysteriously ended up on their porch. Ray had the front page section first. The headline read, "Terrorist with AK-47 Military Weapon Shot Dead."

The detailed article read,

"A young man holding an AK-47 Military grade weapon high over his head confronted the sunset crowd at Malory Square last night. He claimed to be an innocent Muslim man being tortured by the American infidels. He would kill all of them for their sins against the Middle East. 'You Americans have ruined my country because of your lust for oil, which fuels your economy. While you travel all over your country in big oil-guzzling vehicles, my people are starving to death. Well, death to the oil-lusting Americans.' He began to lower his weapon to begin shooting when a single shot rang out. The bullet struck the terrorist close to his mouth leaving a baseball sized hole in the back of his head propelling his hat high in the air. The spent bullet, after doing its job, sailed into the ocean where it harmed no one else. The terrorist fell backward stiff as a large plank, bounced once about an inch, and his hat landed on his still chest.

A man wearing a backpack and a young woman were seen fleeing the scene down front street. No one followed. The crowd just formed a circle around the dead terrorist and stared down at him, until police arrived eight minutes later.

Police are looking for any information on the terrorist or the couple hastily leaving the scene. Captain Jenkins of the Key West Police said, "We want the man and woman leaving the scene. We are sure one of them shot the terrorist in self-defense exercising his second amendment rights. We want them just for questioning so that we know all the details. In the meantime, we thank the couple for stopping the slaughter of hundreds of innocent people."

Ray said, "Lucy, did you hear about this news story?"

Lucy replied, "Sure. Mona and Derick told me about it and think that those two people are genuine American heroes. They wish they could thank them in person. I agree with them. In fact, if we hadn't been looking for you, we may have been shot by that awful man with the AK-47! You know, it could have been you that saved all those people. You carry your gun for just such a situation. It wasn't you, was it?"

"No, of course not," said Ray. But secretly he wondered. After all, it could be something he simply is not remembering.

Ray continued, "Lucy, I'm going to bed. Tomorrow will be a big day for me."

Ray went to bed. He lay awake seeing the face of the woman looking up at him this morning from the street below. He would not forget that face. He also thought about the fact that he had not been in this room, but another that looked just the same. He thought about the key that seemed to match both room's front doors. He thought about the picture meta-data that contained nonsense GPS coordinates. Good grief! What was going on?

While Ray shopped for the fishing equipment, Lucy called Steve from her burner phone and arranged for him to come to Key West.

Steve said, "Karen, I've missed you so much. My wife and I are no longer having any intimacy. I've asked for a divorce because we no longer have anything in common. If we had a child, it might be different. However, I love you, and I can't wait to see you in Key West. We need to find places where Ray will not be."

Lucy replied, "That will not be a problem. He is going fishing for two days west of here in the Dry Tortugas."

Chapter 12 – What Happened

Ray fell asleep thinking about the anomalies in his life. Some he sensed but didn't yet know about for sure. When he woke up, it was 4:30 a.m. He knew the time had come for action. There was no time to waste. He began getting ready for his self-imposed undercover work. He dressed in his normal clothing which everyone had seen him in before. The other clothing, he had carefully packed in his backpack for use when he needed to be unrecognizable to everyone who knew him. Once he was undercover, Ray had to make sure that he was unrecognizable.

He disabled, "Location Services," on his phone. The police could still track him, but he would be back before they became involved.

He packed all his toiletries for the two-day fishing trip he had told everyone he had arranged. He also packed his S&W M&P gun and ammo.

Lucy and Ray had discussed the trip's two-day length. When he kissed her goodbye, she barely woke up. He had talked to Derick and Mona before they headed to bed the previous night. Ray put his backpack on and proceeded out the door which he carefully locked.

He had no idea how to proceed on his quest to find out what he had done that evening he had left, in a drunken state, leaving Lucy, Derick, and

Mona with no idea where he would be. He had very little information about his whereabouts on that evening because he had no memory of it. The article about the terrorist who had been shot and killed in Malory Square after threatening everyone there may not even apply to him.

The woman he recognized as she passed by the room and looked at him from the street seemed to be looking for him. He hoped that to be the case and now was making himself available to be found. So, he headed back to the bar on the wharf where he remembered drinking too much and leaving his girlfriend and friends that evening. He walked to the public restroom facilities on the wharf and changed into his disguise complete with wig and beard.

He sat down on a bench near the restaurant on the wharf walkway and began reading the article, again, about the terrorist and the shooting at Malory Square. He couldn't believe that had happened near here.

Ray started daydreaming about how he would have handled the situation. In an inebriated state, he would have been struggling to take a great picture of the sun setting. The sun, the ultimate backlight, would, due to atmospheric influence, appear larger than normal. It would be a large golden sphere and the clouds surrounding it would also illuminate gold in various shades and forms.

One thing led to another and Ray remembered a morning, while he watched a sunrise near home, when orange clouds appeared in the shape of a lion standing on his hind legs trying to touch the top of the universe. Cutting into the orange clouds was the profile of a four-masted sailing ship with sails full of wind. On the periphery of this scene were some bright visible stars and a crescent moon. Briefly, he forgot all about the terrorist while he mentally took a picture of this wonderful sight he had once witnessed. Then he did a hard stop, wondering why he daydreamed like this. "Ray," he said, "Get back to reality."

Ray decided to walk around looking for that woman. He had an idea that he might find her around Malory Square if she spent any time looking for him. If she did look for him, she might not recognize him because of his disguise. The walk to Malory Square brought him past boats of all sizes and types docked to his right with restaurants and hotels on the left. The early hour ensured that the crowds would be non-existent. Only the early breakfast people would be on the move. Ray tried to concentrate on what the walk had been like when the dinner crowds moved from place to place looking for the perfect restaurant and bar for their mood. He examined every building and sign on his way, trying to activate his memory. He didn't even know if this is the way he walked that early evening. He had to leave the dock area for a while when a couple of large hotels restricted the walkway next to the docks. His mind held nothing but blanks on the evening he drank enough to lose his memory.

Eventually, he found his way near the water again. He watched as birds attacked a homeless man sitting on a bench near Malory Square. The man, obviously very old, sat on the bench wearing a straw hat. Something about him, perhaps a very ripe straw hat, attracted several birds. The birds flew at him pecking at his head under the hat. He barely could fight them off. Ray, with plenty of time, and feeling sorry for this pathetic human being, walked over to talk to him.

Ray said, "I've never seen anything like those birds attacking you. Do you have any idea why?"

The old vagrant said, "I jest try ta mnd my own business. Dey try ta kill me. I dunt do noton to dem. I dnt hve na choice to go inside. I got na money. I got jst what ya see here in ma soppng crt. Ma whol life. I aprciat your cncern mstr."

Ray asked, "Where have you come from?"

The vagrant said, "I cme frm Cndada. Take me tree yrs to git here. Most frze te death on da way. Way up north aint na place ta live otside."

Ray said with raised eyebrows, "You hiked all the way from Canada to here. There aren't many people who could do that. You should sell your story and earn enough to buy a small house."

The vagrant replied, "I caint read or write ar even talk ta goode. Ya know."

Ray replied, "If you find the right writer that won't matter. I wish it could be me, but I'm a bit occupied right now. Hey, I've got a question. Were you here when all of the shooting happened."

The vagrant said, "Naw, dey kck uses ot when de big crawds cme around. Dey put us on a bus ouda twan. Den I'ze wlks back."

Ray said, "Are you hungry. Would you let me take you to breakfast?"

"Shew wold," he replied.

Ray said, "How about that place over there?"

The vagrant said, "Dat wld be fnd n'dndy. I tnk ya kndly, msr."

So, Ray and the old man walked into a local restaurant and sat down at the bar. The old man had left his shopping cart and all his worldly possessions outside. Ray could see the disapproving looks on most of the of the people in the restaurant. He could see on the other side of the restaurant a couple that looked to be on their honeymoon. They held hands, and the man's expression seemed passionate. The woman's back faced him, but he felt like he knew her. Something about her gestures seemed familiar.

Ray helped the vagrant order French toast, eggs, and juice. He ordered a three-egg omelet for himself. As they sat there eating and talking, Ray found out that this man had advanced college degrees in physics and engineering. The man had gotten fed up with society, stopped working and started walking.

Per the vagrant's story, he simply walked out on his marriage and his job. No amount of questions could elicit from the old man why he had dropped out. He mumbled some stuff that Ray could not decipher. His family life stood as an incredible example of failure, which he claimed had nothing to do with himself.

So, the old vagrant said, "I jst left dem ta fnd far dem selves. I took al de muny in cash, I had and disappeared. Deys no wy dey could find me. I trew a stroke and now I cnt cumincate too good, na more."

As the vagrant and Ray stood up to leave, Ray saw the woman who belonged to the loving couple as she turned around. She couldn't recognize him, but he recognized her. Lucy walked out of the restaurant holding hands and with another man! On the way out, he heard her say, "I saw a UFO with my telescope the early morning before we left to come down here. But now, no matter how hard I look, I see nothing! It must have landed!"

In a state of complete numbness, surprise, and sadness, he sat down with the old vagrant on the same bench where they had met.

Ray told the vagrant, "You know, you may be better off than I. You are all alone and don't have anyone to depend on but yourself. I wish you a period of good luck to balance out your long record of bad luck. Goodbye, sir. Enjoy the rest of your days on Earth if you can."

Ray imagined the Key West sunset that he must have seen in the evening he drank too much. No explanation could explain why that sunset entered his mind then. He felt himself the star of a movie, leaving an unfortunate human being who somehow helped Ray find beauty in life despite his disintegrating love relationship.

As Ray started to get up, he became aware of her presence. He could feel the warmth of her arm touching his. The woman he kept remembering now sat on the bench between him and the old vagrant and said, "Hi, Ray. That's just the way it was, you know! Here, look at the photo I snapped." She held out a picture on her phone of the sun, sailboat profile, the moon, and stars, just the way he had painted it in his mind a few minutes ago.

Ray said, "Wow, how did you do that?"

She replied, "My name is Zara from the planet Zarnia a light year away."

Ray said, "You must think I'm an idiot. You're from the planet Zarnia? There is no Zarnia. At least, we've never heard of it in this solar system. What have you been drinking? I want some! I've seen you looking at me a few times since I've been here in Key West. Why are you stalking me?"

Zara said, "First of all, I will explain all about Zarnia very soon. Second, I didn't do anything except take a picture of what you just remembered. What you remembered is even more beautiful than the real thing. You can imagine reality through your personal enhancement lens. What a wonderful gift to have. Don't you remember me? We met at Malory Square yesterday. You, in your inebriated state, entertained everyone around you, especially me! We didn't know it, but a terrorist stood just nearby."

Ray couldn't tell for sure but thought that Zara was about 25 years old. Even though she came from a planet far away from Earth, Zara spoke fluent English. This seemed impossible.

Ray said, "I must repeat. I'm sorry. You're telling me that you're from a different planet than Earth. Why would I believe that story? First, your English is much too good. Second, you are dressed like an American tourist. Third, how did you get here?"

Zara said, "You and I spent some time on the intergalactic ship that brought me here yesterday. Don't you remember anything?"

Ray said, "Zara, on a subconscious level I remember you. How do you speak English so well when you're from another planet where your language must be significantly different?"

"Ray," she said. "On the way, here from Zarnia, I studied English. It made sense to do that since I knew we would land near the English-speaking United States. I even studied Spanish because of the Spanish influence in the Florida area."

Ray asked, "But, Zara, how did you get the sunset picture from my mind to your mind to your iPhone?"

Zara replied, "Simple. You and I are ESP compatible. I can read your mind, and if you try, you can read my mind. So, I simply looked at the memories you brought from your brain's subconscious into your conscious mind. Then, I copied it into my conscious mind. You don't know it, but all Zarnian brains are like Bluetooth devices, so I simply connected to my phone to print the picture of the sunset. Neat, huh?"

Ray replied, "So, you and your Zarnian buddies are way more technologically advanced than we are on Earth? What else should I know about you? Do you plan to take over our civilization, for example?"

Zara answered, "We do seem to be more technologically advanced in most areas. However, the reason for our trip here is to find out how you can help us and how we can help you. Our plans are to cooperate, not take over. You should know that I love sports, so baseball, football, basketball, and tennis made sense to study, also. Believe it or not, we have developed games in Zarnia like all the ones I just mentioned. In fact, the only sport that I couldn't match up with one of ours is golf. We do have a game with the same high degree of frustration that could take the place of golf for an Earth person who spends any time in Zarnia. The two games are similar in that they both seem to be living things that can build you up today only to knock you down tomorrow. The game is sort of like a fickle lover if you know what I mean. So, golf says, 'Today I'll love you and you will par most of the holes. Then tomorrow I'll hate you, and you will bogey all day! I'm not like that. When I decide carefully on something, I don't change my mind easily. I like you and don't think

I'll ever change my mind on that. You are quick and tough, especially the way you took out that terrorist!"

Ray said, "So, you were with me when the terrorist started his tirade?"

Zara replied, "Yes, you imagined accurately. We were together because we had just met when you fell in front of me. You had tripped over a carelessly discarded broken parasol. I might add, that you were a bit tipsy. I'm surprised you didn't put a pink elephant in the picture! See, I even know about pink elephants!"

Ray said, "But, I cannot remember yesterday from about 5:00 p.m. until this morning about 5:00 a.m. ?"

Zara said, "That's because you had way over the recommended amount of vodka in your system. A whole bunch of brain cells in the memory area were offline, meaning they did not function or fired in a random sequence."

Ray said, "Can you tell me what happened?"

Zara replied, "I recorded all of it." She took out a tablet PC and started a video which an intelligent drone had taken. Ray felt like he and Zara starred in a movie. "See, this intelligent drone knew you and me and followed us around. This way, I have records of what I did to acclimate you to our Zarnian project."

Ray looked up. A silent drone hovered over them at that moment. "So, you are videoing us now?"

Zara said, "Yes."

That's when the old vagrant chimed in, "ya no dat I trabeled to Zarnia right after rnng frm mi hme and rspnse'bilites! Yu foks r so wy coo! Talk bout lite yrs. I hd one ystrdy. I nead som dat vadka. Gt any Zra. Boy, y'll's buteful."

Zara and Ray looked at each other and started laughing hysterically.

Ray said, "Hey, why don't you follow that couple that just walked out before us. Keep telling them that you want an interview for WSEX. See them over there. We'll meet you here at sunset time, and I'll buy you a few drinks of vodka if you can tell me where they went and what they did. By the way, what's your name?"

The vagrant replied, "I hab no nme. But, I been to the Shining City. Peter Newman's ma bst frend. Ya cn fnd ot mre frm him! Ys, I'all folle dem far ya nd met ya bck hre! I tinks dey are plotting angst humanity. Ah, ned ta deal wid dem anyhw!"

Ray said, "Ok, I'll just call you Vagrant then. Happy day!" As the Vagrant walked away toward Lucy and her lover, Ray thinks he hears a baby cry. He looks but sees nothing.

Zara said, "Ok, let's go to the video."

Ray and Zara watched the video on her tablet together, on the bench in Malory Square.

Chapter 13 – Twelve Hours

The video started when Ray first encountered Zara as he staggered up to her at Malory Square. The sunset began to highlight surrounding clouds as Ray took pictures furiously. She said, "Hi, can you operate that camera in your condition?"

Ray replied, "My name is Ray and, of course, I can. My coordination increases when I drink vodka. What's your name?"

Zara replied, "Zara, from the planet Zarnia. I can explain more about that later."

Then, as they discussed, photo composition together, Ray tripped and fell. He clowned his way back up entertaining the crowd around him who laughed and cheered him on.

The video not only showed the actions of the crowd, Zara, and Ray but, also recorded and now showed an Extra Sensory Perception (ESP) story that Ray had received while standing and admiring the sunset. The images had come from another person via (ESP). Just like the picture in a picture on television, the video showed Ray's ESP video and the surrounding crowd and sunset at the same time. The moving picture he received, however, proved to be quite depressing.

Ray felt like he inhabited another person's body as he witnessed the visions, smells, tastes, touch, and sounds at the same time as the person he inhabited did. One young boy's body now contained two brains. The first brain belonged to the young boy who experienced the following events. The second, Ray's brain, carried in tandem via ESP and experiencing everything the young boy did.

He sat outside at a table near his home on the sand of an oasis in his desert town. A half-dozen good friends sat with him, playing games and discussing everything that their young bodies wondered about. His friends' fathers sat at another table a hundred yards or so away.

Ray felt it as if it was him. His bladder sent him pains of fullness. So, he excused himself and not wanting to leave his friends for very long, he positioned himself behind his parents' old SUV so he could not be seen while he relieved himself.

Suddenly, over the top of the SUV, he saw in the distance high in the sky an object flying toward him and his friends. The object approached at an incredible speed for someone so young to understand.

He had positioned himself so he could see his friends' faces, at an angle. Confusion showed on those faces as they looked at something they didn't understand. The adults did not see the vision, for they continued their discussions without let up about the politics of religion and Jihads, the struggle against unbelievers.

The children had young eyes and ears. They could see and hear better than their elders. The village, full of clay huts, stretched out with other children and adults moving in the regular rhythm of life around the village. Some women fetched water at the community well in the oasis. Some women, close by, washed clothing. Some cooked. Some breastfed infants.

Then, suddenly, one more object came from the first as it shot upward turned and proceeded away from the village at breathtaking speeds. The second object whistled in a high-pitched tone as it flew directly over the children's heads. As it passed, Ray heard the pitch of that sound become lower.

Within a second Ray could see this object slam into the table full of men and explode on contact.

The next thing Ray saw and heard was the surprise and terror-filled expressions on the children's faces. Then he saw those faces torn apart by shrapnel. In less than a second, the missile exploded tearing bodies apart and sending shrapnel into the children. When the explosions quieted down, sand, dust, blood, guts, and other body parts slowly fell onto the desert sands. Bodies of precious flesh mingled randomly with vehicles, outdoor furniture, and pools of blood-soaked sand. The adults were all dead, and most of the children were also.

Only the child Ray inhabited escaped injuries because he had been unlucky enough to have been relieving himself behind his parent's SUV. Unlucky because Ray could see through his child's eyes a headless woman, limbless corpses, charred remains, crushed bodies, and countless more atrocities.

He cried aloud as he looked at a dead and mangled man. He cried for this man whom he called, "Dad." The headless woman he called, "Mom." The boy picked up a piece of metal with the inscription, 'Made in the USA.'

As Ray's viewpoint swooped down surveying the scene, the boy and he walked away toward the village center, then past it, and in ten years all the way to Malory Square on Tropical Key West. In a morphing transition, the boy became a man who, with Ray, looked out at a crowd watching the very sunset in current time that Zara and Ray watched.

As the boy, now a very angry man, looked down at his AK-47, the scene switched to another source who watched the man holding an AK-47 yell threats at the crowd. The man began to raise the rifle and take aim into the crowd. Then Ray could see himself looking at the man with the automatic weapon. He saw himself draw his pistol from his concealed belt holster, click the safety off, raise the gun and expertly put one bullet at an upward angle in the middle of the angry young man's head. The man fell from the bandstand dying on the way with his rifle still in his hands. The spent bullet landed harmlessly in the ocean.

Then, only in his head, he heard, "He only wanted to kill the people who allowed his family to be killed."

Ray said, "OK, did you see that? If so, I want to talk about this now. That innocent boy witnessed a tragedy that sent him on a killer's path. Whoever produced that tragedy should be ashamed and severely disciplined. But, that does not give the boy the right to kill. Somebody had to stop him. This time I stood on the front lines."

Zara said, "I agree, someone had to stop him. Undoubtedly, you saved my life, and I owe you a great deal of gratitude. But, tell me where did the boy learn right from wrong. Where did he learn what rights he had? I maintain that he learned in a place mad with hate that his country helped create. In this case, America helped with its drone program.

What happens in battle when two close friends crouch in a fox hole side by side and a shot fired from a distance blows most of the head of one of them clean off. The other one sees it happen.

"First, the survivor is thankful that the bullet didn't hit him. Then he feels guilty that he felt thankful. Now he is just plain mad at himself and the whole other army.

"He jumps out of the fox hole and runs toward the sound of the rifle that just killed his best friend. He weaves and jumps and crouches to provide a very difficult target to hit. Adrenalin feeds his fury. Eventually, he reaches the foxhole of his enemy, this person he knows killed his best friend. Then he realizes that he did not bring his rifle. So, he jumps into the fox hole, grabs the enemy's rifle and puts it aside while he begins to hit the enemy with his fists. When it is all over, the enemy is dead, with most every bone in his body broken. The living best buddy has broken hands and knuckles. As the adrenaline dissipates, he begins to hurt all over.

"He grabs the rifle, jumps out of the fox hole, and starts crawling from enemy fox hole to fox hole, systematically executing the inhabitants. Eventually, he runs out of enemy to execute and passes out fast asleep. The army he is a member of realizes that something significant has happened and slowly advances on the position, which recently fought them back. They encounter no resistance and wonder why. They find the best friend and wake him. He explains everything. Now, that action was violent. The living best friend is a hero! I am not excusing what the terrorist attempted to do. I just understand his motivation. Hostilities tend to amplify over time. How tragic is that?"

Ray said, "OK, I feel the same way, but I don't want anyone judging me now on what I just did at the last moment. Let's get out of here."

Zara said, "I'm taking you to the ship that brought me here. You will be safe, and I can have you back at the room with your girlfriend and friends whenever you want."

They ran faster than Ray had ever run before down the wharf walkway and jumped on a jet ski with him seated behind her. He held on tightly as she started up the PASSA, plunged it into the ocean as a jet ski, spun it around and headed to a spot in the ocean.

Within a second, Zara deployed a waterproof globe over the PASSA, and she pushed the steering wheel forward to dive under water. The drone taking the video followed them recording the whole event. They went down under water, and not a single drop of water had seeped into this two-person complete spherical windshield.

After about fifteen minutes, Zara approached a structure under water that looked like two oval dinner plates glued together concave side to concave side with a window between the two halves. The closer they got the more obvious this flying starship outsized everything Ray had seen on television or the movies. As they approached, a port opened, and Zara, without hesitation or deceleration, soared inside and stopped on a platform that looked like a helicopter pad under water. Once the water drained out and she pushed a button that moved the waterproof globe to the sides and out of the way. Then the PASSA changed to motorcycle mode and Zara drove to another platform and parked the PASSA.

From the football field sized platform, Zara brought Ray to a door leading to an elevator-sized room. Once inside, she used a keypad to enter the code, "K407."

Zara said, "This is a travelator. A travelator is an elevator that can move from floor to floor and move in the hallways on each floor or sometimes between floors."

The travelator stopped, and Zara opened the door leading to a large conference room.

"Well, here we are," she said. "Let's talk."

Of course, they are still in Malory Square watching all this action on Zara's tablet. The video continues with the action from a couple of days ago.

"This ship is from a planet one light year from here. All the signs that you see on the ship automatically translate to match the reader's strongest language. A Frenchman and a Russian will see the same content in their respective language. Slick, isn't it." She smiled.

Ray recognized her now as the woman that had watched him the evening that he drank too much vodka. This red-haired woman is the young beauty he had seen several times.

Zara said, "Okay, I read that thought. I was the woman watching you dance with your friend, Lucy."

Ray said, "Yes, I do like what I see, especially when you flash that engaging smile of yours. Please, don't stop."

Zara said, "Oh, I won't. I have plans for you. In the meantime, let me explain that you have a special power when you drink vodka. When you drink it, a special organ of the body processes the vodka to enable super powers within you. Almost no one on earth has a vodocon and have an appendix instead. The fact that you have it leads us to believe that this is the planet where one of our astronauts, who became your father, landed many years ago. We think that he began living among all the people on Earth and met your mother here. So, your mother must, also, have had that vodka organ. This special organ comes from a recessive gene. So, both your parents had to possess that recessive gene. I think they had to both come from Zarnia! Anyhow, your reaction time with your pistol is incredibly fast because of this. I'd like to meet your mother and father someday to get their story.

"This organ gives you the capability to react more swiftly and accurately than anyone else known to intelligent beings. The trick is to get the correct level of vodka. As you approach the correct levels, you geometrically approach your quickest and most accurate capabilities. Too much or too little and you're nowhere near as good! We have methods of helping you determine the correct levels.

"Anyhow, that was a diversion. When I watched you, I wanted to make sure that you were ready and that everything in your body functioned at the level I expected. Using my sympathetic telepathic frequency with you, I put the thought in your head to leave the restaurant and your dancing. I could see the terrorist situation developing and needed your help."

Ray replied, "But, why would you need my help? You seem to be from an advanced civilization with sophisticated weaponry to handle a terrorist such as this."

Zara said, "If I used my weapon, everyone would be investigating where such technology had originated. Someone would quickly put the clues together and know that we are here. We must remain invisible or transparent. The only reason I risk sharing with you is that you are one of us by blood. I, also, needed to see how capable you are. You are plenty capable."

Ray said, "But how can you be so sure? You say that my bloodline is a side issue. I don't think so. How can we find out for sure? Can't you perform a DNA test? This ship must be equipped to do that?"

Zara said, "Sure, it is. I guess we can make that happen. Why don't you come with me right now? Follow me, please."

She led Ray into the travellator and pressed a button that to him said, "Clinic." Ray used a small wallet mirror to look at the button. Since the button only reacted to direct human view in which it could examine the brain behind the eyes, it simply showed the dyslexic Zarnian language name for the clinic, "Cicnilc!" It might be fun to learn Zara's language, but he decided that he had to focus on finding out more about himself.

They exited the travellator right into the clinic. It appeared that, at least in the small sample of destinations Ray witnessed, every room in the ship had a direct route to every other room in the ship.

In the clinic, Zara had Ray spit into a vial which she sealed up, labeled, and deposited into an input bin. Zara told him the results would be back in a day. That was the best she could do at such a remote location.

Zara asked, "What do you know about your parents? Did you ever meet your grandparents?"

Ray replied, "You know I never investigated my parents, and I never knew my grandparents. My mom and dad said they died before I was born and were from a very far away remote country. My parents said that they didn't even know much about them."

Zara replied, "That's what I would expect if your parents were trying to hide something from you."

Ray said, "I did discover something strange once. I discovered it down in the basement of our house, behind a sheetrock wall, which I accidentally opened. On huge hinges that I could only see on the inside after this big sheet rock wall swung open, I found it. I triggered the opening in a very innocent way. I used to stand on my head by putting my head on a pillow and then placing my hands and head like three points on a tripod in front of my face so that my elbows formed a right angle to support. First, I raised my back and butt up in the air so that my elbows rested on my knees. Then, by raising my knees while keeping my balance, I could get my legs straight up with my feet on top and toes pointing to the ceiling.

"This time, I went too far and fell over backward into the wall. My left foot hit the light switch hard. Now, a normal switch has a plate with a little toggle on it. Toggle up, and the light goes on. Toggle down, and the light goes off. I had used that switch for the light many times. This time, however, I accidentally put my heel on the switch plate with a good amount of force, and it went right into the wall! This action set off a buzzing sound, and the wall opened!

"There, behind the sheetrock wall was a very solid metal wall with a heavily riveted door. Next, to the door, a small window stared back at me. I tried tracing my index finger on the screen to enter numbers like my parent's birthdays, my birthday, their anniversary, and our house address. Nothing I tried worked. The little window may have been a fingerprint reader. I have no idea!"

Zara asked, "Did you ever confront your parents about what you had seen?"

Ray said, "As a matter of fact I did. They went with me into the basement and looked at the opened sheetrock wall/door. Both acted surprised. They said they had never known about this before I accidentally fell into the switch. The three of us had fun shutting the door and then pushing the light switch plate to open it again, and revealing the very sturdy locked door. My parents said the house, a year old when they bought it and moved in, must have had the secret door already installed.

The door with the keypad next to it could have opened into an underground area adjacent to the basement. My father and I tried digging down a bit in that area but found nothing but dirt, water, worms, and roots! Eventually, we figured that there was nothing on the other side of the door and that maybe the plans for using it were thwarted for some reason against the previous owners' will. Thus, they may have sold it and moved their secret project elsewhere.

With that line of reasoning in mind, we attempted to contact the previous owners. We could not. They had simply disappeared into a non-traceable void somewhere. Their names were on the closing statement, but their identities seemed to be non-existent. My dad, afraid of losing the house because of a title anomaly, decided not to pursue the affair anymore. We never talked about it again.

Now, my dad has Alzheimer's. He remembers nothing. Nor can he ever again learn anything. My mom still lives in the house, and my dad is in an institution until the disease causes him to forget to continue vital processes. It's the most horrible thing I've ever seen. I watched my very intelligent father, over five years, become a vegetable. He doesn't have much time left before he's totally gone. In reality, my dad faded about 90 percent already."

Zara said, "I'm sorry. I know about Alzheimer's disease, and we have a cure. Once we start the procedure, it takes about three months to restore most of the brain to a point where learning can begin again. However, the forgotten stays forgotten. There is no way to get it back again without teaching. Usually, the person is old enough to succumb to other common maladies. If we find the disease within one year, then there is a chance for complete restoration and a very high quality of life. In your father's case, we may be too late."

Ray said, "But, there is a cure. That is fabulous news and a good reason to be tested for the disease. However, I guess that you don't want to share these kinds of technologies with us, mere Earthlings. Your advanced technology would lead to your discovery. Why can't you make yourselves known to my world and help us improve the health of everyone on Earth?"

Zara said, "We plan to do that but are not ready now. Your people are very mistrusting and violent from years of settling problems by fighting with more and more lethal weapons. An example is something like a drone-motivated terrorist that we both just witnessed! That, in fact, is where you come in. You now have a foot in both worlds and can become a catalyst to bring us all together. Then we can share our technology with you, and you can share yours with us."

The sunset finished while the video concluded. Zara brought Ray back to the ship to continue what had been started two days ago.

Chapter 14 – I Must Go

Now, on the ship, after a good night's sleep, Ray and Zara continued their discussion after an omelet breakfast.

Ray questioned, "But what can we share with you that you don't already have or know?"

Zara replied, "In due time you will know all. Just work with me. Please, just work with me."

Ray replied, "OK, I'll work with you. What do you want me to do?"

Zara said, "Well, silly, that's what we are doing. We have escaped detection, and now we are working together!"

Ray said, "Okay, however, I have another question that you can answer for me. I assume you are here with a whole lot of space travelers. As you mentioned before, you want to cooperate with us and not take control of our people from us."

Zara said, "You are correct! We want to work with the people from Earth, by forming an alliance. As far as you go, your abilities are astounding! In fact, I have a test for you. First, drink a bit of vodka on ice. Here is our planet's best. Try it," as she reached into a cabinet and grabbed a bottle of crystal clear liquid labeled, "Askov," their name for vodka and poured him exactly two ounces."

Ray poured the cup over a larger glass containing ice from what he assumed was the lunch room refrigerator. Ray took his time and devoured the cold liquid. That took about a half-hour while they discussed interplanetary politics. Once done, he said, "Ok, what is the test?"

Zara said, "Come with me." She led Ray to a room with a cork surfaced running track that meandered around, over, and under obstacle machines. There were twenty stations each with a strenuous obstacle. One a weight lifting test, one required balance, one accuracy, some endurance like the stair stepper, and one that required untangling fishing line!

The record for this obstacle course had been 15 minutes. Ray completed it in 5 minutes, establishing a new record, which has never been broken.

Ray said, "Here is another question for you. How do you know what I had imagined? The drone incident specifically."

Zara said, "Because, as I stated before, I can read your mind. You and I have compatible ESP radio frequencies. You can decipher my thoughts if you exercise your ability to do so! Want to try it?"

Ray said, "Yes, I do, but first I want to know about your arrival here on Earth."

Zara said, "I'll think it, and you read my thought waves. I must make sure you can read my thoughts."

Ray said, "Why?"

Zara said, "I'll make that clear to you soon. First, however, here goes!"

Zara pursed her lips and raised her eyebrows to indicate she would no longer speak and that he would have to attempt reading her mind."

Zara thought, "Let me get the movie[2] about our entry into your world and play it for you. This movie should answer all of your questions."

Ray thought, "Sounds good to me."

Nothing had been said. Ray and Zara could communicate via ESP without verbal communication!

Zara brought Ray to his room for the night and played the video describing the Sun Chaser's Landing on Earth.

When Ray finished the video, he flopped on the bed thinking about Zara. He found himself attracted to Zara in a very big way, especially since they shared genetic origins. He couldn't wait to see her again.

After the video about the Zarnian arrival, Zara returned. Then Ray and Zara discussed more of the events after the Malory Square incident.

---

[2] See Chapter 2 – Zarnia's Sun Chaser

Zara said, "Now you know a bit about why all of us from Zarnia are here on your Earth."

Ray started thinking about all that had happened since he and Lucy started their visit on Key West. There were still blanks from that lost twelve hours. "Zara, there is more to the half day of my lost memory. What else did I do in those twelve hours?"

Zara said, "Well, I pushed you too much. Still, in those twelve hours, after you dealt with the terrorist and we escaped together to the ship, you passed out into a coma. You were out for five hours, and none of my staff could bring you out of it.

"We simply subjected you to one of our standard exercises for determining the agility and quickness of an individual in a challenging situation. We overestimated the amount of vodka that you needed for this first test. The second one, you already know you passed successfully. By that time, we learned how much vodka to use."

On the first test, before testing you, we served you more vodka to bolster your skills. Instead, you passed out and stopped. We took you to our clinic and had our best phycologists attend to you. The phycologist told us we probably shouldn't have given you more vodka. Even though it's like spinach to the American cartoon hero Popeye, you had just begun to use it as a personal power enhancer. Your vodka organ needed a bit more training. Ultimately, the game which you were winning caused hallucinations and some minor brain damage that needed repairing by the brain's processes. Eventually, your brain repaired itself, and you came out of the event without any permanent damage. We need you to try the game again. Okay?"

Ray said, "What are the risks? Can I suffer permanent damage from these experiments?"

Zara said, "No, if you survive. Our physiologist on board told us to give you half of the vodka we did in the last test; you should be fine."

Zara had Ray lie down on an examination table and strapped him in. Then she attached an electronic probe on each side of his head. The probes plugged into a computer labeled, "Testing Department." She gave Ray two vodkas to start the test and injected a sleeping drug into Ray's right arm. Then she dialed in the "Jake's Island Test" and turned it on. Ray fell asleep, and the test began.

Ray went through the test again. This test, the same as his first, proved very successful. This time through, when he reached the pool, he completed several kayak rolls, pivot turns, and headstands in the kayak. He left the kayak with a forward flip from the kayak onto the pool deck.

The women in and around the pool were elated. Nothing this skillful could have scared them.

Then Jake didn't even bring out his gun. He just clapped. When Jake led Ray to the room, he was wet, but not crazy. He showered, shaved, and dressed in Jake's borrowed clothing. When he couldn't get out of the door, he simply called maintenance, and they fixed the door. He realized that Jake didn't cause any of his difficulties. It had all been brain cell failures, caused by cell damage which happened because Zara had escalated the vodka protocol too quickly. The pool draining women proved to be a simple hallucination that did not reoccur when Ray's vodka levels were brought up gradually as you would when training in any discipline.

The experiments continued as Ray prepared with more vodka. Ray, after consuming more and more vodka became stronger and stronger. Eventually, game challenges to Ray became trivial. Ray didn't need any gunplay. No hallucinations resulted from any of his challenges. Ray simply became more adept at handling people and physical challenges.

Zara said, "Now comes the hard part. I don't want you to leave me. You must stay. I need you to help me with my planet's business here on Earth and back on Zarnia."

Ray said, "But, Zara, maybe nothing keeps me here. My love life seems to have disintegrated, and my baseball career seems trivial to the pursuit you have in mind to save a whole planet full of people. Not to mention the fact that the people of Earth can gain so much from your help with technology. However, I still must talk to Lucy. I must get her story."

Zara said, "If you have any doubts I could replace her for you. Whatever she does for you I can do and better."

Ray replied, "That's a terrible thing to say even though I believe it. You are smart and attractive. I can talk to you, and we can read each other's minds. You and I fit the romantic concept of soul mates. But, what about Lucy and what I do for her?"

Zara said, "I watched an old American-made movie a year ago, called the 'Stepford Wives.' Did you ever see it?"

Ray replied, "Sure, the wives became 'Yes' partners doing only what the husbands wanted them to do. However, they didn't replace the wives of the men who ordered them. What a bad idea. No longer were these men challenged by their wives. No longer could they grow from the conflicts that occurred. That's another terrible idea. I like you a lot, and you are extremely appealing to my intimate senses. But, I'm still not sure you could replace Lucy. And your Stepford husbands could never replace me."

Zara said, "You are wrong on both points. Let me show you a little movie we made in the room you and Lucy are staying. Watch closely. The Ray in the movie is not you. He is a cyborg modeled after you, and we will simply call him his real name Gelzek. You know me by now and my videos. Watch carefully."

Chapter 15 – The Stepford Husband

A man, Gelzek, who looked exactly like Ray used the key to open the room door. He walked inside at exactly 9:30 am and sat down at the kitchen table. He entered a poem in Ray's computer that went like this,

"Fishing I set out with zeal to do,
But soon I began to simply miss you.
So, I aborted the mission,
with fervor to quit the fission,
I came home to you begging forgiveness,
Please, let us do something with togetherness.
Today, tomorrow, and forever."

Gelzek had waited for eight hours before Lucy walked into the room after her shopping trip, in which she carried on the illicit liaison with her other lover. Lucy, with a look of shock, said, "Ray, I thought you would be going fishing?"

Gelzek replied by reading the poem.

Lucy said, "I am elated that you should come to that conclusion. What would you like to do?"

Gelzek simply looked up at the top of the stairs. Lucy got the message. They walked up the staircase together, hand in hand. Derick and Mona heard the bed squeaking next door accompanied by moans, heavy breathing, sighs of pleasure, for at least an hour. When Gelzek and Lucy came downstairs to the outside bar, they blushed like newlyweds.

Mona said, "Ray, what kind of fishing was that, what did you use for bait, and how stiff was your rod?"

Lucy said, "He fished for intimate exhaustion for both of us, used a poem for bait, and his hot rod was skillfully deployed!"

Derick said, "Now I've heard everything. Do you have any energy left to walk to dinner?"

Gelzek replied, "I am ready to walk to dinner. I am ready to eat a huge full-course meal; whatever Lucy would like to do. We could try, Commodore Waterfront for surf and turf.

Ray watched the video of his girlfriend getting it on with a very sophisticated robot. Feelings of shock flooded his entire body. Obviously, Lucy had no idea that this machine was not him. Everything about Gelzek perfectly mimicked him, the real Ray. Even the terrible and corny poem is something he could have written. Obviously, Lucy had no idea, so she had done nothing wrong. He was furiously disgusted, mad, and ego-deflated. But, he also recognized from this little experiment how advanced they were. Ray's scientific inquisitiveness got the better of him.

Ray said, "Okay, this little experiment really has me in sort of a bad place. I could easily break your neck for putting me through this. I don't think I want to cooperate with you any longer. However, before I leave this ship and your project to merge our two worlds, I have some questions. The cyborg's likeness to me is exact. I suppose it was easy to do since I'm on your ship being constantly observed. But, it's not just a 3D image copy that you did. Somehow, you must train this thing to move like me, talk like me, make love like me, and even write like me. How did you train it?"

Zara said, "I apologize for putting you through this, and I hope I can convince you to help us. I don't believe any damage has been done to your relationship with Lucy. Hopefully, she will never find out that her lover today was not you. By the way, that is a live feed of events this morning. So, we had to observe you before you spent any time on board and yesterday. I hope you can appreciate the significance of this.

The process is simple in concept, while beyond complex technologically. We have developed a production machine that processes a set of videos of the subject to be copied. The set of videos are taken of a subject, you in this case, from the top, bottom, left, right, rear, and front. We used the situation when you were dancing with Lucy by rigging the dance floor ahead of time. How we made that happen is beyond the scope of this discussion. Do you agree?"

Ray said, "Yes, we can cover that in the future. Wait. What I mean is, we don't have to cover that part."

Zara continued, "OK, this video data is fed into our cyborg production machine which uses it to build a cyborg out of plastic, metal, human stem cells, in a couple of hours. This cyborg has an onboard computer and sensory network. The software which controls all functions of the cyborg is a learning artificial intelligence system. So, he is as you suspect, not simply a clone of you. The cyborg watches your every move using a video feed from a drone that follows you constantly. When the drone cannot get a good feed, like in your condominium interior, we have installed video cameras. The cyborg's observation of you is 95% complete, including showers and restroom visits. Again, I apologize for the intrusion into your life. But, I maintained to my colleagues that this was the best way to convince you of our capabilities. We used you and Lucy as subjects."

Ray said, "Do you mean that you have a Cyborg Lucy?"

Zara said, "Yes, and you can test her if you want, right now. The difficulty for us is to obtain all the memories that the subject has. Obviously, we don't have access to all the data from all your life. So, when speaking to Cyborg Lucy, it would seem like she has a long-term memory problem because we have not had access to her as we have had to you. You, however, are a different story. I can read your mind. We have already established that, right?"

Ray replied, "Yes, and I know where you are going. You have executed a process by which using your ability to read my mind; you have downloaded a complete history of my life. In fact, I'm betting that Gelzek would perform better than I on a trivia test of my life. I'm embarrassed to think that you have found out some of my deep and dark secrets."

Zara said, "You are very intuitive. I love that about you. I have accessed your memory extensively and am amazed at how much alike we are. Your scientific capabilities are as good as mine. The only difference is that I have had access to more sophisticated technology. Our social and intimate tendencies are very close when you adjust for my female state. Unlike you, however, I do not have a significant other. My parents recognized my scientific abilities at an early age, and I spent most of my time in special education classes to develop those abilities. My social engineering did not happen. Yours did. I'm like a teenager now going through some of what I missed when I was an adolescent. To me, while you are part of a scientific pursuit, you are also a social pursuit. That language is hard to understand. What I mean is that I have a crush on you. I'm having a harder and harder time separating you from my thoughts as a subject and a possible lover. I hope that doesn't make you too uncomfortable."

Ray said, "I'm not uncomfortable with that, Although, I am pissed at you for the things you have done to my Lucy and me. I recognize on a scientific level how much I've learned from you. Of course, there is a distinct possibility that Lucy is cheating on me, as I seem to have witnessed yesterday. That complicates my feelings. I need time to sort all of this out!

"My exposure to the possibilities of technology has turned me on. I feel so fortunate that you picked me as your subject in your quest to join our two civilizations. From an intimate point of view, I am attracted to you in a big way. But, there are social limitations on what I can do without violating my conscience. Does that make sense? I have a long-term commitment to Lucy, which may be over."

Zara replied, "Yes, that does make sense, and I will respect those limitations. However, I must say that our social conscience is more like the love movement in the early sixties in America. So, I don't think you, and I are too much different on that subject. I know that while you were not part of the free love movement, you were certainly sympathetic to it."

Ray replied, "Yes, I was sympathetic to that movement. However, when I did have the chance to stray from my relationship with Lucy, something held me back preventing me from following through. Lucy never did start to stray, or did she? I am so confused. I suppose when the truth is no longer the truth and a new truth emerges the transition is painful and confusing."

Zara replied, "While watching the movie of Lucy and Gelzek, I noticed her wearing a distinctive diamond ring with the large blue diamond set with pink and white diamonds all around the platinum silver setting. When did you give that to her?"

Ray replied, "That was her Great Grandmother's engagement ring many, many, years ago. Look, I'm not sure I'd leave her. A commitment is a commitment. Don't you see that? Or maybe I see something that has been invalidated based on information gained today!"

Zara didn't know what to say. Ray had only seen the tip of Lucy's cheating today. Wait until Ray finds out about Lucy's shopping-with-benefits days. Lucy and Ray needed to have a serious discussion and Zara might have to be the catalyst for that discussion.

Ray said, "I don't disagree! But, I came to Key West with a girlfriend, and we freaked her out with Gelzek. I have no idea what she felt, but we did trust each other for a year or so and made love to each other many times. I broke that trust with her. Now she's gone."

Zara replied, "When I dug into your past, I dug into Lucy's past as well. We have very sophisticated techniques for watching people. For example, we have developed a stalking drone which will follow a person based on their aura. All human auras differ the way their fingerprints do. Look at this little movie. It proves that she violated your trust first. What you thought you had, you didn't. I'm sorry."

Ray watched the movie. He saw with his own eyes, the masquerade that took place at Bed, Bath, and Beyond. The drone had the ability to perch, like a bird, on a window sill and record the events inside. There could be no doubt that Lucy had been physically loving someone else. He knew he could be guilty of the same thing with Zara, but so far had not.

The feeling he got watching Lucy tangled in the throes of passion with her secret lover could only be described as a non-lethal lightning strike to his whole body. Ray experienced a draining of all his power. He felt anemic symptoms of weakness. The violation of their relationship seemed so complete. The violation of his trust in her seemed so complete.

Ray had almost proposed to Lucy during this visit in Key West. His plan had been to take Lucy on a sailboat ride during sunset. There would be a guitar player who would play dance music for them. Ray worked out with the guitar player to play, at the peak of sunset, a pre-recorded DVD of Ray playing a beautiful guitar solo instrumental that Lucy loved. While the crowd on the sunset cruise watched, he would stop their dancing and get down on one knee to formally propose while the sun set in the background.

He would say,

Every day the sun rises.
Every day the sun sets.
But never will it set on our love.
Will you be my companion in life?
Will you hold on to me,
through the rest of our sunrises
through the rest of our sunsets?
For the rest of our lives,
will you be my wife and bear our children?
Will you accept me as your
husband, partner, and lover for
the rest of our lives?
Will you marry me?"

Ray had, in fact, made some of the arrangements already. Now he realized that there was another in Lucy's life. Now he realized that there was another in his life. He thought to himself, *Life happens. No plans are safe. No relationships are safe.*

Zara said, "Please, call Lucy and talk to her about your future together. I need you to decide. If you want to stay with me, we need to train you immediately. If you decide not to stay, I'll return you to Key West, and figure out something else. Okay?"

Ray replied, "Okay, I'll call right now."

Zara said, "By the way, the DNA test results on you have confirmed that you are full-blooded Zarnian! That fact may help you make a decision."

Ray replied, "Well, I'm glad to hear that. It explains a lot of things that have gone on in my life!"

Chapter 16 – Ray's Parents

Zara had to know more about Ray's parents and how they became stranded on Earth. She decided to research the captain's logs from previous trips to Starlight, a.k.a. "Earth," as the Starlight inhabitants called it. She knew that Ray Berger had been born on October 22, 1991, if his American license could be trusted.

All of the captain's logs were stored on a web server on board the ship and contained vital information from all the ships and all journeys to other solar systems and planets in the universe. Via Wi-Fi and a Google type search server, she located a trip to Earth on 1960, Earth time. They traveled in a much smaller and less sophisticated ship that landed right in the St. Lucie channel in Florida those 56 years ago.

Jerry Berger had applied for teaching jobs at the local high school.

Captain's Log – May 27th, 1960

Jerry Berger is one of our passengers destined to remain on Earth after we complete our mission and return home. Jerry was an athlete when he attended school. He, like many of our young men, was equipped at birth with a vodka organ located in his body where most Earthlings have what they call an appendix. The vodka organ seems to be evolutionary in our young men. The fact is that a boy or girl with this vodka organ is almost guaranteed to survive past reproductive age. Without it, many young men do not survive because they are subjected to all kinds of deadly activities when living on the remote planets we must now colonize.

This vodka organ or vodocon is very new in our evolutionary biology, so it is worth discussing a bit more and including that information in this log. During Jerry's first trip to Earth, he landed just outside of the city of Moscow, in Russia. While there, our folks that remained in Russia began to drink a great deal of the local inhabitant's favorite beverage. They called it vodka and soon the benefits became famous as young men began to perform physical and mental feats beyond their previous capabilities.

Our young men benefitted more than the Russians even though the Russians originated the beverage vodka and the idea that it enhanced performance. The vodocon enhanced Jerry's performance when compared to the Russians' performance.

I inquired as to why vodka and not some other alcoholic beverage resulted in such performance gains? Apparently, vodka is formulated in a distillation process to make a beverage of ethanol and water. Vodka is the best way to consume ethanol or drinking alcohol. Lack of purity, in other beverages, causes a geometrically degrading performance in that beverage compared to vodka. Vodocons are specifically tuned to use vodka.

That also means that straight shots will work the best without a recent past, current, or future meal!

Jerry Berger realized that the vodka would be his key to a bright future in college with the athletic support provided by the Soviet Union. Jerry experimented with the amount of vodka that would optimize his performance. It was during this process that our scientists realized that Jerry had a very advanced vodocon, the vodka organ. He began to train as a hockey player, hoping to play as a member of the Russian team in the next Olympics. However, he never made it because our men had to move to another country on Earth to handle an emergency.

Jerry, however, could not be deterred. He worked out in fine detail how much vodka would be needed for him to be in peak condition. He worked out lifting weights, running sprints, running hundred-mile races in the mountains, swimming miles in the ocean, bicycling where and whenever he could, playing basketball, baseball, and everything else you could imagine.

Then on September 4th 1960, he was given the new assignment. The pay would be extremely good because of a hazardous duty component. The ship landed and parked due east of a place called, by locals, Bathtub Beach on the Sun Coast of Florida.

He found a job teaching at a local high school. This job was ideal because he could teach his best disciplines - math, and physics. He would also teach the Physical Education classes and coach the high school teams. He was so well rounded and physically sharp that his colleagues asked him many times if he came from another planet, the one that provided Superman. "Jerry, how could you be so good at everything?"

Jerry responded, "You guessed it. I came from another planet where supermen were just ordinary folks." One day a voice behind him said, "Hey, Jerry, the wise and strong. Would you like to play tennis with a very little girl?"

When Jerry turned around, a petite five-foot-five woman, with dark black hair in a ponytail, dressed in a white tennis dress with a racket in her right hand and a ball in her left looked back at him. If she weighed a hundred pounds, it would be way over any estimate he could make. Her breasts thrust forward like high caliber artillery shells. Her waist was just right to go along with those breasts and her tiny waist just north of her perfect sized hips. Her tight-lipped smile and brown eyes melted his heart. So, he said what every good male would say, "Sure. I'll take it easy on you."

She said, "My name is Julia, and I'm counting on you taking it easy on me!" Her brown eyes focused somewhere into his brain, and he knew he had met his match. He would not be able to avoid taking it easy on her.

The next day, the day of the match, the tennis court's bleachers filled up before Jerry and Julia made it to the court. Everyone wanted to see Jerry pummel Julia. High School students placed bets on Jerry. Just about every student bet his allowance and savings on this sure thing. However, none of the students knew the secret.

Parents came from miles around to see this agile male teacher, and this small woman teacher battle it out with racket weapons and tennis ball projectiles. All the parents bet on Julia, however. Why? Because, before challenging Jerry, Julia had contacted every parent while the students attended school. Julia showed a video in a local movie theater that advertised a matinee titled, "Samson's Daughter." Most mothers attended and many fathers also did.

The video was a recording of a tennis match between Julia and world champion, Tony Trabert. Julia, of course, with her vodocon, had an edge.

But Tony, a big guy and world champion, looked awesome. This match, a well-kept secret, between Tony and Julia could only be viewed when Julia and Tony both agreed. In this case, they both agreed if the parents agreed to a non-disclosure.

Julia wanted no fame or fortune from this match. Her whole motivation centered around impressing Jerry. She beat Tony handily not by high velocity serves and powerful forehands and backhands, but by spinning the tennis ball so effectively that it bounced almost at right angles. Julia could make the ball bounce in any direction she wanted. She used so much spin that they had to use new balls every couple of serves! Tony had never been up against someone who could do this so successfully. He lost like a true champion and learned from Julia how to defend against her type of game.

Tony attended the match between Julia and Jerry. Jerry had won the toss to determine who would serve first. He tossed the ball straight into the air directly over his head with his left hand and with his right hand swung the racket hitting the tennis ball with incredible force sending it an inch over the net on Julia's side of the court. The ball hit the pavement in the opposite quadrant of the court and bounced up at a great speed, possibly over 150 mph and very low to the court.

Julia saw the ball come off the racket immediately heading for her inside track. She swung instantly at the ball as if her racket was a hand doing a karate chop. The ball and racket hit, sending the ball up in the air and just barely over the net. The ball hit the pavement just behind the net on Jerry's side and spun back into the net giving Jerry no possibility of getting his racket on the ball to return it.

What Jerry didn't know was that Julia had secretly been brought to the planet to prove that a female with a vodocon could perform better than a male. The whole video and betting strategy made a huge statement that only the Zarnian women's organization knew about. Yes, women's rights are a concern on every planet.

Jerry lost the game in straight sets. Julia had more tricks than he could understand, let alone counter. Julia, of course, had tweaked her vodka menu to perfection., Also, Julia didn't want to remain superior to Jerry. She wanted to be an equal so she could share this part of her life with him. She wanted to share all parts of her life with him. She wanted to have children, exceptional children, with him. And so, she had her way. She taught him all her strategies, tactics, and tricks on the tennis court and a whole wonderful repertoire in bed. People would flock from miles around to see them battle it out on the tennis court, as well as, hold each other tightly on a bench near the tennis court. They married in 1970 after a long courtship. Apparently, they didn't feel the need to hurry.

These two incredible athletes, however, could not seem to get pregnant. This problem went on for over twenty years until January 22, 1991, when, for no apparent reason, Julia conceived. Julia and Jerry, in their fifties, had a child, Ray Berger, on October 22, 1991.

All this information had more than satisfied Zara. She now knew that Ray ultimately would become the best athlete that ever lived. She secretly hoped he would use his athleticism for more serious pursuits than sports to help their home planet of Zarnia survive its current crisis. She had a plan, a plan she shared with no one.

Chapter 17 – Ray and Lucy

Ray called Lucy via cell phone, "Lucy, we have to talk. I'm not on a fishing trip. In fact, I disguised myself so that I could walk around Key West without being recognized. I wanted to walk around alone trying to remember where I may have gone after I left you the night I drank too much. I attempted to jog my memory of that evening. I wore a really good disguise so that no one would recognize me, and I've discovered many things in the process."

Lucy said, "Wait. Ray. I know that you didn't go fishing. You showed up here yesterday and told me. We had a great time after you read me a poem you wrote, and we made love for an hour. I thought you had just gone to get us a table for dinner tonight. Where are you?"

Ray said, "Lucy, that person you made love to yesterday is an imposter. He is not me. I can't tell you everything yet, but will sometime in the future. I have been recruited by a secret agency to help with some very sensitive and serious homeland security issues. I can say no more about that. The only thing I have to talk about with you right now is this."

Lucy quickly jumped in, "Wait. Are you telling me I spent the day with an imposter? That person looked, felt, and acted just like you, only better!"

Ray replied, "Forget about the imposter for now. Do you remember seeing a bearded guy having breakfast with a vagrant yesterday morning?"

Lucy replied, "Yes, I did. I thought they watched me constantly."

Ray said, "My disguise as a bearded fellow worked, apparently. You didn't know the vagrant's friend was me, did you? We observed you being really chummy with another man."

Lucy replied, "Well, the truth had to come out eventually. You know that vagrant followed me around all day. He even peeked in the window to see what Steve and I were doing!"

Ray said, "Well, what were you doing? Am I to assume the worse?"

Lucy said, "OK, here comes the truth. I'm glad we are on the phone. Steve has been my other lover for many years. He and I were together before I met you. I worked for him, and one thing led to another. He's married, so we met in a clandestine fashion.

"Then about a year later, I met you and couldn't have been happier. I told Steve, and he understood that he and I had no future until he divorced his wife. But, he couldn't do it. From my perspective, it didn't matter anymore. You became my obsession, and I loved you, even though I never forgot Steve. By the way, his name is fictitious to protect him and his wife. For a long time, I didn't see him.

"You and I made a loving and happy life together. However, I felt from you a lack of commitment. You never proposed marriage. Something held you back. I wanted to get married, settle down, and have children, but you didn't. Your baseball career became an all-consuming endeavor for you. I understood that, so I waited and loved you for what you are, and there is nothing wrong with what you are. Don't ever change.

"Also, my Roman Catholic beliefs kept nagging at me. Our lovemaking without a marriage put me constantly in the state of sin."

Ray said, "Ah, what does the church say about sleeping with another woman's husband?"

Lucy said, "It is forbidden. My actions are indefensible, but I ended up loving you both!"

Ray said, "I get what you are saying, even if I don't understand it. You had both of us hooked even though your religion forbids both extramarital relationships. It doesn't sound like you are serious about this religion of yours. First, there was him, then there was me, and then there were both of us. What changed that you began meeting him again?"

Lucy said, "This may be hard to believe, but I left my seat at one of your more important home games to get some food and visit the restroom. While waiting for my burger, I saw a couple having a quarrel, with their two children witnessing it the same as me. When the man turned around, I realized that it was Steve, and he recognized me instantly.

"When the argument ended, he looked at me in kind of a pitiful way that made me feel needed. Then they left the ballpark. He called me the next day from his office, and we set up a lunch meeting for that day. We had lunch. He committed to leaving his wife within a year. I forgot all about right and wrong. We simply, turned each other on and ended up in a no-tell motel for a couple of hours. From that point on, we met regularly to make love and plans.

"However, I'm not a man, so I don't know why, but leaving his wife became a logistical nightmare for him. I, being the coward I am, didn't want to leave you to go to him, and end up with no one. I'm sorry, I'm not a good person.

"Several, times I've confessed my extramarital affairs to a priest at confession. However, I couldn't get myself to leave either of you. Now, I've broken up a marriage and am leaving you. Steve and I will be doing the best we can to reconcile with the Catholic church.

"Frankly, I'm fond of you, but I truly love him and am ready to go all-in with Steve. When I met with him yesterday, he showed me the signed divorce papers. That did it for me. I committed to having this talk with you before we headed back home. You beat me to it."

Ray said, "OK, I get it. I will not be going back with the three of you. I will be making a different commitment shortly and not return home for a very long time. I'll notify the team this afternoon. Please, put everything of mine in storage. I will be disappearing for a minimum of two years."

Lucy said, "OK, I can't ask you what you are going to be doing. You made that clear. But Ray, I still have feelings for you. Please be safe. When you can confide in me, please visit Steve and me and tell us what you can. You will like him.

"This may or may not interest you, but I suppose it should. Using my telescope, I have spotted more UFOs. I've watched four faint specks of light moving around Earth as if looking for something. They separate and then get back together again, over and over. What do you make of that? Why, again, is there not news coverage about UFOs except some social media segments with terrible videos? I pray to God that these are not dangerous aliens!"

Ray could not get over the irony of Lucy witnessing the Zarnian ship arriving at Earth through her telescope before he knew anything about the Sun Chaser. He decided that someday he would tell her and her husband to be, Steve, all about what he has been going through. But now, she is seeing more alien ships wandering around Earth!

Ray said, "Lucy, it is beyond my comprehension that you believe in a supreme being, you call God, who is somehow hidden in the heavens somewhere waiting to save us from aliens in space ships. Could it be possible that extraterrestrials are the ones who initially populated planet Earth? Some people believe that."

Lucy said, "There is no way that God is an extraterrestrial. I don't care how many people are misguided enough to even think about that crazy idea. Goodbye!" Lucy hung up the phone.

Ray decided to drop the whole idea of convincing Lucy of anything. He began to wonder why they had stayed together as long as they had. Lucy's commitment to the Catholic church caused him to wonder how the Sun Chaser, Zarnia, and Zara would fit into the truth per the religions of Earth. He guessed he knew the answer.

The churches of the world would not ever consider that a superior intelligence from another planet could have populated both Earth and Zarnia, leaving similar humans on each planet. Logic might lead you to believe the superior intelligence could be called God.

But, if that superior intelligence was God, then it still existed somewhere. Someday the answers would come to everyone as irrefutable evidence. Maybe that someday would be very soon.

Ultimately, Ray didn't let his past life interfere in any way with his commitment to Zara and Zarnia. If Lucy took care of his possessions, it would be great. If not, then he lost some stuff. He had another mission now, and that would be paramount to his efforts.

The very next hour, Zara began training Ray as a Sun Chaser pilot.

Chapter 18 – What Evil Lurks?

If you watched from space, the planet Zarnia (Gliese 581g), a planet in the remote Gliese 581 solar system, seemed healthy. There was very little evidence that it is wobbling on its axis. The measurements are irrefutable, however. The wobble is increasing daily, and if it continues to increase, the planet will wobble to pieces in about ten years.

The ship with men looking on at the site of Zarnia didn't seem evil. It didn't matter, however, because evil intent soaked the ship and its inhabitants like maple syrup on pancakes.

The shadow the ship cast into the universe by Gliese 581's Sun knew of the evil lurking in the human minds aboard the ship.

Two men strategized while looking out the operation deck's 50-foot-high window circling the middle of the ship.

Rankin said, "Do you think they have any idea of what is happening to their planet, that we made it happen, and they can easily fix it?"

Keratins said, "No way. They are getting ready to evacuate before Zarnia rocks off its axis and explodes. At this very moment, their best ships, occupied with all their best people on board, are spread all over the universe to find a planet to move to. They are attempting to determine if they can coexist with the people of other inhabited planets. Can you believe that they want to move their whole population?"

Rankin said, "Our ships should be at Starlight soon. Four Dragoon ships against one Zarnian should give us an easy victory, even though their ship is bigger and has a few more sophisticated systems on it. Then we can find the other ships and destroy them in the same way."

Ranking said, "Have the people of Starlight been alerted to the fact that an Alien ship is hiding under water at one of their favorite vacation spots?"

Keratins said, "Yes, it is only a matter of time before the Starlight military forces discover the Sun Chaser and destroy it. Then the fun will begin. Once we help destroy their best scientists, the inhabitants of Zarnia and Starlight, we can expand our population into both planets. Our planet may destruct, but we the Dragoon people will survive! We will kill whom we must to win, and then those left living will be slaves until they enter our food bank. To quote the famous Starlight expression, 'Life is good!'"

In the meantime, back in Key West, the question of what caused the Zarnian wobble came up in a discussion between Mona, Lucy, Derick, and Gelzek.

Lucy said, "Derick, as I now understand it, you are an expert at interplanetary physics. What could cause a planet to violate its rules and wobble on its axis? It seems to me that anything like that would evolve over thousands of years. Per the Zarnians, the wobble went from zero to considerable in one day. What could cause that."

Derick replied, "Nothing natural could do that in such a short time."

Gelzek said, "As you all know, I am a cyborg. Like real people, we also have feelings. Just like humans, we vary in our sensitivity to situations. Since I must react to situations as if I am Ray, my sensitivity is like Ray's. However, I have an interesting ability that Ray does not possess. It may or may not prove to be helpful, but I'd like you to know about it just the same. Here goes.

"First, there is a network of subconscious thought and knowledge in existence all over the universe. You may or may not have heard or witnessed it, but it surely exists. We, cyborgs, have access to it just the same as you human beings. It's like a collection of computer servers, where each server is a human being with his or her subconscious database. Whatever goes on in your life and whatever you learn is stored in your individual subconscious database.

"As you might expect, however, with so much information, it might be impossible to access quickly. It would take far too long to find out what everybody thinks about a specific individual, for example. Everything is like nothing unless you have a good way to find a specific piece of data in the entire universe of subconscious information.

"Google is an example of a search across computer servers. There is, also, a search across human subconsciousness. All you must do is think of the search criteria as if you were going to perform a google search. You can do it for yourself without me, but it takes, maybe, an overnight for the standard human to view the returned results. Tell me the search criteria and the results will be returned almost immediately. Try it."

Derick asked, "Who is the greatest baseball slugger of all times on the planet Earth?"

Gelzek said immediately, "Babe Ruth. Believe me, I had no idea, but my retrieval speed hit instantaneously."

Derick said, "OK, let me try something a bit more difficult. Who had the highest career batting average?"

Gelzek replied, "Ty Cobb at .366!"

Derick replied, "Ty Cobb. Yes. Correct."

Derick said, "What is causing Zarnia to tilt on its access."

Gelzek thought with his lips pursed together, and his thumb and index finger spread over his mouth. "To save time we need to translate into the Zarnian language. That may … No, I'd better not. Maybe someone knows in a different language. Hmm … Mostly what I'm getting is the fears of a whole planet of people who are fearing for their lives. One little boy tells his friend that when his top starts to wobble, he just picks it up and starts it spinning again. But then listen to this curious one. This is a quote taken from a discussion between two men somewhere, 'Do you think they have any idea of what is happening to their planet, that we made it happen, and they can fix it easily?'"

Mona replied, "That can't be possible. Who would do such a horrible thing? Who would scheme to kill a billion people? Is there anything else you can tell us at this point?"

Gelzek said, "Well, the individual who is saying this is looking at another man. They are both on the bridge of a space ship with a window all around it. Here is another quote from the man on the bridge. 'Our ships should be at Starlight soon. Four against one should give us an easy victory, even though their ship is bigger and has a few more sophisticated systems on it. Then we can find the other ships and destroy them in the same way'""

Lucy said, "An intelligence determined to take over the planet has caused the wobble so they can take over the planet! Don't evacuate anyone. We have to alert everyone!"

Mona said, "I don't know. How can we verify this information? What if Gelzek simply imagines these statements? Who made the statements and where are they from?"

Derick chimed in, "I will spread the word around to my colleagues. Maybe they have some ideas." Derick started to punch keys on his solar impulse phone.

A solar impulse phone is a device that sends voice and data information over a very short atomic wave, not unlike waves of energy that emit from every sun and star in the universe. The impulse waves are relayed from one sun to another sun and eventually are received by the impulse phone dialed. The most current solar phones can use any technology that is available including, satellite, cell, VHF, shortwave, radio, and voice waves. Transmission speeds are limited by the speed of light, however. A conversation from Earth to Zarnia would take one year to ask a question and one more year to receive the answer.

Gelzek said, "You don't believe me because I'm a cyborg, do you? Even in the case where the person may now be dead, the data can reside in someone else who retrieved it based on some information he or she looked for. Contact Ray and Zara. They will help us. Try Zara's cell phone."

Chapter 19 – The Battle of Key West

Zara and Ray sat in the control center of the Sun Chaser discussing what they should do next. Due to circumstances beyond their control, they sat alone, the only two people on the ship. No one thought that Ray and Zara seriously wanted to test Ray's abilities using the simulator systems and then a live test using the ship.

But, enemy ships might be on the way, so, they had to move forward and prepare for the worst.

Zara said, "I'm glad you learned how to operate all facets of the ship so you can become an effective captain. Until the real captain, Captain Damara, who has run off with a couple of Key West body painters, can be located, I must teach you the best I can. Right now, we have no one that can manage the ship in a combat situation, and we may need someone with those skills any time now. You are Zarnia's best chance right now.

"Yes, as unbelievable as it might be, all the crew have fallen prey to the Key West playful atmosphere and did not respond to my request for them to help train you as a backup captain. You are more than qualified and should learn quickly with the potential to far exceed Captain Damara's skills. I've coached several captain trainees, and you are the best I've ever worked with.

"In defense of the Zarnians, nowhere on Zarnia can you find the Key West philosophy of celebrating with food, music, booze, and lust. None of us has been tested against that level of temptation. Temptation resistance has never been developed by any of the Zarnian people, including me.

"The captain of the ship, for example, as I just mentioned, has last been seen with two women who body painted each other so that you could not tell they were naked, but they are. All they are wearing is paint! Then the captain gleefully disrobed so that they could body paint him. Each of the women has been painted like colorful flower gardens with one big butterfly on each of their chests. Each of their butterflies has one wing per breast. I'm not even going to tell you where the butterflies feet are painted. I'm sure you can guess.

"The two women painted the captain like a big butterfly net. With the captain in the middle, the three of them danced down Duval street headed to the Southernmost point on the keys, like Judy and friends in the Wizard of Oz. Where they have gotten to from there, no one knows."

Ray said, "I cannot believe that the rest of the crew is involved in similar pursuits instead of managing this ship? It seems like very poor discipline in your defense forces. I don't care what you think are justifiable reasons. Do you really feel like the two of us can get the job done without their help?"

Zara said, "Yes, we Zarnian people are tricky and imaginative, but we give into temptation quickly. That's why our rulers do not allow anything but strict business on board or anywhere for the crew. We are constantly watched. However, on this trip, they have loosened up a great deal, so that we can learn the most we can about the people of Earth.

Can you imagine coming from the Zarnian atmosphere to that of Key West? But, I'm here and confident that we can get you trained with all of the tools at our disposal! Probably, our biggest asset is the ship itself. You don't need a complete crew because this ship is fully automated. You just need to do some computer programming in our Defense Automation Language. I showed you most of it already."

Ray said, "Yes, I see your point. But let's get back on our predicament with the assumption that you are the only one who is available to train me. It is a fact that I have learned much in a short time thanks to the simulation that the ship provides and your help. We may have a chance!"

For training purposes, the Sun Chaser had a red switch near the control center door that puts the ship in simulator mode. In this way, the trainee becomes used to the actual controls. No possibility exists that the simulator controls do not feel, look, and handle like the real controls because they are the same.

The indicators in simulation mode and those in real mode showed the same information. The ships windows were made from computer monitors. They could show the real outside world or a realistic fabrication constructed by the simulator from video of places the ship encountered before.

The control room consisted of an array of keys for entering data and commands via fingers, like a computer keyboard. Zara had replaced the Zarnian keyboard with an American one because Ray could touch type without looking.

Most captains, however, used microphones for verbal commands. After a simple and quick training session, anyone could talk to the control systems on the ship and make things happen. A command like,

Take us to 'Fort Jefferson' in the Dry Tortugas,

would put you on autopilot from takeoff to landing in the fort provided the maps were installed and up to date.

Cameras were also used to control the ship when speed was of the essence. The ship's computers could parse camera input to identify ships, planets, suns, missiles, and much more. The ship's control systems possessed the most advanced artificial intelligence systems in the universe, including the ability to learn from its mistakes and correct itself.

Simulator mode scores the trainee on the length of time he or she survives competing against the simulator. It hurls situations at the trainee until the simulator wins.

Ray worked with the simulator for a couple of days. On the first day, he used his standard performance-oriented methodology before testing. That's the day when he lasted for an hour before losing. That length of time quadrupled other captain's best scores, including the missing captain's.

On the second day, Ray did not use his performance methodology and noticed the difference. He consumed no vodka at all. His scores were miserable, and he only doubled the others who had worked with the simulator. He realized that he needed to consume just the right amount of vodka to keep his performance at a peak.

Ray asked, "Zara did you ever test on this simulator?"

Zara said. "Yes, I have, and I obtained close to what everyone else before you obtained. You're great at that simulator, showing multiple levels above everyone else. You are gifted and motivated, especially when you prepare properly. Your use of the automation really helped. Most don't understand the automation which should be a requirement.

"Now, you need to operate the actual ship. Although kept at a minimum, there are subtle differences between the ship and the simulator. You'll have to get used to these as soon as you can. Start practicing before it's too late. Why don't we go up now?"

Ray said, "I understand. Now is better than later when later might be too late." He had switched the simulator mode off and now when he touched the controls the actual ship would respond accordingly. All challenges would now come from external forces and not the simulator's creativity.

Zara continued the discussion, "Yesterday, I received a desperate message from the Zarnian Armed Forces leader who is now hiding in his remote fortress. Forces of the planet Dragoon have taken control of our planet. Five ships engaged one of the Sun Chaser's sister ships, the Star Blaster, and destroyed it. No one knows the details of how we lost the battle. Our ships are far superior but, apparently, cannot handle a five to one disadvantage!"

Ray replied, "Well, what can we do. That message probably took a year to get here, right?"

"Yes," replied Zara, "At the speed of light that's how long it took. If we leave right now, we'll get to Zarnia in a year. That means that the Dragoons will have been in control for two years before we get back to attempt retaking the planet. That's not the only thing, however. As you know Zarnia, a year before we came to Earth, had developed a strange axial wobble.

"We came in peace with the idea of settling some of the Zarnian population here if our planet looks like it will blow apart. At our last observation, before coming here, Zarnia remained stable except for a 2 percent wobble increase per year. On top of everything, one or more of the Dragoon ships may be on its way here. Since the message is a year old and it takes a year to get here at the speed of light, the Dragoons may just be arriving here."

Zara answered a telephone call.

Gelzek was on the line and spoke to her briefly. Zara yelled to Ray, "Hey Ray, listen to this. Per Gelzek, there is some evidence that Zarnia may not be fatally flawed and that someone has temporarily caused the planet to wobble on its axis! Join the conversation."

Zara said, "Tell me again so that Ray can hear."

Gelzek answered, "Zara and Ray, there is some intelligence on the sub-conscious network indicating that our planet is not permanently flawed and that this wobbling is just a ruse to get us to leave. How did someone do that? And what devious person would pull such an enormous deception? The Dragoons are mentioned in the discussion that I retrieved from the sub-conscious network."

Zara said, "So, let's get going to complete your training before it is too late. We must train you so that you, without the help of our body-painted captain and a team of recluse crew, can be ready when we get everyone back together again! Thanks, Gelzek, and goodbye. Talk to you later." Zara hung up the phone.

Ray said, "During my simulation runs I developed a battle procedure that engages our ships automation. This is what it looks like:"

- *Name: Computer Battle Automation Procedure*
- *Start:*
- *Set: All steps are interruptible;*
- *Set: All steps can be overridden via human commands;*

    REM Define errors
- *Define error: human intervention required;*
- *Define error: offensive hit on one of our ally ships;*
- *Define error: offensive hit on us;*
- *Define error: offensive miss against enemy;*

- *Open: Data;*   *REM open automation Data Base*
- *Load: Earth jet;*   *REM load jet ship description*
- *Define ally: Earth jet;*   *REM define as ally*
- *Load: Zarnia ship;*   *REM load Zarnian ship description*
- *Define ally: Zarnia ship*   *REM define as ally*
- *Engage: video feed;*   *REM open video input*
- *Define others: enemy*   *REM enemy is default*
- *Proximity ally:*   *REM Identify order to ally ships;*
- *Avoid:*   *REM Execute avoidance protocol;*
- *Fire:*   *REM fire offensively at enemy;*
- *Cloak: off;*   *REM Cloak off;*
- *Wait: Random seconds:*   *REM Wait random seconds;*
- *Cloak: on;*   *REM Random amount of time*
- *Wait: Random1 to 10 seconds;*
- *Interrupt: Inbound ordinance;*
  - *Avoid;*   *REM: complex maneuver to avoid hit*
  - *Fire Offense;*   *REM: fire default weapon on Enemy ship*
  - *Exit;*
- *If Error: Adjust coefficients of decision polynomial;*
- *Go to Start*

Figure 1. Computer Automation Script

Zara said, "We are on our own. React. Defend us! This is no longer a training run. We are alive, at least, for a few more moments!

"Do you want to help me? Do you want to leave your life on Starlight to captain this craft back to Zarnia and enter the fight with my people and me against the Dragoons? Or would you rather remain here on Starlight to live life as a happy member of the Key West culture?"

Ray replied, "I'm with you all the way for several reasons: One, someone needs to lead the efforts of the Earth to catch up technologically. You and your people are the best chance we have. Second, I enjoy being with you and the idea of spending a year together seems very attractive. Third, I'm into the whole hero idea for me. Compared to baseball it seems to be a much better way to spend my time saving a whole planet-worth of nice party-going people who could visit Key West someday! Key West businesses will love me for it!"

They laughed together until, suddenly, an explosion rocked the ship. Both Ray and Zara fell to the floor from the tremors that rocked the Sun Chaser.

Ray yelled, "Damage Report?"

The ships audio response unit, or ARU, responded, "Rear hatch number three blown and taking on water."

The ship now under the surface of the ocean had proven to be an easy target. Ray couldn't wait for answers to questions that neither Zara nor he could provide. Any action had to be instant.

Ray said, "Fasten your restraints now! Damn, they are here and have located us."

Ray said, "Alex. Depart Water for altitude three miles.

Start 'Computer Battle Automation Procedure.'

Alex. Out."

The ship launched out of the ocean dragging ten tons of water in seconds as it headed for an altitude of three miles. The water came back down as vapor trail.

People out sailing in the morning light saw a spectacle seemingly from a science fiction movie as the ship broke through the surface of the water close to Key West, Florida in the United States of America.

The ships automation kicked in right after breaking water. It twisted and turned the whole way up automatically firing missiles at the alien ships firing on them. This spectacular display of automated warfare took place at low altitudes while everyone partying on Key West witnessed it in all its splendor. Then the battle, suddenly, became high enough to be hidden by clouds.

The computer automation flew the ship quickly to a higher and safer altitude while correcting all damage it could, without manual assistance by;

1. Triggering compressed air to blow all the water taken on, out of the hatch-water-exodus port.
2. Closing three emergency doors that blocked compartments of the destroyed hatch.
3. Injecting enough foam insulator compound into that same compartment to fill it, including most of the ragged and damaged port opening.
4. Filling the hatch opening with quick setting rubber skin from foam insulation to air.
5. Informing the captain, "Rocket Launcher Three no longer functional."

All that processing had been included in the ship's default computer procedures. No manual intervention had been required. Then, the computer automation gave control to the Battle Automation that Ray had developed.

First, an error interrupt occurred because of the inbound rockets that the Sun Chaser had experienced including the one hit. The computer caused the ship to move with the random speed in a random direction based on an x, y, z three-dimensional axis.

The ship also fired back to the ship that fired on it, several spread-area rockets, not unlike a shotgun blast of rockets instead of sniper fire. The enemy ship went down hard exploding in the ocean three-hundred yards west of Malory Square. There was no way to know who had fired on them.

Soon, Ray noticed on the radar, hundreds of tiny blips approaching their location, half a dozen bigger blips, and four huge blips. The ship suffered more minor hits which could be handled by the computer automation. By themselves, the damage, caused by these hits on the ship, did not threaten the integrity of the ship. Cumulatively, the hits threatened to destroy Sun Chaser gradually.

However, the Sun Chaser's automation was a learning system, so avoidance became more intelligent, hits became less often, and of diminishing consequence.

Ray said, "I see four large blips on the radar. They seem to be together, flying in a diamond formation. I guess that those are the four Dragoon ships.

"There are hundreds of medium-sized blips which have emblems of a pink and black bikini-clad woman sitting on a WWII swastika. What is that all about, I wonder?

"Then, there are the small blips that I'm betting are American fighter jets. The fighter jets probably are in the air to defend against the four large, and the hundreds of medium-sized ships. Now, we are in the mix and appearing gigantic compared to the others! Everybody must have seen us because they are all headed this way!

"The American fighter jets have no idea who we are, so we may become their targets unless we can contact them and explain that we are on their side and they believe us!"

The view from the ship revealed mainland Florida to the northeast, Key West in the southeast, and Cuba ninety miles away to the South. Ray pressed the maximum speed button, engaged the throttle, and the Sun Chaser quickly disappeared from sight. Some of the early morning sailors and other tourists videoed the takeoff, and many of these videos ended up on YouTube or news channels. No one realized the seriousness of what happened in front of them. Social networking became flooded with UFO claims. A couple of members of the crew, enjoying the fun carnival atmosphere in Key West, put on extraterrestrial costumes and let people take selfies with them.

Now, temporarily safe, Ray and Zara realized they must go back to help the fighters from Earth. At least now they could cloak the ship to transparency and sneak up on one of the larger Dragoon ships at a time. Ray headed back cloaked to be as invisible as possible.

This worked well except that almost every Dragoon ship probably had a type of radar that could "see" even when their target was cloaked.

The Dragoon ships could also cloak, but the Sun Chaser had the radar to see the Dragoon ships anyway.

Ray suspected that the Earth Jets could not see cloaked Dragoon and Zarnian ships. As he flew toward the action, he tried to communicate with the Earth Jets to let them know the very large vessel was on their side, but could not reach them.

In any case, Ray wanted the Earth Jets to see Sun Chaser fire on the Dragoons, so the people of Earth knew that Sun Chaser was allied with Earth. Earth ships would not be able to see what the cloaked Sun Chaser fired on. To cloak or not to cloak seemed to be a big question. Cloaking had to be turned on and off at random times so that Sun Chaser could be seen firing on Dragoons and the others if proven a threat and then disappear to avoid being seen and tracked easily.

Zara and Ray looked at the radar and started counting dots on the radar scope.

Ray said, "We now have about 100 jet fighters from Earth, four Dragoon ships, hundreds of medium sized ships, and Sun Chaser. The Dragoon ships were smaller than Sun Chaser, but there were four of them.

As this ship got closer to the medium-sized ships, Ray noticed two things: One, these ships had the image of a woman clad in a pink-and-black-striped bikini reminiscent of an image you might find on an American WWII military plane. Two, the four large Dragoon ships were firing on the medium ones, as well as the jets from Earth. The Dragoon ships, apparently, wanted to clear the skies of everyone but themselves.

The bikini ship fired an array of rockets at Sun Chaser. Ray began shouting a command, "Alex. Execute avoidance ..."

Ray never completed the command when, Sun Chaser began on its own, due to the already running, *Computer Battle Automation Procedure.* Sun Chaser flew in random directions perpendicular to the approaching missiles and firing back at the ship that fired on them. Missiles passed over under and around the Sun Chaser, but only one hit causing minor damage to the ships landing gear door. Suddenly, the ship attacking them burst into explosive light, flames, and ship parts.

Lucy, combing the skies above Key West with her telescope, saw the blast and began watching that area of the sky. She saw the Sun Chaser and recognized it as the ship she had seen the morning they left for Key West. She set the telescope on auto mode to follow the current object it could "see." Then she plugged the telescope via an HDMI cable into the television and began watching with Mona, Derick, and Gelzek.

After firing the array of missiles at the attacking bikini ship and destroying it, the other's fled. The four Dragoon ships and the Earth Jets remained with Sun Chaser. The Earth jet airplanes fired many missiles at the Dragoon ships. Ray and Zara looked out of the ship's window to watch as thousands of missiles headed at each of the four Dragoon ships.

Ray had overridden and interrupted the procedure flow seven times because of things he saw might be going wrong. He realized that meant he had to do it correctly the next time or lose everything. Ray knew what to do but honestly didn't know if he could make it happen on time. He had to try.

Ray had prepared with a couple of vodkas and now knew he had to simply react to every situation with the utmost speed and precision. Most times the computer automation of the ship's offensive and defensive systems sufficiently defended and offended the Dragoon ships, but Ray occasionally had to react quickly.

At these times, Ray, with renewed determination, turned into a whirling dervish of hands, arms, feet, legs, and head. No time could be afforded to think. The thinking had been completed. Now, he just had to act with speed and feel. He hoped the simulator logic had prepared him sufficiently.

Ray left the automation running because it corrected its mistakes, defining a mistake as whenever Ray had to interrupt or override the procedure. If Ray did not catch an error, it could be a disaster, so he had to spot everything.

He couldn't tell you exactly what he did or why. He just reacted, and the automation did the rest. Ray looked a bit like a random light show produced by a hundred non-concentric rotating colored-mirror balls with a rainbow of moving colored-laser beams focused on them.

Ray had to make sure that he didn't shoot down one of the Earth's jet fighters. He wanted them to be his allies when the day was over. He, also, had to make sure that when he protected his ship, he protected the Earth's ships from the alien enemy fire. Again, the automation accomplished a great deal of this work with Ray filling in the missing pieces.

Eventually, the Earth fighting ships realized that the oval spaceship did not target them but did target the alien ships, so they began to protect the large starship that Ray navigated.

Ray said, "Zara, look at that. It's like watching clouds of mosquitos headed toward a bright light that just turned on!"

Then Ray and Zara saw the mosquitos (missiles) swarm around the four Dragoon ships whose captains had kept them too long in their high-speed, close-in, flight pattern.

Ray acted quickly saying, *"Fire: REM fire offensively at enemy"* sending an array of atomic missiles at the preoccupied Dragoon ships. Twenty out of the fifty missiles hit the Dragoon ships already suffering from ordinance fired from the Earth Jets. Everyone in North America and the Caribbean could see the atomic explosions light up the sky like all the fireworks for the Fourth of July celebration at the same time.

Colonel Roger Battier, in one of the American jets, described the scene after he fired his missiles and looked on, "My battle cameras are turned on, and I'm adding this voice track describing a battle scene like nothing we have ever seen, even in movie sci-fi battles! The alien enemy ships made a strategic blunder by remaining in tight formation way too long. The hundreds of ships under our command have fired several missiles each at the four enemy ships, whose attention seems focused on the larger ship that just rose from the ocean! That ship is an ally! He has fired large missiles at the four smaller enemy ships.

"At the same time, the ally ship fires countermeasure devices between us and the missiles headed in our direction to intercept the enemy missiles fired at us. I'm just sitting here making a battle movie and not being threatened by any ordinance! Nothing gets close, as the countermeasures from our allied ships, explode enemy ordinance at a safe distance away.

"While our missiles and the enemy missiles head toward their respective targets, the very large allied ship rotates clockwise and counter clockwise, dives down thousands of feet, darts up thousands of feet to avoid being hit by the four enemy ships. The allied ship reacts with such speed and intelligence that I cannot keep track. Only in slow motion will we be able to effectively analyze the battle action.

"The time is here as our missiles, and the ally missiles are reaching the enemy ships whose countermeasures have not protected them sufficiently. Our missiles hit with little impact. However, they are doing some damage which is accumulating, and the allied ship's ordinance is blowing the hell out of the four enemy ships."

Suddenly, one incredible blast created the light and heat of another sun in front of Roger. He closed his eyes to protect them from the excruciating blast of light and heat. When the light diminished, two of the enemy ships no longer existed.

Derick, Gelzek, Lucy, and Mona, watching on a TV attached to Lucy's telescope, gave a loud cheer at the sight of the Dragoon ships exploding out of sight.

Roger continued his description of the battle, "That ferocious blinding blast has annihilated two of the enemy ships! In the meantime, the odd little bikini ships left in haste. Apparently, they understood that they were outgunned and outclassed.

"The two remaining enemy ships have performed a complete about face, warped out, and can barely be seen. Wait, one more atomic blast has caught up to the fleeing ships and the ball of fire that resulted probably destroyed both!

"I have never witnessed anything like this, ever. It's been a beautiful view, especially since I've survived!"

Finally, no more offensive fire could be detected by the Sun Chaser. The battle had ended with the Zarnians and Earthlings victorious.

The commander of fighter jets from Earth, Colonel Roger Battier, began broadcasting over all known frequencies hoping to speak to the captain of the ship that destroyed or chased away all the opposing forces, "Captain of the immense starship that rose from our ocean, please identify yourself."

Zara had been monitoring all frequencies for Ray in case she heard something that might help. She heard on one frequency what may have been a human message.

She said, "Ray listen in."

Ray tuned into the radio transmission, "My name is Colonel Roger Battier, of the 125th Fighter Wing of the Florida Air National Guard. Somebody just saved our butts. I'd like to thank you. Please tell me who you are. Are the hostilities over? I never thought I'd see the day that extraterrestrials would bring sophisticated war on a grand scale way above our abilities in my corner of the universe. But, here we are, and everyone on Earth is clueless. You seem to be an ally, and I hope it stays that way. Can we sit down and find out what everybody's motives are?"

Zara replied, "This is Zara of the planet Zarnia here with Captain Ray Berger, a citizen of The United States. We are glad that we helped you, but now we must organize and leave immediately to save our planet which has been taken over by the forces that followed us here. We must prepare to leave immediately. Once we are gone, I predict that you will be safe from further acts of aggression. Someday, we will return, and we will, specifically, look for you, Roger Battier."

Roger Battier said, "But how did an American citizen become the captain of a Zarnian ship and such a good one at that? Why are you here? What precautions should we take? What else should we do? We obviously need help. Help us. Please."

Zara said to Ray, "What can we tell him? How can we help without being here? Those aliens with the bikini emblems may be big trouble. Do you have any ideas?"

Ray said, "Yes, I do. I'm going to talk to Roger. Interrupt whenever you deem necessary."

Ray spoke into the mike with Zara listening. "Roger, we have twenty-four hours to get you up to speed so that you can execute a plan that might protect Earth while Zara and I rush back to Zarnia. Can you land that jet of yours on an aircraft carrier? I'm going to make our ship visible and open a large door into our docking area. If we both maintain the same speed with you a bit faster, you can safely fly into our ship and land. Then we can meet and go over the details. Want to give it a try? We cannot do anything else because we don't have time to meet with half of the world. We must be on our way to save ours.

I'm mostly speaking on behalf of Zara and the other Zarnians."

Roger replied, "OK, I'll give it a try. Hell, if it weren't for you I'd be crispier that a mosquito in a 'lectric zapper." Ray stopped the battle procedure, decloaked the ship, and opened the docking station door. "OK, I can see it and will approach with landing gear down at 300 mph."

Roger docked the fighter jet successfully and followed Zara to the ship's main conference room. Roger asked Zara on the way, "How do two of you operate this massive ship?"

Zara replied, "Computer automation. Our systems are learning systems which learn from their mistakes and ours. In fact, in some cases, they can learn from other computer's mistakes. Most times a verbal command will suffice. For example, we just told our docking system that a ship would be docking shortly and it did the rest."

When Roger and Zara joined Ray in the conference room, Ray presented his plan, "Zara has a complete list of the Zarnian people that inhabit the Earth. Each person's address, phone, physical description, age, pictures, DNA, fingerprints are listed. You should be able to find them all. Start with Captain Damara and make him second in command. You are to remain first. Currently, we don't know where he is, but I'm confident you can find him. Zara, I assume you can cut formal orders for everyone to cooperate with this effort, especially that Roger oversees the forces on Earth while we are away."

Zara said, "Yes, I can. Formal orders have always been my function while on this trip to Starlight."

Ray continued, "With Zara's permission, we are going to hand over the schematics and plans for this ship. There are enough Zarnian people with the background on that list to build one of these ships. If not, you should be able to equip your defenses with some of the features. The gravity-focusing engine may be a bit too much. At any rate, that is the best we can do. I'm only worried about the ships we saw with the bikini emblem on them. They may come back when we are gone. But then, they didn't seem to have the sophistication that the Zarnian ships have, so that you may be lucky there. Do you think you can do that? If you can't, there is nothing we can do at this point."

After that Ray, Roger, and Zara talked for hours about details. Finally, Roger undocked from Sun Chaser and returned to his base in Jacksonville, Florida to explain everything to his upper command. He had expressed his concern to Ray and Zara about getting the job done considering that the top military brass had not participated. However, he understood that they did the best that they could do.

We are going to have to talk about it and plan. We have a year to put together our plans to save both Zarnia and Starlight! Let's get busy!"

"Wait," said Ray. "I just thought of something that might save us some time and prepare us better for the trip back to Zarnia. We should be able to get most of the crew back. We are going to land at Fort Jefferson."

Mona, Lucy, Derick, and Gelzek had watched the whole event from Lucy's telescope feed on her TV. The battle speed only afforded visibility when a ship exploded and fiery pieces fell to Earth in a final destruction of a ship and crew.

Ray landed the Sun Chaser in the middle of Fort Jefferson in the Dry Tortugas. No one objected. He landed it there so that battle damages could easily be determined and repaired, while all the Sun Chaser crew headed to Fort Jefferson to help on the trip back to Zarnia. The Zarnians who had assignments to visit individual countries on Earth continued to their respective assigned country. All of them had been contacted, and most felt that the research should continue in parallel to the defense of Zarnia. Zara allowed anyone who wanted to travel back to Zarnia immediately to do so. Zara, also, collected messages from all the Zarnians to family and friends back in Zarnia.

Chapter 20 – The Truth About Zarnia

Ray and Zara, still aboard the Sun Chaser, in the Dry Tortugas, had just been through the most nerve stimulating adventure of their lives. As soon as Ray landed the ship in Fort Jefferson, he and Zara embraced and kissed. When two people survive an adventure of the significance they just did, they tend to become very close very quickly. Now, with no one else involved, Zara and Ray had become very close. This led to physical intimacy and lovemaking with a release of emotions beyond their expectations.

The others joined them in the Tortugas. Lucy did not. She joined Steve back home. His life became hers, and her life became his. They married a year later. Lucy never forgot, though, the sight of fighting ships that she had viewed with the help of her telescope. She had captured movies and still photographs. She wished she had met the aliens that won the battle, and saved many fighter pilots from around the world.

Ray realized that his subconscious had tried to warn him of something. His brain while scrambled after overdosing on medicinal vodka, kept getting this image of Zarnia as a boy's toy top that is tampered with and then cannot spin again unless it wobbles. So, even when his brain is a bit confused, the subconscious network, of which he is a node, keeps sending input that can be useful in the future. There also seems to be some intelligence to what the network sends to you. His subconscious mind knew that he had become tangled up in the affairs of Zarnia and retained the wobble information that the subconscious network presented to him!

In the future, Ray vowed to take the subconscious network more seriously. The information sent to Ray proved to be too important to miss. He needed a way to clear his brain of all other input except the data from the subconscious network. So, he vowed to spend an hour a day alone with ear plugs in and blindfolds on sitting up in a crossed leg position, meditating. When thoughts came to him, he simply spoke them in a shorthand fashion with his cell phone recording. Then, later, he could fit this information into his activities, hoping it would help. What usually happened is that a piece of intelligence would come to him during these meditation sessions that completely replaced the need for meditation and cried out for action. In these circumstances, Ray opted for the action.

Having realized that meditation had a permanent place in his life from now on, Ray immediately began to spend an hour a day, when he first woke up, meditating. He had to be totally awake to meditate effectively, so it made sense to do it as soon as he woke up in the morning. The day after the battle, Ray, therefore, woke up, grabbed a cup of coffee, did a few calisthenics, and sat down in the ship's gym to meditate.

Of course, the biggest thing on his mind was who put the wobble in Zarnia and how could it be undone. A whole planet full of people depended on the solution. He could not ignore these thoughts that flooded his consciousness and supposed that this is what meditation is all about. Let the conscious mind dump questions on the sub-conscious network and move on, even if nothing is currently available on the conscious questions.

So, for one hour that is what he did. He let his mind muddle over conscious high priority information. Whatever came to mind must, somehow, be important. He decided not to record anything and let his brain work the way human brains had worked since humans evolved from the missing link. He thought about his love for Zara and complete respect for her abilities. He thought about the loss of Lucy with whom he had spent a big segment of his life. He was shocked to realize that he had remembered the toy top image from his brain-rage spell. That was not supposed to happen. Life is full of questions and surprises.

After his meditation, Ray, Zara, Mona, Derick, and Gelzek gathered around a conference table.

Ray had called this meeting of everyone on the ship, currently, to begin a plan for restoring Zarnia to a state of health. "OK," he said, "We need a plan. Someone must solve the wobble problem on Zarnia. Who did it? If man caused the wobble, how can they find the answer to removing it? If a solution exists, let's get it done. I'm not a physicist. I'm a fighter. Who can take this one?"

"I'll take it," replied Derick. "I have intergalactic resources at my disposal. Maybe I can find the right person. The problem is that communications take so long that resulting information may be worthless once we get it."

Zara said, "OK, Derick, when the rest of the Zarnians return to the ship, I'll introduce you to them, and we may find help amongst them. In the meantime, we must head back to Zarnia to look for ourselves. I will communicate back as soon as this meeting is over to start those physically on the planet Zarnia looking for something, even though we don't know what the something is! The problem is that my message will get there only a bit ahead of us."

Mona said, "What can I do? I've spent my adult work life teaching history. I want to help, but I can't figure out how. It is just not coming to me."

Ray said, "Just stay with us, and maybe something will occur to you. Okay?"

Mona replied, "Okay."

"What about me?" asked Gelzek.

Zara and Ray in unison replied, "The same thing that Mona is doing. Something will occur to you or us."

Ray added, "Colonel Roger Battier is locating volunteers from Earth to join our crew. What criteria can we use to pick these folks?"

Mona said, "Let me provide them with a standard set of questions, and we can all review the answers together to pick the ones that might help. I'll develop the question form, and all of us can add or subtract from it. The questions will be online a few hours from now."

Ray said, "Good idea. Okay, let's get back together in two hours."

Everyone walked away with a very positive attitude.

Ray and Zara silently walked back to her room entered and closed the door. Once in with the door closed, Ray said, "What have we done?"

Zara replied, "We made mad passionate love. It was a good thing. The emotional release with each other was just what we both needed. During that battle, I learned to trust you. That, for me, was the first step toward our love making. I'm not ashamed that I look forward to more."

Then he looked into Zara's eyes with a question. She looked back with the answer he wanted. They embraced with a bond of loving trust and passion. Ray said to Zara, "You are filling the vacuum of my lost love. We should not hurry. We should learn all about each other. We should experience the vacuum filling with our togetherness."

Zara said, "Ray, you are such a romantic and I, in a very practical sense, enjoyed our orgasmic experiences together. Now, there is no one else in my life, but let's be practical. Our lives may be very short if we cannot resolve the impending disaster on Zarnia! Let's take some time to get physical together and then get down to business! We must get back to Zarnia quickly and figure out how to save the planet. I love you."

Ray said, "And I love you. Are the repairs to the ship complete and is everyone on board? If so, let's do what you said."

Zara said, "Yes, to both questions. Captain Damara, who has finally separated himself from his body-painting friends, will take control of the ship until we are in a combat situation. Then, he will hand over the controls to you. Also, you should teach him everything you know about the automation. Make sense?"

"Yes," replied Ray. "That is a good plan, but I want to delay our departure to Zarnia for a day or so to check something out. I have a theory about a mysterious room in my Mom and Dad's old house."

Chapter 21 – The Secret Room

Sun Chaser had been repaired and everyone on the crew, who could, had returned to the ship. The political-committee people, however, would remain at their locations around the world to finish their analysis. The new knowledge that their planet may not be in permanent peril gave the Zarnian people hope that they could reverse the wobble in their planet and live there for the foreseeable future. However, if they could not restore the health of Zarnia, then the study would be completed so that the first plan of moving some of the population to Starlight could be completed successfully. Everyone hoped that another few planets had been discovered by the other Zarnian ships that were either underpopulated or ready to take on Zarnian people regardless of overpopulation. They would not know until all the ships had returned to Zarnia.

Because the political committee would not be returning, plenty of room on the ship could be used for Earth citizens to go along. Planetary physicists with the knowledge to help find a solution to Zarnia's axis wobble issue were asked to go along.

Colonel Roger Battier had made good on his promise to organize the Zarnian resources on Key West. His command had given him anything he wanted to get the job done, and Roger located all the wild and crazy Zarnian crew on Key West. He explained all about the current Zarnian situation. Roger found Captain Damara first. The captain and his two

body-painting experts had found an inexpensive house at the Truman complex on Front Street. From that location, they hosted a series of non-stop parties in which people came in normal bodies and left with very creatively-painted bodies.

Roger attended one party in which he isolated Captain Damara in an upstairs room long enough to explain the seriousness of the Zarnian situation. Once the captain had been completely informed, he cooperated immediately, by leaving the body painting enterprise to his two female associates.

Roger and the captain then organized a team of US servicemen to locate and explain everything to the remaining Sun Chaser crew. Everyone rode the catamaran to the Dry Tortugas to get to and board the ship now sitting in Fort Jefferson.

Captain Damara gave the orders the next morning to begin the flight from Fort Jefferson to Bathtub Beach so Ray and Zara could follow up on Ray's hunch about the secret room in his Mom and Dad's house.

The battle in the skies above Earth had been watched by everyone on earth. Some witnessed only a fiery object falling from the sky. Some, with telescopes, saw more. The news media had received many recordings from many sources and had their own recordings.

Roger had put everything from Sun Chaser's battle cameras and various meetings on the ship on YouTube. He and Zara posted their own explanations of the Zarnian people and their quest to either save their planet or find another planet to inhabit.

So, everyone on Earth knew about Sun Chaser and trusted the Zarnian people, so they had no problems landing offshore at Bathtub Beach. In fact, while Ray and Zara took the PASSA to the old house, many on the ship spent the time fishing from the ship.

While the Sun Chaser sat offshore a huge raft up occurred with hundreds of small boats tied together in a parked flotilla of party people. When the Sun Chaser had to leave some folks had to be shuttled to shore because they couldn't figure out how to get back to their own boats! Some folks walked aimlessly about with empty glasses on sand bars and beaches close to St. Lucie's Inlet. They were rescued by the Coast Guard who kept an observation vigil around the Sun Chaser. Eventually all boats became reunited with their owners.

In the meantime, the amphibious PASSA that had been specially built for Zara became Ray and Zara's transportation to Ray's parent's house. Once there, Ray knocked on the door, and his mother answered.

His mom, Julia, said, "Ray, I thought you were in the Keys. What happened?"

Ray replied, "Mom, I'd like you to meet Zara. Zara is from the Planet Zarnia, which I believe is your home planet. Am I correct? You have no reason to hide anything from me now. I know many of the details. I know that you and Dad came to Earth, separately, from Zarnia to help keep track of events here and report back to Zarnia. I also know that you and Dad met playing tennis, fell in love, got married, and after some difficulty had a child. The child is me. Am I correct so far?"

Julia replied, "Yes."

Ray continued, "Mom, Zara and I are trying to avoid a crisis in Zarnia. You must trust me on this. You and Dad have a room downstairs with a fake door that has another door with a lock on it. I believe that if we unlock that door, we will find something that will help us in our efforts to save Zarnia. Can you help us in any way with this?"

Julia replied, "Yes, your dad and I did not want to tell you anything, but we left Zarnia for a new life on Earth. Eventually, we lost contact with Zarnia and didn't want to risk your happiness by linking you to Zarnia. But I gather that you are in a hurry, so let me move on to the important stuff. Your dad had access and used the device downstairs. I did not. We filed our reports to Zarnia's military offices using the devices downstairs. But, only your dad has access now, and you know he can't remember a thing."

Julia led them down into the basement to open the door. They opened the sheetrock door exposing a small window on a very sturdy door.

Zara said, "What do you suppose we do with this?"

Ray said, "I don't know. My dad never admitted that he knew anything about it. I don't think he told me the truth. Did you ever hear of agents on Earth or Starlight? Maybe there is something in the Captain's log. Mom, do you have any ideas?"

Julia said, "No, I don't. I'm sorry, but I thought that part of my life had ended many years ago!"

Zara said, "I never heard of any agents already here. Let me call Gelzek and get him to patch me into the Ship's servers so that I can have access to the Captain's log." She dialed Gelzek's cell phone, and he answered. Without waiting, Zara said, "Gelzek. No time for explanations. Patch my cell phone into the ship's network. I know you have a device to do that. Quick!"

Gelzek responded in five minutes, "Done. Bye. Good Luck!"

Zara said, "Wait. Do searches on Jerry Berger, Starlight agents, Julia Berger, 1960 agents, agent communication techniques, or anything else you can think of."

Gelzek responded, "Okay, I'm on it."

Zara accessed the "Zarnian Ship's Log" app and started punching keys rapidly sounding like a machine gun. After five minutes, she said, "Okay, I have something."

Just then, Gelzek rang her phone. She answered. Gelzek said, "Agents used a long-distance communication technique, called in English, 'Turbo Access.' Engineers ran lines through the fifth dimension of the universe where time and space become irrelevant to the movement of short wave transmission and reception. I don't understand it, but a working one is on Earth, and it can be used to communicate directly to our defense center on Zarnia. Response time should be instant in each direction!"

Zara said, "I just found the same thing. Unfortunately, the damn thing has a lock on it. It's a little window that must be used to enter a password or something else to gain access."

Gelzek replied, "Yes, you need both hand prints and a retinal scan of the agent that controls it."

Ray said, "That has to be my dad, who is hospitalized with Alzheimer's. We must get him, bring him here, and use his hand prints and retinas to get access to whatever the facility is."

Zara said, "We'll go get him. In a pinch, we can fit three on the PASSA. I'll have to sit on your dad's lap on the way back, so you'll have to drive the PASSA and do whatever you do to get him out of the hospital and on the PASSA."

Ray said, "Mom, can we use your car? Can you come with us?"

Julia said, "Sure, let's go."

Zara said, "Ray, that is a much better way to go. Why do I sometimes miss the obvious?"

When they arrived at the hospital, they found Jerry Berger sitting in the corner of the main social room. He didn't move, appearing to be in a state of catatonia. No amount of encouragement seemed to get him going.

Ray said, "Hey, dad, let's get going to your house. Mom is here to see you. Don't you want to see her?"

Ray's dad did not respond.

Zara tried, "Jerry, you have to be at a meeting in an hour. Let's go." No response came back."

Ray tried, "Dad, you are the only one that can use the device down in our room. Dad, Dad, Dad, … "

Zara said, "Okay, I'm going to try something," Zara started singing while forcing a couple of shots of vodka down Jerry's inert throat,

Oh, Zarnia, Oh Zarnia,
how beautiful you are to us.
From snowy mountains, oh so high,
To fertile valleys wide and low.

Suddenly, Julia joined in followed by Jerry who smiled at her deeply,

Do not forget the crystal seas,
With sandy shores to frolic in.

Ray interrupted, smiling broadly, and said, "Thank you, Zara. All together now from the beginning,"

Everybody started singing,

Oh, Zarnia, Oh Zarnia,
how beautiful you are to us.
From snowy mountains oh so high,
to fertile valleys wide and low.
Do not forget the crystal seas,
with sandy shores to frolic in.
Steadily through dark space
We ride our magic carpet ride,
Our Magnificent Universe,
upon your body, steadfastly.
You provide us with the place,
to grow the food that nourishes us.
The people of your land guide us,
into technology that keeps us safe.
We will always care for you,
as you have always cared for us.
So, Zarnia our Zarnia,
please hear us sing to you today!

Ray added, "Dad, do you know who I am?"

Jerry replied, "Yes, Ray, I know who you are. I love that song, and I love our planet. And, who is this young lady who started our chorus?"

Zara replied, "Jerry, I am Zara, your son's good friend. We need your help. I don't understand why that anthem combined with life-giving vodka is so powerful, but I don't care. Please, Jerry, come with us and help us use the secret room in your old house. Tell us about its power. Tell us how to activate and use it."

"Hey," shouted a guard, "what did you just give him to drink? It's time for his medication, and you may have compromised his treatment if that beverage is alcoholic."

Zara said, "On second thought, let's get out of here. We don't have time to explain everything to this guy, and I suspect that your dad's drug regimen might be responsible for some of his symptoms. We need to go."

So, the four of them ran as fast as the ninety plus Jerry could run, and Ray hopped into the car first followed by Jerry with Zara and Julie helping him. As soon as their seatbelts clicked on, Ray gunned the car. The guard had taken the time to round up more guards thus losing the race to the parking lot. They trailed behind until lost in billowing dust rising in the rear window view.

As Jerry gave them the back-road directions to the house, Ray and Zara discussed Jerry's sudden change for the better by simply singing a Zarnian motivational song.

Zara whispered into Ray's ear, "I had a feeling that song might help, especially with the vodka that used to power him years ago. But, I had no idea how well it would work. By that logic, I have no idea how long it will continue to work! Again, maybe they intentionally kept him under!"

Ray said, "Well, the main thing is that we take the next step and get the lock opened. Dad simply must show his palms and his face to open the lock based on what we have learned. Then we can take the next step."

They arrived at the Berger house, ran down into the basement, opened the false sheetrock partition, and shut it behind them. Then Ray pointed Jerry to the window, and Jerry responded by putting both palms flat down on the glass and putting his nose and forehead just above his palms. Somewhere behind the glass, a light flashed.

Ray said, "Hey, Zara, do you feel what I feel and see what I see? My whole body seems to be numb or in a euphoric state of well-being and satisfaction. I see you, my dad, my mom, and me moving in dark space. There are no walls to restrict us. I see dim white streaks instead of stars against a dark sky. We must be moving at an incredible speed."

"Yes," replied Zara, "it is much the same for me."

Before any more conversation, all four stood facing a cave with rock walls, floor, and ceiling. They faced a heavy wooden desk. Behind the desk sat a large man dressed in a military uniform with medals and ribbons attached. A sign on the desk read, "General Franco."

Zara looked at Ray and said, "Ray, are we on Zarnia?"

Ray replied, "I don't think so. Look behind us. See the sheet rock wall of the house. We are coupled with the cave across space and time. General Franco, can you see and hear us?"

Franco replied, "Why son, I certainly can. And there are my good friends Julia and Jerry! It's been a very long time, hasn't it? How are you doing? Who are the two with you? Wait, she looks familiar! Young lady, are you Zara who is helping to lead our expeditionary force to Starlight?"

Zara replied, "Yes, I am!"

Franco continued, "How did you link up with Jerry and Julia? We haven't heard from them in thirty years and thought they had died! What a pleasant surprise."

Ray replied, "Sir, my name is Ray Berger, the son of Jerry and Julia. Your expedition force, through their thoroughness, located me. I knew about my parent's home and the façade that hid this special portal. My parents hadn't told me about it. I guessed."

"Franco," Zara interrupted. "let me tell you everything that has been going on, a sort of status report."

Franco listened while Zara explained everything.

Then Franco told them about everything that had transpired on Zarnia since the expedition had left. He thanked Ray for his part in destroying the four Dragoon ships and everything else he did to help Zara.

Then Zara asked the big question, "Franco, can Jerry and Julia cross this threshold and join you on Zarnia?"

Franco replied, "As a matter of fact, you cannot. This is a video and audio link only. You're going to have to travel for a year suffering all the perils of space travel. Someday maybe we will be able to dematerialize people, transmit the data and rematerialize them on the other side of their travel. Our scientists are working on the technology now. We've had some pretty ugly test cases up till now."

Ray said, "Then they need to travel on the Sun Chaser with everyone else. What can we do now to help? Is this a fixed link that we cannot bring with us on the ship? Can we move it onboard?"

Franco summoned his technical assistant Captain Huxley. "Captain, how can they move the old Dimensional Communicator for use onboard ship?"

Huxley went back to his desk and returned with a piece of paper which he lay flat on the communicator screen. "Here, take a picture of these instructions. Follow them exactly. We've had to do this only one other time, and it worked, but there are no guarantees. Besides removal and installation on board the ship, these instructions describe the calibration process which you must repeat every time you use the communicator on the moving ship."

Ray, after using his phone to take a picture, replied, "OK, if it works you will hear back from us today after we board the ship. Otherwise, we will keep trying until we either get through to you or meet you face to face on Zarnia.

"Hold on a second, it looks like we have a duplicate system here. That makes sense, I suppose. This communication would be extremely important and parts, even if available, would delay an important message if the device failed. The time to repair would certainly risk everything. There is a sheetrock partition between the two systems so, they are totally separate. We will, then, remove one and take it with us and leave the other one here. Zara, get ahold of Captain Roger Battier. See if he can fly into Stuart Airport and get over here so we can grant him access to the backup Dimensional Communicator. Then we will be able to get Earth status reports and perhaps help him and our Earth Allies."

Then Ray tested the backup DiCom, as they would call these devices for short. It worked fine.

About that time, Zara returned to say, "Roger Battier is on his way. He is already in the air and should land at Stuart Airport shortly." She raced out of the room and the house.

Ray said, "Franco, hang on for a while. We need to authorize our main contact on Earth before we let you go."

Franco replied, "Okay, I look forward to a 'face to face.'"

After the end of the conversation, they could hear voices in the room behind the sheetrock partition. A man said, "I hear them on the other side of this wall. How do we get to the room on the other side?" Others tapped on the wall at different spots. Heavy shoes could be heard walking everywhere carrying men all around looking for a way in.

In the meantime, Ray followed the removal process for the first DiCom. Once shutting it down, and sliding it out from a cement cradle, they removed it from house power. The whole unit ended up being the size of a large desktop computer. Now they had four people and the DiCom to get past their pursuers to the ship.

Ray said, "I'll call Captain Roger Battier. Maybe he can call off these guys."

Ray called Roger Battier, was patched through to Roger racing over 600 mph toward him and explained the situation. On another line, Ray could hear Roger query several people, one after another, until they could hear him begin talking to the lead guy just outside the sheetrock partition. "All set," said Roger. "I'll be there shortly."

Ray said, "OK, Zara it is safe for you to use the PASSA to pick up Roger." Zara opened the partition and blew a kiss to everyone on the way to the PASSA.

In a half hour, Zara and Roger showed up. Ray trained Roger and Franco authorized Roger to use the DiCom.

Roger said, "OK, I have clearance to do whatever you need me to do. By the way, if I ever get to hang out with Zara again, I can make her into a jet pilot. The way she drives that PASSA is an inspiration. She has the reflexes of a Karate Master! It's almost unnatural."

Ray said, "I know, she is really something. Roger, I'll contact you in a week from the ship. That should give you enough time to secure this house and make yourself comfortable. The house is yours for the foreseeable future. Please, do not share this with anyone. I trust you. Keep us informed whenever you can. Coordinate work on you own starship and include as much of the Sun Chaser technology as you can. You may need it, sooner than we think. We can help with information and training."

Their pursuers then helped transport Ray, his parents, and the DiCom to the ship. Zara left the PASSA for Roger.

With everyone assembled onboard the ship, Ray and the ship's technical staff began installing the DiCom.

Chapter 22 – Return to Zarnia

Captain Damara launched into Earth's atmosphere by focusing on Zarnia's sun and neutralizing all other gravitational influences. Slowly the ship rose from Bathtub Beach straight up to an altitude of about sixty thousand feet. Then, after leaving most of the heavy atmosphere under the ship, Captain Damara engaged high-speed drive.

Ray and a team of electronic engineers on board the ship installed the DiCom on one of the command center walls and patched it into the ship's electrical system. Ray's dad opened access and began the calibration process that he had captured on his phone.

The calibration process worked fine. It had been developed for a planet that rotated in space, revolved around the sun, in a solar system that itself traveled through the universe. A ship traveling directly toward the target location presented an easier calibration.

With the calibration completed, Ray's dad successfully began to communicate with General Franco. The technicians at Franco's location helped give Ray, Zara, and some other crew members access as well. From then on, they could communicate almost real time with Zarnia's military leadership.

The DiCom had been tested to and from Zarnia to General Franco's secure hideout in the mountains. Now, Ray and Zara decided the time had come to attempt a contact with Earth and Captain Roger Battier. They had gotten all the information they needed from General Franco and his technicians. Ray, dialed from the newly installed ship's DiCom to the backup DiCom in his parent's old house.

Captain Battier appeared on the screen. Roger said, "This location has been secured by my command and some National Guard Troops. Some fighter jets are being kept at Stuart Airport ready to scramble in seconds. Work is proceeding on Earth's Starship, called Starlight Hope, which will emulate Sun Chaser. They will name it Starlight Hope. I have been promoted to Colonel with no other responsibilities than this one.

"I have one major concern. We have had many sightings of ultra-fast, F-14 Tomcat sized UFOs. One amateur astronomer captured several clear images of these ships and their insignias. It's the same insignia every time. A woman wearing a pink-and-black-striped bikini is sitting on top of a German swastika. The inscription is, 'Herrenvolk.' When we approach within twenty miles, they race away at an incredible speed that we can barely reach. Attempts to contact them always fail. What do you think they are? Where do you think, they came from? What is their motivation? How do WWII Germany Pinups fit into anything? Are they Nazi sympathizers? Anyhow, if you have any ideas, please contact me!"

Ray said, "I sure will! I'll get some research people on it right away! These sound like the same ships that ran away as soon as we destroyed one of their ships. Based on my knowledge of history, the swastika cannot mean anything good for America."

Chapter 23 – A Terrible Step Backward

In the meantime, Ray and Zara continued their love affair, in between sessions with physicists and Earth scientists trying to determine how the planet's rotational axis could be wobbling and how to stop the wobble.

The ship had traveled about a year bringing them almost into the gravitational field of Zarnia. Zara called a meeting to discuss Zarnia's axial tilt with the expectation that someone would now have some idea what had happened.

In the main conference room on the ship, a group of scientists gathered. Some came from Earth and some from Zarnia. An air of cooperation flooded the room as the discussion began.

Ben Hagen from the United States of America said, "Did you know that the Earth wobbles on its rotational axis?" The Earthlings rotated their heads left and right uttering a "NO" or up and down uttering a "YES." The Zarnian members noticed the body language and tentatively responded the same way with all "NO" s.

Ben continued, "Yes, Earth's axial tilt moves from 22.1 degrees to 24.5 degrees over 41,000 years. Then it moves back. Other planets in our solar system have varying degrees of axial tilt. How pronounced is the axial tilt variation on Zarnia?"

Jarmon Karenin from a country on Zarnia whispered to Zara who translated to English, "Jarmon says that Zarnia's axis used to move from a tilt of 15 degrees to 18 degrees over a period of 20,000 years. One of our years is about twice one of yours, so the time is close to being the same. However, when we left Zarnia two years ago, the axis tilt moved from 2 degrees to 3 degrees in just one year. Our measurements are being broadcast to us and are now about a half year old due to the delay in a broadcast over this vast distance we are from Zarnia. However, Ray helped us use the DiCom to get the latest numbers. The data seems to indicate that the rate of wobble is consistent. The effects on climate are profound. This increase in tilt happened almost overnight. It's only after the climate change that we started looking at the axial tilt."

Ben replied, "Very interesting. Something dramatic happened to cause that change. I guess you have no idea what happened."

Zara replied for Jarmon, "We have no idea."

Ben continued, "Japan's Earthquake in 2011 changed the Earth's axial tilt by an extra 6.7 inches and then shortened Earth's wobble by 1.8 microseconds."

Derick said, "There is no way that the tilt of the Zarnian axis suddenly moved to 2 degrees per year from natural causes. That's what all of my sources are telling me."

Suddenly, the lights went out on the whole ship, and the computers went down as well. In fact, the power in the ship completely failed. None of the backup capabilities recovered even the most necessary defense systems.

Then, an explosion rocked the ship. Captain Damara realized that the ship had suffered a glancing blow from a missile. He handed the ship's controls over to Ray, "It seems we are under attack. You must take evasive action immediately."

Ray began looking at the radar which no longer functioned. Then he manually raised the nonfunctioning window television screens to uncover the ship's real windows. He didn't see anything soon enough. An explosion rocked the ship violently even though the shields had been on. They failed with the general power failure. Five people were knocked off balance. Two fell down stairs. One suffered a broken leg and the other a broken neck dying instantly.

One person working out in the ship's gym dropped a heavy bench-pressing barbell on himself crushing his chest and killing him instantly. All other injuries proved minor.

Ray reacted by putting the ship into a series of manual avoidance maneuvers which required several times the effort required of an automobile that lost its power steering capability.

Ray had not kept his vodka regimen up to date. He had not taken even the minimum amount required to keep his performance at an exceptional level. He said aloud, "Why the hell didn't our detection systems discover this alien Dragoon ship until it may have been too late."

A voice in perfect English came over the ship's intercom preceded by a healthy laugh, "I can answer that question! We tracked your progress for a day and realized that you thought all our ships had been destroyed back on Earth. You did pretty well, but this one survived!"

While the voice continued, Ray motioned for someone to get Zara and his vodka supply.

The voice continued, "First, we were able to transmit a signal to your ship that was received by one of your less-intelligent cyborgs. With our help, he figured out how to cut your power completely. You are now floating helplessly in space and will eventually enter Zarnia's gravitational field. This will cause you to fall at terminal velocity while in the thin atmosphere and eventually burn up when you slam into thicker atmosphere.

"With first cyborg's help, we have taken control of about twenty others. They are armed and guarding various parts of your—no—our ship.

"We have all of our offensive weapons systems trained on your ship. We can vaporize you all with these weapons whenever we want or deem necessary.

"So, we will simply use a tractor beam to tow you into Zarnia, if you follow us in peace. You have no choice but to give up now and live."

Ray thought, "Where is Zara. I need her, and I need my vodka power. What a stupid mistake I made. First, I didn't keep up the vodka regimen. Second, I assumed we would be unopposed for most of our journey to Zarnia."

Zara had read his mind and began to think back at him, "I'm on my way, but your vodka supply is gone. Perhaps we have a Dragoon sympathizer on board."

Ray looked over the radar and other detection systems that Sun Chaser had been equipped with. Nothing worked. He thought hard about this and Zara received his thoughts. We have no choice but to surrender."

Ray knew she was right and wished he was back in Key West with nothing else to do but eat, drink, and be merry. But he wasn't, and reality had to be reckoned with.

Ray kept thinking there must be something he could do. He yelled into the ship's non-functioning intercom, "Everyone, we are about to surrender. We have no choice. This is my blunder. I should have been more diligent."

The Dragoon representative responded, "Just don't move a muscle. We will board immediately and take control."

Ray bowed his head down. He had failed miserably and let everyone down. Just then Zara passed through the door with a crew member on either side of her. He thought, "You are so beautiful, and I love you so much. What are we going to do? I'm sure we will become slaves or worse."

Zara got the message, "I love you, too, but …"

At that moment, one of the men at her side held Zara tightly so she could not move while the other reached into her hair and seemed to push a button. Zara stiffened like a mannequin. Her thoughts had ended.

The voice from the Dragoon Ship said, "She is a cyborg, and we simply turned her off! It was simple. Only her thought processes have been shut down. All circulatory systems that support the human flesh on her are still running. We will, for the time being, continue to feed her. We will copy everything in her memory, all RAM, Hard

Drive, and cloud storage. Then we will decide whether to keep it or destroy it. Boy, did she have you fooled! All of the rest will be similarly processed."

Ray felt his pulse reach terminal velocity while adrenalin reached every cell in his body causing electric shock symptoms. His vision turned into a dark tunnel with a light at the end that shrunk quickly but not quite completely dark. He had never even thought of this possibility. She or it had been so convincing. It had been his lover. He started to vomit all over the carpeting. What did it matter at this point, anyhow? The visual tunnel opened up, and he ran as fast as he could to the first door he could see and out of the room.

During the process of installing the DiCom, he had learned of hidden passageways on the ship and ducked unseen into the first one he encountered. The doors to these passageways required facial recognition for a small and select number of crew members. He became a member of that list just a day before. He knew he would be abandoning everyone but could think of nothing else to do. He also believed that the now occupied ship would not be destroyed because the technology could be reverse engineered by the Dragoons. As he suspected some Dragoon sympathizers had snuck onto the ship and helped in the takeover. But there were few, and he figured he could get away on one of the small landing ships.

Running as fast as he could, Ray reached a juncture point in the passageway, opened a door, and entered a small eight by eight conference room. This room with four doors joined four intersecting passageways. Inside paperwork with diagrams and photographs covered a small table. This is where he and Zara spent many hours discussing Zarnia and Earth. He taught her about Earth, and she taught him about Zarnia. He paused as he thought about those happier times in contrast to the recent events now causing his facial muscles to involuntarily contort his mouth into a near crying frown.

But now he had no time to reflect. He had to be fast to escape the clutches of the Dragoons. As he passed by the table, he saw one of his vodka flasks. He picked it up, opened the cap, drank a swig of the contents, recapped it, and stuffed it in his pocket. His vodocon processed the elixir as he rushed through doors and passageways toward a promise of bitter, lonely freedom.

The secure and secret passageway only got him close to one of the landing craft. The rest of the way, in the open and guarded, presented a real problem. He had only a small laser weapon to fight with against two guards. Ray walked out of the protected passageway and crouched into a kneeling position with his laser gun ready. The two guards instantly turned toward him. Ray fired first hitting the guard to his left sending him into the air and rotating into the wall on the opposite side of the room. The guard on his right started firing at Ray who now rolled and ran in a zig-zag pattern toward the landing craft. Laser hits blasted all around him. One nicked his ear. Another burned his hip. But, his random stop and go, zig-zag track, and slow, fast movement, kept him from a serious laser hit. He made it to the landing craft and dove under it to the other side where he instantly climbed the ladder to the landing craft door. He swung it open and dove in just as the Dragoon's laser creased his head and put a hole in the landing crafts aft and forward partition. The door slammed behind him, and the whole landing craft began receiving hits which did little against a robust adamant outside skin.

Ray jumped into the captain's seat and taxied the landing craft toward the ship's door. As he turned, he fired on both guards who each, in turn, vaporized instantly. Then he blew the hatch door out and soared through it breaking the sound barrier only a mile away from the ship. He and he alone had gotten away, for now, at least!

Mona and Derick became very silent residents of a cell within an hour after witnessing many cyborgs being switched off in front of them.

Finally, Mona said, "I wonder if Lucy has any idea what just happened?"

Derick replied, "Probably not. We are out of sight and out of mind."

Mona said, "I've been wishing we were back in Key West, simply drinking and eating and drinking and eating. How foolish we have been to end up here in this predicament! Instead of our remaining life being full of eating, drinking, and being merry, we will probably be starving, thirsting, and being miserable. Ultimately, we must all pay for our decisions, good, bad, and deadly!"

They pondered that statement in silence as the ship began to move. Of course, Derick and Mona didn't know where it was going or how they fit into the plans of the Dragoon natives.

In a day or so, the Dragoon victors came to get them out of their captivity. Each had an operation which installed an implant in each of their skulls. Then after a day of healing back in their cell under mild anesthesia, both were put to work taking care of every need the Dragoon people on board required.

They waited on tables, cleaned restrooms, shined shoes, washed and ironed clothing. Mona was taken away repeatedly. She wouldn't tell Derick what they made her do, but she always washed thoroughly after returning. Daily, she became more and more depressed. Derick asked her over and over, "Are they making you perform intimate acts?"

Mona replied each time, "I don't want to talk about it. Just leave me alone."

Then one day they discovered Mona hanging from a support beam at the end of her belt. She was cold and stiff but would suffer the indignities no longer.

Without Mona, Derick simply gave up. He refused to move on his own and no longer performed any chores for the Dragoon people. He wouldn't talk, and he never ate again. One day they came and took him away. Derick never returned.

In the meantime, soon after escaping, the small landing craft captained by Ray had begun to fly erratically after reaching the lower altitudes of Zarnia. Apparently, one of the guard's lasers had hit it in a vulnerable place, before Ray had evaporated both guards.

Ray flew the landing craft as well as he could, but the engine quit just as the craft, which was totally under the influence of Zarnia's gravity, began an accelerating fall toward the planet's surface.

As the craft's speed increased, and Zarnia's atmosphere increased, heat accumulated in the heat shields. Ray deployed the emergency parachutes to reduce his speed of descent, but the heat shields had caught fire which in turn ignited the front of the craft. When flames heated the cockpit enough, Ray's feet began to burn. The smell of his smoking shoes reached his nostrils. A terribly painful death would come soon.

Ray, looked around as he thought about life, death, and the decisions in his life. He wished he had not consumed so much vodka on his first day in Key West. He wished he had somehow reconciled with Lucy. He wanted to be back in Key West, eating, drinking, dancing, and making love in Key West.

Then, as his face began to heat up, he spotted a green lever with no label on it and pulled it just because he had nothing else to do as he continued to burn from the bottom up.

He felt his seat explode under him and a whole pilot capsule blew out of the landing craft. After an agonizingly-long free fall when Ray had no idea whether the parachutes would deploy, he could see individual branches in the trees below. Finally, the parachutes did deploy jerking him violently but happily into a slowing decent. In the distance, he could see nothing but forest. The landing craft wreckage, visible miles away, burned vigorously in the thick underbrush!

Ray had never parachuted before, but on the way down, he figured out how to pull two levers inside the capsule. On lever for left and the other on the right. He guided the capsule to a clearing the size of five football fields, landing and being dragged for two hundred yards until the capsule came to rest. He was free and on his own without a clue about what to do next!

Chapter 24 – Alone and Going Places

As Ray looked around, he could see no mountains higher than the one he had landed on with the parachute capsule, and where he now stood wondering what to do next. He was at the top of the mountains and thought of the old movie, "The Sound of Music," where the hills seemed alive. He could hear Sleigh Bells, "Comeback Kid," lyrics echoing in the hills, "…You gotta try a little harder, you're the comeback kid…"

OK, if he aspired to be the comeback kid, what should he do first? Simple, he had to investigate the contents of the large survival backpack he noticed in his ejection capsule. He found the following in the backpack.

flashlight
lighter
Knife or Multi-tool
Small stove and extra gas
Water
Tent
Sleeping bag
Canned meat and vegetables
Canned eggs and milk
One aluminum pot with a pot grabber
One aluminum cup
Spoon, knife, fork

Long Nylon cord
Backup water treatment
Flashlight
Waterproof jacket with hood
Wool Knit Hat
Gloves
Hiking Boots hung off either side of pack
Socks (synthetic or wool) plus spares
Biodegradable toilet paper
Hand sanitizer
Insect repellent
Tear gas spray
Small saw
Two full vodka flasks
Hammock

He knew several key facts. One, I'm on Zarnia where I may find allies in my quest to survive and help take the planet back. Two, Sun Chaser is on the planet. He knew he could fly it if he could get back to it. Three, he had friends and his parents on that ship!

As a practical fact, he knew that the faster he got to a lower altitude, the better, except for the bounty hunters he figured he would encounter. The Dragoons would be looking for him and probably had a good fix on his location because of the landing craft wreckage. Bears might become a problem at lower altitudes. Zara had told him about the Zarnian bears. Then his inner self-buddy said to him, "How long will it take you to get over her? You may be the first man to ever fall in love with a cyborg not knowing she was a cyborg. You probably never will get over her or the fact that your sole-mate is a machine! Isn't technology wonderful? It made a fool out of you. Okay, I'll shut up so you can get on with your survival project."

So, trying to stop with the self-inflicted regrets, Ray started walking downhill all the time looking for a creek to follow. The terrain, trees, and bushes reminded him of the North Carolina mountains where he used to hike and bike. This is beautiful land he thought. He kept looking for the bounty hunters who would be looking for him. His laser gun was dead and out of power from so much use during his escape, so he had no weapon until he could figure out how to charge it. He supposed, he at least, needed a sharp stick.

He found a sturdy green branch and began to cut it from the tree. To his surprise, a small feminine voice spoke out to him, "Oh, thanks a lot, barbarous creature. That hurts so bad. Don't you think we trees can feel?" Right about then another branch whacked him in the back of the head. "There, that might teach you a lesson!"

Ray said, "I'm sorry. Trees never talked to me before. So, they never voiced their pain when I cut them down."

The tree replied, "I don't know a damn thing about trees where you come from. But, we are very intelligent and alive on this planet. Plenty of us have died of old age or lightning storms. Can't you use dead wood for your purposes?"

By now he knew the voice came from somewhere close but not the tree itself. The tree had become a ventriloquist's dummy. He played along. Ray said, "I can't believe I'm talking to a tree. Okay, I simply wanted to make a weapon from green wood so it wouldn't break in the heat of battle. That's all. I'm sorry."

The tree replied, "Look, we do not like the forces of evil that are taking over our planet. In fact, we don't ever talk to them. Work with us, and we can help you. We would love for you to help us in a war against them and return our planet to us. Please, figure out the wobble that the evil forces have installed on our planet."

Ray said, "OK, I've got a very open mind and will cease from hurting live trees. May I use dead wood for my spear?"

The ventriloquist's tree replied, "Look for a tree that is short and snarled. There is one just fifty yards toward the sun. Short and snarled indicates a cranky tree whose appendages would make great weapons. Look on the ground for a dead limb and use it for your spear. Sharpen it on both ends. That gives you more flexibility during a battle. Talk to all the trees while on your quest to overcome the evil empire. I'll pass the word all over the forest about your quest and the trees will help you when they can."

Ray said, "Thanks, and goodbye. I'll remember to ask for help along the way."

He walked the fifty yards toward the sun, found a dead limb from the short, squat tree, trimmed it, carved a point on each end, and asked the tree if everything was okay.

The tree replied, "All is okay. That was one of my favorite limbs by the way. A very big storm blew it off. Can you imagine how it would feel to have a leg blown off your body?"

Ray replied, "I'm sorry for your loss. If this limb that you so painfully lost helps me, I will come back to let you know. Maybe your sacrifice will not be in vain."

"Thanks," said the tree.

Ray began to walk downhill again, with his spear at a ready. He tried to follow valleys that would eventually lead to a stream, then a river, and then civilization.

With Zarnia's sun setting, Ray decided to camp out for the night. He found a level spot inside a group of evergreen trees. He would be hidden from anyone walking by. Ray asked the trees, "Can you please let me know if someone is approaching?"

A few trees began to speak at the same time and then backed off letting one tree speak. "OK, we will keep lookout for you. Enjoy a good night's sleep."

Ray, while in his tent, wondered what the ventriloquist did at night. He examined the fabric of the tent and realized that although it might be waterproof, it had a coarse enough weave to be partially transparent to the point where the snooping eyes of a bounty hunter could see him moving about in the tent. He shut off all lights and got a fitful night's sleep.

He woke up when the sun came up. He couldn't tell whether the sun came up in the east as it did back home, but thought it must. That voice inside him said, "Dummy! East is defined as where the sun rises at dawn!" That made sense! Ray crawled out of the tent and began making breakfast, by opening one can of steak and eggs. He added water and heated it in the pot over his camp stove. It was delicious.

Ray packed up the tent, cooking gear, sleeping bag, put the backpack on, picked up his double-pointed spear and walked out of his tree screened protected area. He caught site briefly of the ventriloquist as he did. He began walking downhill looking for a stream. He looked to his right thinking that he had heard something. When he did, he saw something. He spoke to the tree next to him, "Do you know what that is?"

The tree responded, "It is a person. I don't know what his motivation is, though."

Ray took no chances. He hid behind the tree and silently waited with his spear at the ready. The person very quietly advanced toward the tree that Ray hid behind. When he thought, the time was right Ray jumped out from behind the tree and jabbed his spear at the figure in front of him.

The figure jumped backward ten yards with amazing speed and said, "Wait, I mean you no harm! Let's talk. Okay?"

Ray put his spear down after seeing no weapon in the figure's hands. In front of him stood a man a good eight feet tall, with a beard, and long scraggly hair, who began to talk. "Look, I know who you are, and I know you have a bounty on your head which I could sorely use. But, I will pass that up because you are far too important to my home planet. You know how to win it back. So, how may I help you?"

Ray replied, "Surely, I don't know. If you have any ideas, I'm open to them. How is it that you speak my language? Come to think about it, so did the trees!"

The big guy said, "okay, you are speaking our language. How are you doing that? Wait, did you have a relationship with a cyborg? They know how to rearrange your head, so you speak and understand languages that you never have before. Just don't worry about how it is happening. We have enough problems! And what do you mean by the trees talking to you?"

Ray said, "Well, someone has been following me using trees to communicate. If you are not him, then he is still close to us. Besides that, we must avoid or beat all the bounty hunters while locating the Sun Chaser, one of Zarnia's technologically superior warships. Then we must take it over, resolve your planet's axial wobble, and free Zarnia's people. So, I think I need a better weapon, we need more men, and we must find the Sun Chaser. Got any ideas? How far from civilization are we? What is your name?"

"My name is Benumb Bulger," said Benumb. "We have about a two-day journey to my place. If we go there, then we can ask around town about strangers and then proceed from one town to the next being careful to watch for strangers."

So, Ray and Benumb walked together away from the rising sun for some time. Occasionally, a tree would comment on their progress. So, three of them hiked together. They came to a river too wide to cross on foot and walked downstream on a dirt path for several miles until the path abruptly turned right onto a narrow dirt road over a covered bridge and the river. They walked about halfway over the bridge when a couple of men climbed from opposite side of the river bank onto the dirt road and blocked their way. They both turned around at the same time and of course two men were blocking their way on the side of the bridge they had just come from. As the four men neared them slowly, Ray threw his two-pointed spear hoping to make the odds 3 to 2 instead of 4 to 2. Ray missed completely, and his spear ended up in the river.

"Benumb," Ray said, "Do you have any weapons?"

"No," he replied.

Ray said, "I noticed that they are all holding big knives. I suggest we jump into the river. Can you swim?"

"No," Benumb said, "But, I can float good, and the stream is swifter than a fast walk. By the time, they get off the bridge to chase us, we will be long gone."

So, they looked on both sides, and the men were within one step of knife range. Benumb jumped first, and Ray followed. Benumb's huge splash came up to catch Ray who then had a very soft landing. Benumb put himself in float mode, and Ray swam downstream as quickly as he could. Ray passed Benumb as he floated. The guys who were after them, or maybe just after

Ray, screamed and yelled, but, of course, Ray and Benumb were in no position to respond in any way, except by flashing the occasional obscene gesture as they outdistanced the frantically running bounty hunting thugs.

Of course, Ray noticed, Benumb's obscene gestures in Zarnian did not match Ray's in English. This fact, which occurred to Ray as he swam with the current, made him wonder. Since his verbal language translated automatically, would sign language, also, be translated automatically? This conscious wondering, Ray realized, went out on the sub-conscious network. He could expect a flash of insight sometime in the future. Ray's wondering turned into sudden concern as the river suddenly became very rough.

The river turned into rapids. The rapids flowed into a big U rock face which gave way to a spiral downslide of rock. Ray abandoned his count of the cycles when the river hurtled him off a gigantic waterfall. This turned into a thrilling ride. If he had known the eventual outcome, he would have challenged the four knives on the bridge upstream. Ray safely came to rest on the sandy banks of a pool of deep water, crawled out and waited for some sign of Benumb. He waited until dark and still no sign of him. So, Ray crawled out of the river bank and found a place to pitch his hammock.

Of course, he was lucky to have been wearing his survival backpack. It took a couple of hard shots that would have broken Ray's back. However, everything was very wet, and his stove never worked again. So, cold canned goods would be his diet until he ran out. He did have his supply of vodka which he was saving for a special need.

He slept well and then packed up everything. For a good couple of hours, he looked for signs of Benumb but saw nothing. Ray kept going back to Benumb's statement that he could not swim, but he could float. Perhaps his lack of swimming ability had killed him. Or maybe without a pack on his back he had suffered a terminal whack on the back. Whatever, Ray could not find him, so he proceeded down the road that followed the river. Ray had always been taught that when lost in the woods, follow a river downstream.

Ray had lost his double-pointed spear, so he carved a new one out of a very hard branch that had fallen from the nearby tree. He carved the branch on both sides into a point for his double-edged spear using the knife included in his backpack. While working on it, he heard a voice speak to him by name. The voice said, "Ray, you're a bit down on your luck, aren't you? Your ship is gone, both of your girls are gone, and now a new friend is gone. What's wrong with you?

Anyone who knows your history would certainly stay away from you. I'm probably the only one who might want to be your friend."

As Ray continued carving, he looked around and saw no one. "I'm over here dummy!" said the voice. "Can't you see me. I'm in the tree. If you didn't know better, you would think the tree is talking to you, wouldn't you? I fooled you good way back there on the first day, didn't I? Look carefully. Come closer."

Ray walked closer to the tree, and sure enough, a man leaning back on the tree exactly mapped the tree to his front. Only if he moved would you see him in front of the tree?

Ray said, "That is an amazing camouflage job. What is your name?"

"My name is Walkout Bellyacher. Is there something I can do to help you? I can be almost invisible in front of anything given enough time, and I can make you invisible too. It just must be planned a bit and in enough time. I use body painting technology," said Walkout.

Ray said, "Walkout, I have to find the Zarnian ship that has been captured by the alien force that now occupies this planet. I'll recognize the ship when I see it. I was the Captain when it was taken. Where is it likely to be?"

Walkout said, "Well, I'll come with you, and we can walk to the biggest city on this planet.

Its name is Chibouk and is about 100 miles away. If you are walking, that takes a long time. Maybe ten days or more. Do you have any money? We could rent an air car maybe?"

Ray said, "I have nothing."

Walkout said, "If you can ride a bicycle, we could do it in two or three days? Or if you can fly a gravity-focusing landing craft, we can be there tomorrow. I know where we can get one, and this little delight has weapon systems that might be very helpful."

Ray said, "The landing craft is the way to go. I haven't found one yet that I cannot operate. Where is it?"

Walkout said, "We have to steal it!"

Ray said, "Oh great! Maybe the owner will let us borrow it if he knows why we need it."

Walkout said, "Well, the owner is dead. Before he died, however, he hired three full-time guards, who spend all their shift time watching the craft. They get paid so well that they don't want to advise anyone that the landing craft could be sold and the owner's heirs wouldn't lose all of the money to guard the thing!"

Ray said, "One solution is to drive one of the two guards nuts so that he doesn't see what we are doing. You're good at doing that. You had me all confused when I thought the trees were talking to me! If I can put you in the correct location, so they don't see you and you just talk to the guard to distract him, then I should be able to steal the landing craft. We should catch them when they are changing shifts."

At 5:00 am two things happened near the landing craft. First, the first shift guard walked into the guard house. The two guards socialized for a time. It turned out that the two shared a pyramid marketing system that demanded constant attention. During that half hour, Walkout body painted both him and Ray to look like potted plants. Then they simply walked in, occasionally stopping, so they looked like the landscape. When the guards were only giving each other attention, Ray and Walkout moved until they entered the landing craft.

Since the landing craft was meant to be used only to shuttle people to and from an Intergalactic space ship to the ground and return to the ship immediately, there were no key locks or any other kind of security. Ray simply climbed into the pilot's seat and took off. The landing craft was identical to the one that he crashed a few days ago. Ray could see the two guards still writing and drawing as he guided the landing craft into the pre-dawn darkness.

Chibouk was 100 miles or so downstream. So, Ray followed very low over the river. This kept them out of site to most of the countryside.

Walkout commented, "What's that floating downstream. It looks like a raft shaped like a huge pile of flesh."

Ray looked and couldn't tell until he got within 10 feet of the raft. "Wait!" he said, "That is Benumb's body. We must recover it. This guy and I hiked a day together and were accosted by thugs. We fled from them together by jumping in the river. I survived, and he didn't! Walkout, can you look for something we can use as a hoist?"

As Ray hovered over Benumb's body, Walkout searched under seats and in compartments. The landing craft is small, so it didn't take long to find nothing that could be used as a hoist. Walkout said, "We are going to have to land. There is no other way. Then we'll have to tie him on somehow. He is just too big to fit in the landing craft unless he can get himself in. He looks to be over three-hundred pounds of muscle and bone. The two of us can't handle that weight."

Ray replied, "Well let's land downstream and wait for the body to get to us." Ray flew ahead about a mile or two and found a field big enough to land in. They landed, got out, and waded in shallow water with each one about one-third the distance from each side. In the distance, they could see a shape in the middle of the river which slowly became bigger and bigger bouncing a bit in the undulating water. When the body was close enough, Ray and Walkout grabbed it from either side and began pulling and pushing it toward the landing craft. When they had it grounded, and began to roll it, the body suddenly stiffened and twisted. Then it opened its mouth and uttered, "What the hell are you two doing. Let me float. I'm almost home!" Then looking in Ray's wide-open eyes, Benumb said, "Oh, I thought I lost you. What's going on, and who is this?"

A half hour later the three of them were in the landing craft and flying toward Benumb's residence. Benumb said, "My wife and I can speak to each other using only our thoughts. She is expecting us and preparing my favorite meal, roast pig stuffed with brain and other left-overs from the fridge."

Chapter 25 – Katy Bulger

Benumb's wife, Katy, although very sweet, was almost as big as he was. When they hugged, it was like the final winning touchdown in an NFL game. After dinner, they all gathered in the Bulger's living room filled with overstuffed chairs and a large coffee table in the center of the room. Benumb's chair was twice the size of the others, and Katy Bulger's chair was a half size bigger than the others. Ray and Walkout had no problem fitting in theirs. The room glowed golden from a roaring fireplace and oil lamps. Heavy drapes with floral patterns hung on all the walls, while curtains, tied back, partially covered the windows. Both Benumb and Katy puffed on long pipes filling even remote spaces in the room with smoke.

Katy brought out a carafe of her, "Special Brew," for all to sip on. Ray sipped on the brew and noticed his mind going to pieces immediately. He described it as, "A short walk in a long nightmare!" The other's felt the same way. Pieces of their day dream seemed missing.

Katy explained, "This brew helps us to dream pieces of the same prophecy. None of us has the whole thing. We must put our parts together for any sense to come out of it.

Katy said she got this message,

The problems she now suffers are man-made, like you and your friends. To resolve many wrongs that exist in the universe.

Ray said his prophecy went like this,

So, drink the vodka of Zarnia. This new you will go on and can be repaired by better men.

Benumb said,
Do not fret for Zarnia. She is a living thing with courage in limitless amounts. Zarnia will never be afraid. Do not ever quit, for the processes you undergo will become you and get on with the task.

Walkout said,

You or someone you will know can initiate that repair. Like Zarnia, you and your friends have courage in limitless amounts of repairing what has been damaged.

Ray said, "What the heck is all of that nonsense?"

Katy said, "Let's just write it down and see if we can make sense out of it later."

Walkout said, "No, let's write it down, cut out all of the words, put them in a pile, and begin making sentences until we have something that works.

As if time were of no consequence they worked on this most of the day and night while Benumb and Katy drank the special brew and smoked their pipes.

Eventually, they solved the puzzle which turned out to be an encouragement to them all.

The final prophecy went like this,

Do not fret for Zarnia. She is a living thing with courage in limitless amounts. Zarnia is not afraid. The problems she now suffers are man-made and can be repaired by better men, you and your friends. You, or someone you will know, can initiate that repair. Like Zarnia, you and your friends have courage in limitless amounts.

So, drink the vodka of Zarnia and get on with the task of repairing what has been damaged. Do not ever quit, for the processes you undergo will become you. This new you will go on to resolve many wrongs that exist in the universe or will in the future.

Ray said, "Ah, I don't know if I needed to know that or not! But, I'd like a bottle of that brew to keep with me. It might come in handy in the future. By the way, what is the vodka of Zarnia."

Benumb said, "You are drinking it."

Katy said, "We will provide you with plenty of it."

Then Katy offered Ray and Walkout pipes of their own, but both declined because there existed enough second-hand smoke to cause a three-alarm fire! After being sufficiently mellowed out by smoke and brew, they began to focus on tomorrow's mission to fly to Chibouk, locate the Sun Chaser, and steal it back. Could three people manage that mission or should they look for more team members? They decided to find the Sun Chaser and see how many people were aboard and how well guarded it was. Ray said, "Fewer people are easier to trust and coordinate. If more are needed, we must visit some local establishments looking for sympathizers, who want their planet back and are not afraid to die attempting to get it back!"

The landing craft had been hidden in Benumbs barn amongst hay, chickens, pigs, and horses. After the discussions, Ray took a very close look at the landing craft trying to understand all its controls and weapons. There were quite a few buttons and computer options that he didn't understand. The computer display had so much information on it in the Zarnian language that it seemed impossible to understand any of it.

It was one thing, in an emergency, to use this landing craft to get to Benumb's house, and another to prepare for battle. Ray needed to understand as much as possible.

Katy came outside and struggled into the landing craft to see what he was doing. Katy said, "I can translate for you. That might help. You could try to use an Internet facility to translate the whole menu system into English. Whatever doesn't translate, I can fix manually."

Ray said, "That's fabulous! But, why doesn't this menu appear to the reader in his primary language automatically?"

Katy said, "I don't know. Apparently, we need to upgrade the software. We don't want to do that, however, as it might alert the wrong people if we download the updates from the Zarnian defense server."

Ray and Katy worked on the translation all night. He found out that Katy had worked on flight and weapons system's automation for Zarnian armed forces. She knew the computer programming language for the landing craft and had some good ideas for automation on the landing craft.

They were not done in the morning, but their progress had been significant, and Ray decided that they should delay a day to complete everything he and Katy were working on. So, he told Walkout and Benumb that they would have another day before risking their lives with him and that they should use the time to prepare for the hazards they would soon face.

While all of them were at breakfast, Benumb said, "Katy, I missed you in bed last night. Is this alien from Earth trying to put moves on you?"

Katy responded, "If he did, I'd probably crush the tiny creature. You're the only one for me, big boy! However, he is not really an alien. As I understand it, his parents both originated in Zarnia."

Ray laughed and said, "While Katy is lovely, I'm only interested in her for her technical knowledge. I'm in love with another whom I found out is a cyborg from your planet, and the pirates that stole the Sun Chaser turned her off, of all things. I miss her so much, but I don't think I could love a cyborg. I think I missed her when she was a real person to me."

Katy said, "You know, while I worked on weapon and guidance systems, I knew folks in the cyborg project. Cyborgs operate like sophisticated stuntmen in movies. The Cyborg stands in to take all the physical risks for the person it represents. The cyborgs lived with the person they were modeled after for a year to learn speech, habits, knowledge, memories, value systems, morals, religious views, political views, and just about everything they could about the person they would replace on long and dangerous expeditions to other planets. So, there is a very good chance that if you fell in love with a cyborg woman, you would fall just as much if not more with the real woman the cyborg had been modeled after."

Ray said, "Wow, you have given me hope that I never would have imagined I should hope for!" Ray didn't say much more, but he ached for the possibility that there could be a real Zara that he might meet and fall in love with. He started directing thoughts to this other person. When he talked to himself, he included her. He had absolutely no feedback to suggest that he was being heard. He described his whole relationship with Zara the cyborg. Still, nothing came back.

After the second day, Ray and Katy understood all the landing craft's systems and had automated many of them. Ray figured it would be helpful to take Katy with them, but the landing craft might be too small if they found someone else to take along. Ray figured that he had learned enough from her and he needed her husband based on physical size and power, and he needed Walkout for his deception capabilities.

They left the next morning after drinking a bit of Katy's Brew, Zarnian vodka. Ray, not taking any chances, had begun his vodka regimen with his supply, in case he needed a boost in coordination and speed for a combat operation. Therefore, Ray was flying under the influence and just plain feeling great. He kept mental telepathizing to the real Zara in the hope that he could reach her.

As they flew off all of them looked back to see Katy waving from her and Benumb's little farm in the wilderness. Everybody wished they didn't have to leave. However, all realized that the wonderful life represented back there was under attack by the aliens that had taken over Zarnia. The life back there would end unless this landing craft of brave friends succeeded.

Chapter 26 – Chibouk

Chibouk lay perhaps seventy miles away straight down the river. They would be there in an hour. Ray, as he recently learned how to do, cloaked the landing craft. It looked like the sky from below and the river and land from above. The cloaking simply lets the sky imagery through from the top and the ground and river imagery through from the bottom. He had used this function on the Sun Chaser, but Katy had helped add the functionality to this landing craft.

As the miles went by more and more signs of civilization popped up. A boat or two followed by several boats followed by more and more as the river widened. The road along the river got wider, and then it became paved. Eventually, it became four lanes. They saw automobiles with advanced aerodynamics on the road, and they saw more and more flying over the roads and everywhere in general. All vehicles carried crash avoidance systems that kicked in based on the distance between and speed of approaching vehicles. The newest cars could be left to drive themselves. Benumb told them that he knew of people who sent their new car, unmanned, to pick up a friend at the spaceport.

The crash avoidance system became a lifesaver for them when a big cargo carrier decided to cross the river at the same altitude and location as the landing craft was flying mostly invisible. The cargo carrier headed right at them. Everyone flinched except the drivers of the cargo carrier who never saw the landing craft. When their avoidance system did kick in the cargo carrier drivers thought it had been an anomaly. Because of their low altitude, the system sent the cargo carrier up and to the right rather violently. They saw nothing in their way and surely talked at great length of their adventure when a malfunctioning crash avoidance system saved them from a collision with a non-existent object.

Ray said after the narrow escape, "How did the cargo carrier's guidance system 'see' us. We are invisible."

Benumb replied, "I don't know. Perhaps Katy can answer that question. Maybe it is a sonar technology that bounces sound waves off objects in front of the vehicle."

When they entered the city, the roads became three dimensional hung in the air to great heights. The raised roads were not physical roads. They were images that visually let all driver know what path cars would follow.

People could drive into buildings on almost any level and park on the same level. Ray had to be very careful to avoid roads at the higher levels.

He approached this by flying at an altitude that became higher than the highest road.

No one had any idea where the Sun Chaser was parked. No one had any idea if it was parked in Chibouk. They were going to have to land, get out, and ask questions in a way that would not arouse suspicion. Ray circled the city for some time looking for a place to land. He finally spotted a piece of undeveloped land and put the landing craft in a dive right to this piece of land. Benumb and Walkout both vomited on the way down. Ray pulled up and landed softly. They left Walkout to tend to the landing craft while Ray and Benumb walked into the first building they could find.

The plan was to let Benumb do all the talking to avoid Ray making a language mistake or some other SNAFU caused by not being a long time fluent master of the Zarnian language. The technology that took the English that Ray spoke in his head and automatically translated it to Zarnian for his vocal cords could be easily detected.

The inside of this building was loaded with shoppers who had no idea that a hick and an alien just entered their protected domain. After walking around for about fifteen minutes, Ray spotted a bar, only because a few patrons were walking out in single file with a uniformed man coaxing them out. They were being sent out of the bar for drinking two drinks for the night. Ray found out that you had to use your driver's license to buy drinks and could not drink more than two per night. There was a whole computer system to keep track of the number of drinks you had per night! That is exactly how Zara described her fellow Zarnians!

Per Benumb, however, he had ten licenses. He could then order 20 drinks per night, and no one cared. If the bar could list one valid license per two drinks, no one cared or checked.

Ray and Benumb entered the establishment called, "Frolicking Fencer." Above that inscription sat a hologram of a swordsman in drag holding a deployed laser light sword in one hand and a gigantic mug of something liquid sloshing over the mug's rim in the other. He fenced with a dragon-looking animal who had already lost a couple of limbs and part of his nose in the fight. The significance of this evaded both Ray and Benumb.

The two had walked in, separated and then sat down at the bar with a couple of seats between them. They hoped they could entice a person to sit on either side of each one of them becoming six in a row at the bar discussing some topic that eventually would lead to the subject of the Sun Chaser and her Dragoon aliens that everyone should hate. Benumb took two seats for himself. Thus, the whole troupe would take over seven seats! Eventually, people sat in the four seats that they had left opened. A woman and a man sat between Ray and Benumb with the woman next to Ray and two men on either side of them. The woman asked Ray where he was from. Ray not prepared for this question hesitated, and Benumb said, "Bounder, about 70 miles north of here. We're looking for a job working with the new government from Dragoon. Do you have any idea where we should go to apply?"

The woman furiously replied, "You traitors. Why would you volunteer to associate with those alien intruders? They took over our planet in the most insidious way. If you cooperate with them, you're as bad as they. I should hope you both die at their hands."

The inebriated guy on the other side of Ray slurred his words, "You can talk like that bar fly, but they're gonna hep us git rid of the wobble in our planet's rotational movements. They are heroes ya follow."

Ray just smiled and didn't dare talk yet. But, the man on Benumb's right said, "Well, what if they caused the wobble. Shouldn't we kill them all or at least resist. We should be able to figure out the problem ourselves, shouldn't we?"

Then the guy to Benumb's left said, "Hell, there are not that many of them. They just have four of their own ships and the one of ours that they captured. All we need is a few good and brave pilots to jump into our other ships and shoot the Dragoon ships out of the sky. In fact, I'll bet one good crew that recaptures our own Sun Chaser could put them all out of the sky. Then we'd be free again."

Ray couldn't help himself asking, "Do you know where the Sun Chaser is right now?"

Benumb's left said, "Hey mister you sure do sound funny. Where ya from?" Then he began to whisper. "Hey, you're not the one they're looking for, are you. The one from Earth. You got a million-dollar bounty on your head. Boy, I won't tell no one. I'll bet you could take them all, from what I've heard, if you are piloting our Sun Chaser. Tell you what. I'll take you there if I can be on the ship when you shoot them all down."

The other three, even the woman told Ray and Benumb that they wanted to help. So, Ray invited them all to squeeze into the landing craft and have a private discussion over some of Katy's special brew, which tended to evoke the truth from most people. As instructed, they left the bar one at a time in two or three-minute intervals so as not to arouse suspicion. Then they met outside the building's door to be led to the landing craft where Walkout awaited. They all fit inside with the woman and one of the men sitting on

Benumb's lap. Then the discussion began with each person introducing him or herself.

"My name is Victoriana Butanoate from right here in this beautiful city until the Dragoons showed up. I'm a sort of chef who can make wonderful tasting desserts. Sometimes, for special events, I mix in some very active ingredients with special properties that can cause very desirable effects on the consumers. I defined desirable as whoever is purchasing my services. This could be the ones consuming or the ones plotting against the consumers. You tell me the results you desire, and I'll make them happen. I am only awake for 20 hours a day. Time up." Victoriana, suddenly, was asleep on Benumb's lap.

"My name is Collegiately Devonshire from a town 50 miles south of here called Bankable. I can use a pistol faster and more accurately than most. However, what makes me special is my silent and accurate use of a slingshot. My victims hear nothing and see nothing. After I strike, they hear nothing and see nothing, forever. My price is high, but Dragoons are on special forever."

"My name is Baklawa Goldendale from right here. That's my apartment over there. I can solve any puzzle known to Zarnian people and possibly other planets as well. Whatever I can do to defeat the Dragoons, I will gladly do! Unfortunately, the easier the puzzle, the more time it takes to solve. That may seem weird and non-intuitive, but that has been my experience."

"My name is Parathas Languor, and I can time travel. I live nowhere. I have no known birth date because time is irrelevant to me. Living for today is meaningless. My age is meaningless. While the time is irrelevant to me, the place is not. I have a machine that amplifies my time travel abilities. Without the machine, I can travel alone in time. With it, I can bring others with me including the surrounding structures. All Dragoons should be transported to our sun for processing!"

"My name is Benumþ Bulger, and I'm big and tough. I am immortal. For example, I broke my back recently while floating over a waterfall and drowned. In twenty-four hours, my spirit reentered my body, and I was again alive and well, floating down the same river. Dragoons must go."

"My name is Walkout Bellyacher. I am a body painting expert. With my multicolor spray paint gun, I can make your naked body invisible in front of any background. For example, Ray over here and I met when I convinced him that the tree he was near could talk. Otherwise, I'm good at fooling people. One less Dragoon never hurt anyone."

"My name is Ray Berger who until recently lived my life on Earth, a light year from here. All I wanted to do was eat, drink, and be merry. During an overdose of vodka, after many adventures and a love affair, I ended up here! It's a long story that I won't burden you with now. The right dosage of vodka makes me quick and accurate. Somehow, given half a chance I can pilot the Sun Chaser to defeat hostile ships against very tough odds.

"I would like to try my abilities against those of Collegiately. However, that is not a good idea since I don't want to waste his time and I don't want to find out I'm wrong. Using all our combined abilities, we will defeat the Dragoons and return your planet to you. Then we must get rid of the planets wobble. Only after that can I return to eat, drink, and be merry back on my own planet. Is everyone ready?"

They all replied positively except Victoriana who slept on. It was Parathas who said he could take them to the Sun Chaser. Ray started the landing craft and listened intently to Parathas. Parathas led them back to the river and south for two miles or so keeping low to avoid all elevated roads and flying traffic. Then he told Ray to follow a canal to the right for about a mile. That's when a voice came over the landing crafts intercom, "Identify yourself, please." Ray set the landing craft down in the trees, and all kept quiet. He put Walkout on the mike. Walkout said, "Hey I'm one of your landing crafts. Don't you know I'm out?"

The other end of the conversation said, "No, I don't. I've checked our log and don't see any landing craft out. Give me your serial number please."

Walkout started working the intercom controls so that feedback and crackling and other noises that he generated using his tongue, lips, and teeth made it sound like equipment failure. Then he shut the whole thing down.

Ray said, "Good move Walkout. We found out the Sun Chaser is well occupied but, in the process, strayed too close. Now, they will be looking for us. Parathas, take us back to the day they landed here."

Parathas opened what he had called his guitar case. This was not a case shaped like a guitar. It was rectangular and thicker than a normal guitar case. Inside the case was nothing that looked like a guitar. Instead, it looked more like a folded-up case made of sections of electronic gear. He slid the device carefully out of the case and set it on the ground near the landing craft. Then he pushed a button releasing one section which unfolded into a coil of springs about four feet by four feet by four feet. He pulled at this four-foot cube of spring steel until it formed into an eight-foot sphere of springs intertwined with each other in a very complex pattern of spring steel. He pulled here and there unfolding section by section of this device until it looked like a large mechanical tree about sixteen feet high. Then he pulled from one compartment of the device a foil tarp that he used to cover the device, the landing craft, and all of them. The tarp connected to a USB port on the bottom of the device. Then he connected the device with two cables to the atomic battery on the landing craft. "That's it he said. Are you all ready?"[3]

"Well," said Ray, "I suppose we'd better be ready. Let's do it before the Dragoons get here." They couldn't see them but could hear them yelling obscenities and getting closer and closer.

Parathas opened a monitor from the main unit, a keyboard, and a mouse. He started entering computer commands. For the date to go to, he entered, based on Zarnian time to go back, 9 days 11 hours 49 minutes, the exact time in the past one hour before the Sun Chaser landed in that spot. "OK, brace yourself. Sometimes the ride is very bumpy." All, took a deep breath as Parathas

---

[3] You have seen up above the reference to a USB port. I, the author have taken the liberty to use common names in technology to make this book understandable without delving into the differences in earth and Zarnian standards and architecture.

set his mind to travel and disappeared briefly. The machine kicked in and Parathas re-appeared signaling that all the rest began to travel back in time with Parathas.

Parathas had a following of people whom he regularly took into the past. He could travel alone without the elaborate machine he had just unfolded. But, to take his friends with him, he needed the "Time Travelling Amplifier."

The ride ended up being very smooth. Parathas folded up the metal tarp. When they looked for the ship and furious Dragoons, neither appeared. Parathas carefully folded up his time machine amplifier and put it back in the case.

So, everything inside the metal tarp moved in time. Everything outside the metal tarp did not move. This left a big hole in the future cut out of the three-dimension reality fabric. The future travelers had to hope that nothing filled that hole until their return. An hour passed as the ship approached and eventually landed.

Ray said, "OK, Victoriana, I see you have awakened. Walk over to that grocery store and get the ingredients for one of your delicious pies. The drug store next door can provide you with any drugs you need. Can you fix the ingredients so that those who eat the pie need, suddenly, to take a long walk away from the ship? The active ingredient must be timed to activate as soon as you get back here with us. We can watch them leaving and then travel."

"Sure," Victoriana replied.

Victoriana went after the ingredients, returned with the grocery cart as Ray suggested, and baked the pies.

Ray said, "Wait an hour and bring the pies to the Sun Chaser as a welcoming committee. This means that everyone who eats your goodies will leave the ship an hour before we arrive back here."

After an hour or so, she loaded the grocery cart and brought the pies to the ship. Victoriana said to the guards, "I'm part of the welcoming committee. We are so glad you are here to lead us into resolving our poor planet's wobble issue. We are so lucky to have such wise neighbors. Please accept, on behalf of our whole planet, these fine pies. They are made from berries grown on Zarnia. Eat them today for their freshest and best flavor. While I'm here, may I have a tour of the ship?"

Victoriana had her tour of the ship. Throughout she passed out pieces of her pie. When consumed by one, others tried. Everyone raved over the pleasant taste of the pies. She estimated that nearly everyone consumed some of her pie. Once her tour was over, she returned to the others standing near where the landing craft would be in the future.

It had taken three hours and fifteen minutes for their work in the past. With the work done Parathas used the time machine to return them to their actual time by jumping into the future to their real time. If they had done all their calculations correctly, the Sun Chaser would be much lighter in staff than before when they first landed the landing craft in the area.

In fact, the flood of Dragoons was non-existent now, and they organized to board the Sun Chaser by force if need be, believing that there were few aboard to oppose them. All of them carefully walked up to the Sun Chaser's main door, looking for a way in or a signal alert for someone to let them in. No amount of knocking or looking around the ship gave them any hope of getting into the sealed ship. Apparently, Victoriana's treats had been too effective. There was absolutely no one on the ship!

Ray said, "This might be a very simple puzzle, Baklawa, but you have to figure out how we can get in and any other combination locks or protection devices we need to bypass in order get this ship in the air and in combat. Can you do that?"

Baklawa said, "I'm working on it." After a half hour, he said, "Crap, I don't get it. I don't see what the hell is here to even work with. Until I see the puzzle, how can I solve it?"

The whole time that Baklawa moved all around the ship, Walkout stood staring at one location on the side of the ship. Finally, after Baklawa's declaration, he turned around and said, "I see something in that area of the ship. I can't explain it, and I don't know what it might be." Now, everyone looked at the area that Walkout had pointed to except Walkout who was still looking at all of them, having just addressed them with the fact that he thought he saw something.

Just then the ship's laser gun covers opened exposing all forty of the laser guns on their side of the ship. All the guns rotated left or right and raised up or down until everyone pointed at the whole team that Ray had organized. Three lasers pointed at each of them.

Victoriana yelled, "Let's get out of here. They are going to vaporize us!" She turned around to start fleeing. As she did the lasers began to power up, at first dimly, and then brighter and brighter."

Parathas said, "Ray, what should we do?"

Baklawa declared loudly, "That might be a place where a facial recognition camera allows only certain people in. That would be a big problem. None of us will match! Do we have any pictures of anyone that would be authorized to open the door to give access to everyone else? Can we get one before being vaporized?"

The device that Baklawa and Walkout saw aimed at each one of them for a second at a time and then moved to the next.

Ray said, "That is a good question. Let me try. You don't know who Zara is, but she said she gave me unlimited access to the ship. I'm not sure what the security protocols were when I flew it, but I'll bet they haven't changed at all. The Dragoons did little more than fly the ship here."

The facial recognition camera, if that's what is was, focused on Ray last. If he did not satisfy the ship's criteria, then something awful would happen. They could all hear a high-pitched whine that got louder and louder as the ship's security prepared to eradicate the intruders it faced. When the device focused on Ray, he tried moving up and down, left and right, forward and back, and the whine got louder and louder. None of them moved because they sensed that they couldn't possibly react before the lasers reached out and vaporized them.

Finally rotating his head around like a bobble-head, loose at the neck, the camera recognized Ray. He didn't know which head movement resolved the issue, but finally, he satisfied the facial recognition software and a very big door opened. As they all walked inside, the lasers dimmed, and the covers closed.

Once everyone moved inside, Ray looked around until the doors closed and stayed closed. Only someone else on the access list could have opened it again. However, if they didn't take him off, they probably didn't put their own pictures on the access list.

Chapter 27 – Preparation for Battle

Ray said, "Today we've been smiled upon. Let's make the most of it. Benumb, the immortal one, I want you to fly in formation with us. I'll give you commands depending on what happens in the battle that we are about to encounter. Keep sharp and stay close. Let the power and wisdom of our ancestors be with us."

Ray and crew in Sun Chaser followed by Benumb in the landing craft ascended through elevated roadways, around buildings, and south along the river, leaving Chibouk behind and below. Both ships moved silently with nuclear-powered gravity-focusing engines. Ray realized that he should not try to take out the four Dragoon ships without a plan and a very well-organized team. He, also, knew that within a very short time the Dragoons would be looking for Sun Chaser and them. He had to hide somewhere undetectable to put his team together. In a flash of intuition, he knew he needed Katy, Benumb's wife. She had the expertise in combat computer systems that could give them an edge.

Ray contacted Benumb in the landing craft, "Benumb, we need your wife. Pick her up and bring her to us. I'll keep you informed about our location."

Ray didn't realize that while he thought about all of this, it was like having a conversation with himself, which, via his conscious mind, tried starting a telepathic conversation with someone that might be sensitive to his telepathic wavelength. Deep down inside, he wanted it to be the real Zara if she existed.

Ray kept asking himself the question, *"How can I defeat all of the Dragoon ships. It's four to one. I know I've got to try, but how can I maximize my probability of success? If I don't act quickly, I'll lose the element of surprise. If I act too quickly, we will not be ready. Okay, there has to be a way. Is there anyone who can help me figure this out?"*

Finally, from somewhere in his head came a question in a telepathic way, "Hey, do you want some help?" The question came from a woman, at least it sounded like a woman. Telepathy is different than the subconscious network. Telepathy is a point to point communication between the sender and someone who can tune into his or her telepathic broadcast.

Ray thought, *Sure, I could always use some help. This is going to be so difficult that I can use all the help I can get. But, who, the heck, are you, haunting my thoughts?*

She replied, "What do you mean, who am I haunting your thoughts? You are the one haunting my thoughts. You started it. I have been sitting here trying to read about battle tactics and strategy, and I can sense your questions. I don't know why, but I thought I'd inquire before you make me crazy! And now you're giving me a hard time about contacting you."

Ray telepathized, "OK, it doesn't matter who started our telepathy conversation. What matters is that you are studying battle tactics. That's the information I need. Are you any good at it?"

She replied, "I said I was studying battle tactics. I didn't say I was good at it. How does one, he or she, get good at something if he or she has never, actually done the something?"

Ray telepathized, "I have been in one battle with this ship and won. So, I have some success, and you have some knowledge on the subject. With your help, I should be better off, at a minimum. Look, I have a whole team, a team with special attributes that might help. Why not you, too? Can I come to get you somewhere? Or can you come to us somewhere?"

She replied, "I live on the planet Zarnia. Do you know where the town of Slazenger is?"

Ray replied, "No. I have to add that my ship is bigger than three football fields. It needs to be hidden. Never mind, I'll send a friend in my landing craft to pick you up. Would you share your GPS location? Wait, do you even know what GPS data is? If you have it here, it must be called something else."

She interrupted his thoughts, "Yes, I know what GPS is. It stands for Global Positioning Satellite. Are you from the planet Starlight or Earth to the residents there? Did you get the ship you are on at GPS location, 24°36'26.33"N and 81°51'42.33"W, called the Sun Chaser?"

Ray said, "That is correct. How did you know?"

She asked, "Did you know a woman in her thirties named Zara?"

Ray replied, "Yes, how did you know?"

She replied, "Never mind. Have your friend pick me up at Chibouk, in the new establishment called, "Wobble Pot." I might have an interesting surprise for you. I'll be sitting at the end of the bar wearing a T-shirt with the inscription, 'Wobble Lots or Wobble Not at the Wobble Pot'"

Ray contacted Benumb's wife Katy and asked her to direct Benumb to the "Wobble Pot" on his way back from picking her up and to look for the T-Shirt girl at the end of the bar. "Then I'll meet you somewhere where we can hide the Sun Chaser, the landing craft, and all of us until we have a battle plan that will work."

Benumb said, "How about if you circle around to just west of Chibouk and then head due west for eighty miles. Land in the very large and deep canyon on that spot, and I'll catch up with you there. Make sure you are fully cloaked top and bottom."

The Sun Chaser found the canyon and landed seemingly undetected. Then the landing craft showed up with the mystery woman. Ray had Benumb fly the landing craft into the Sun Chaser and dock it there. That way they could, at a moment's notice, take off with everybody on board. From the top, the Sun Chaser looked like the bottom of the canyon complete with a river flowing through it. It was a seamless cloaking. Electronic means of detecting it were thwarted by the high canyon sides. Detection from straight up over the Sun Chaser would be difficult because of the scrambling beam being used, and the ever-ready missiles and lasers pointed straight up.

Everyone would meet in the central conference room to begin planning and learning about each other. Ray and the team that had been on Sun Chaser arrived first. Then Benumb let the mystery woman walk in, in front of him. Ray looked at her, now wearing a tight T-Shirt with "Starlight Prep Team" written on it. Ray read the shirt, studied her face, and gasped.

Ray choked out, "Zara!"

She said, "I'm not the Zara you knew back on your Earth. She is a cyborg meant to protect me from harm. While she fulfilled my duties on Earth, I remained here safe and sound. I, also, am called Zara, but when I talked to her I called her Zara Cyborg, and she called me Zara. I trained her for a year before her flight. Pretty much, whatever she thought or however she reacted in each situation, I would have. I'll look forward to discussing with you how she helped you or you helped her on Earth, and what her disposition is now. We have had almost no information about the project on Starlight. Everything has gone silent. Perhaps we need to cover all of what you know about the project before moving on the battle plan development.

Ray spent the next two hours explaining everything he knew, without covering the close relationship between Zara Cyborg and him. That would best be left for a private conversation with Zara.

By the time that the organizational meeting of Ray's team was over each person had the following responsibilities.

Benumb Bulger would man the landing ship, now called Stinger 1, while in battle. Everyone felt that Benumb in the landing craft could deliver decisive blows to a ship distracted by the Sun Chaser. They felt that a missile well placed could take out a Dragoon ship.

Katy Bulger was put to work immediately to automate combat processes. If a ship could simply react without human intervention, it would more quickly respond to threats and take advantage of weaknesses.

Baklawa, the puzzle solver, manned the data gathering station. He had access to all intercepted communications, and computer systems to help process that data. Systems on the ship gathered data about everything that moved around them. The closer to Sun Chaser that something moved, the more data the Sun Chaser's systems gathered. Motion data could be analyzed on any other moving object that could be tracked.

Walkout Bellyacher, the camouflaged man, was put to work looking for something to do. No one could figure out how his talents could be used other than convincing Dragoons to do something dumb in the battle. His workstation would be the immense communications desk where all contact with other ships could be controlled.

Victoriana Butanoate, the baker of fine desserts containing brain altering ingredients, was put in charge of keeping the crew fed. Ray told her to make everyone keep a positive attitude and be quick and efficient.

Collegiately Devonshire, nicknamed the Gunslinger or slingshot man, was assigned to defend the ship from onboard threats.

Parathas Languor, the time machine man, was put in charge of time travel. It was generally felt that he could redesign his time machine to include the whole Sun Chaser and it's landing craft if on board.

Cruet Roemer and Keego Owlet, who Benumb met and recruited at the Wobble Pot, would fly Stinger 2 and Stinger 3, which had been found still docked in the Sun Chaser. These two men had divulged to Benumb that they knew how to fly the landing craft like the Stingers, and could use the weapon systems.

Now, with the Stingers, the Zarnian freedom fighters had four ships to challenge the Dragoon's fleet of four. Things began to look brighter.

Ray had the whole group meet in front of the DiCom to contact General Franco in case he had intelligence data or other ideas that would be useful to them in the upcoming battle.

Ray had thought about his parents and feared that they had perished after the ship had been taken over. Luckily, he had the authorization to use the DiCom. After letting the DiCom read his facial features and hands, General Franco appeared on the screen.

Ray said, "I assume this is a secure link to your location."

Franco replied, "Yes, no problem. I thought you were lost somewhere. I heard about your daring escape from the dragoons. Your parents also escaped by avoiding some drugged pie that a resistance member passed out on the ship right after they landed. Then, as the drugs in the pie set in, and Dragoons hurriedly left the ship, your parents managed to fool one of the guards into letting them go. In fact, all our people managed to escape in the same way. Your dad and mom are in an assisted living facility on this compound. Your dad is undergoing treatment for Alzheimer's and is progressing rapidly. Apparently, the drugs the medical staff administered to him caused most of his symptoms. The vodka you administered in the absence of his drug regimen pretty much cured him. We are doing the rest here. Your mom and dad's vodocons are working just fine. They are both looking younger every day!"

Ray replied, "Oh my, that is fabulous news. Do you have any idea what happened to the cyborgs that had been deactivated?"

Franco replied, "No. Some of our survivors said they saw them destroyed. Others said they saw them reactivated to help with some technical aspects of the ship. It could be that the ones with technical knowledge were reactivated to help. The reports are not clear." Ray asked, "You said that most of our people escaped when the Dragoons abandoned the ship. What about Derick and Mona Clark. Do you have any status on them?"

Franco replied, "Yes, and it's very bad news. The Dragoons used Mona as a sex slave. To escape she committed suicide by hanging herself with her own scarf. Derick, without Mono, simply wasted away, committing suicide in a different way."

Ray replied, "If it weren't for me, they would still be alive! How can I ever forget that fact? How can I ever forgive myself for bringing them to this dangerous place? The universe lost so much when they died. It's tough to believe that we have no way to ever exchange ideas and conversation with them again. It's tough to believe that they are not in another place where beauty abounds, and we can join them again when our lives are over. We must stop injustices like this forever. We are making a good beginning by taking back Zarnia from the Dragoons."

Ray then explained the whole battle plan to Franco to get his feedback. Pretty much they agreed. Franco said that some of the other ships modeled after the Sun Chaser were on their way back and could help if they got back in time. All the other ships had DiCom devices installed as standard equipment, and he couldn't understand why the Sun Chaser hadn't had one.

Ray said, "Zara, do you have any idea?"

Zara replied, "No. It was in the plan. I don't understand why Zara Cyborg would not have known. The DiCom should have been installed on the bridge near all the other communication equipment. It should be in cabinet C4. Hold on, I'll look." Zara left and then returned. "It's there, but covered up with a piece of sheet metal on which is printed the layout of the whole ship! We know that some Dragoons snuck on the ship as crew members, but Zara Cyborg would certainly have spotted the problem. It's almost like she conspired with the Dragoons to hide the DiCom and cut off communications back home."

Ray said, "I can't believe that she conspired against the Zarnian people. The Dragoons had deactivated her before I escaped."

Zara said, "Well if we find her we can dump a trace of everything she did and knew. Then we will find out if she became a traitor! It's a mystery why no one on board the ship knew about the DiCom, even the technical people. It's as if from the very beginning the DiCom had not been included on the ship! We must find out about this, but we have other priorities now. Let's move on!" They broke communications with General Franco who wished them success.

They discussed the Vodka Paradox after the strategy session, and everybody had their optimum recommended amount of Zarnian vodka using the formula developed by their scientists. Some of the crew had never heard about this biological fact in Zarnia. Apparently, the vodocon created so much controversy that it had not been included in any biology classes. For now, the new vodka users received the least so as not to overdose. The vodka made them all very happy, philosophical, and talkative. Benumb and Katy left for their room, together, a half hour before the others did. He carried her out of the room, and both were grinning broadly. Of course, they were very well acquainted with the vodka paradox of Zarnia and adjusted their own vodka intake.

Ray walked with Zara to the room she would stay in. He asked her, "Zara, did you have any communication with Zara Cyborg your cyborg twin while she stayed on my planet Earth or at any time after she left here for Starlight?"

Zara replied, "No, we did not. They never contacted us, and we never knew why until now! Unfortunately, she did not have time to report to anyone before the ship was captured. Do you know what happened to her?"

Ray replied, "Yes, they pulled her shutoff switch, and I saw her go dead! You can imagine my surprise and my feelings when that happened. I had no idea that she was a cyborg. When it happened, my spirits went dead with her. We worked very closely together once she and I met. Then, suddenly, she left me in a most unique way, and our whole relationship became invalid by what I learned in one second!"

Zara said, "I'm so sorry. The objective of our cyborg program was to make them indistinguishable from their human hosts. I guess we succeeded. Why was she so interested in you?"

Ray said, "It turns out that your people have made numerous visits to our planet and that my parents both came from here and that I am full blooded Zarnian. I have the vodka organ or vodocon, for example, instead of an appendix. She worked with me on adjusting the dosage. I was able, with her help, to repel the first attack by the Dragoons. We were very close after that."

Zara said, "How close?"

Ray said, "I loved her very much and had left my girlfriend to continue with Zara Cyborg! We were intimate one time after the first battle with the Dragoons at Key West. After that battle success, we both could not nor did we want to control our emotions and physical attraction to each other. Can you understand how much I loved her and how much I'm attracted to you, essentially her twin? I want to be elated at your presence but can't because you are really not her. It's a major conundrum! I assume that depending on how they treated her after the shut-off, she might be able to be restored to life. But, now the woman I fell in love with is not what I thought her to be and I would not be able to continue my relationship with her. I can't even figure out how to act with you. Part of me wants to kiss you and hug you. Part of me says no. I fell in love with a cyborg! For, universe's sake, I made passionate love to a cyborg. I loved her, but I felt foolish, violated, and lost at the same time. Do you understand what I am saying and how I felt? Would you have allowed that to happen if you had known? She was supposed to think like you, right?"

Zara said, "No, I would not have let that continue if I had known. I am sorry that it happened, and I can understand how you felt. If we can find her and power her up … Well, that doesn't matter. All our cyborgs have recording devices. We can look at the recording to see what she thought, once we have our planet back. If we don't get it back, it may not matter anyway."

Chapter 28 – Battle Begins

Just then Walkout came over the intercom. "Everybody, listen. I think we've been discovered. Looking at the detection systems, I can see two large objects approaching this location! Per our erudite radar, about half the size of Sun Chaser with a vast collection of weapon systems. They are approaching from the north and south at a very slow speed. I see tiny dots approaching from all directions. I'm guessing these are observation vehicles with maybe only one person flying or they may be unmanned drones. It's a net attempting to ascertain our location. Ray, per your orders, everybody should get to their battle stations immediately."

Ray picked up the intercom microphone and said, "OK, everybody, man your battle stations as we planned in our strategy meeting. This is a little earlier than planned, but we are ready."

With the microphone off, Ray said to Zara, "You must concur with everything I do, if possible. I know you have keen tactics and a strategic mind. Zara Cyborg proved that to me. You, being the host partner of a human and cyborg pair, should be better."

Zara said, "Right on, so far. We need to get the Stingers off Sun Chaser and wait for the best time to strike. What about our automation? Can you check on that? Also, if we go undetected, I think we should wait until we initiate the action. Would it be possible to get Walkout onto one of their ships so he can be disguised as part of the ship? Then we can get all kinds of intelligence from him. You should have a small transmitter that he could use. Make sure it is encrypted and not directionally detectable."

Ray said, "OK, you are much more helpful than Zara Cyborg. Your ideas are all very good. Maybe you should be in charge."

Zara replied, "No way. We must be a team. You issue orders, and we both will think things through. The crew needs to perceive one leader."

Ray said over the intercom, "All Stingers prepare for launch. Walkout, I want you to be on Stinger 1 for possible drop off on one of the Dragoon ships. Bring your body painting kit with you. If we can get you aboard one of their ships, we want you to transmit information to us. Pick up one of the walky-talkies with you. Victoriana, I want you on Stinger 2 with the leftover desserts from the other day. You may possibly be deployed on one of their ships. Gunslinger, on that note, walk the halls looking for someone that doesn't belong and interrogate. Then, put the SOB out the space door if he or she is not one of us. Details will follow. Katy, what do you have for us regarding automation?"

Katy got on the intercom, "Most everything was already in place. I just made a few alterations. First, all the Stingers can be controlled from Sun Chaser. Second, once in the air, we can automatically maintain a safe distance from each of their major warships. I'm working on more ideas, so I'll let you know when they are working. I can only test on battle models, but this should catch 90% of any errors in my code."

Ray said over the intercom, "Okay, think, and then email any new and creative ideas to me. Use the ship's intercom to tell us of any new ideas. Zara, work with Katy on her new ideas. Two strategists are better than one!"

Ray said to Zara, "I wonder why they only sent two looking for us? Wait, I know, the other two are looking on the other side of the planet. If one pair finds us the other pair will join quickly."

Zara said, "Probably correct."

Katy said over the intercom, "Hey, let's send Stinger 1 over the horizon and attack the other pair. When the pair here decides to help the other two, we will have an easy shot at the rear of them."

Zara said, "Is there any value in waiting a bit in case they can't locate us?"

Ray said, "No, we've got them separated already. That may not happen again. Let's take out these two, right now! Benumb, in Stinger 1, figure out how to drop Walkout onto one of the ships."

Meanwhile, the Gunslinger encountered a crew member in a remote part of the ship while he looked for Dragoon insurgents. The crew member hastily walking away from him didn't look back when he said, "Wait, stop, I need to talk to you."

She paused for seconds and turned on her heal quickly and said, "Hey don't you recognize me? I'm Zara."

The Gunslinger replied, "Oh, yes, I thought you would be on the bridge by now. You'd better get going. The fun's about to begin! Everything is secure down here."

Zara hastily walked away headed toward the bridge. No sooner had she disappeared out of sight the Gunslinger received a call, "Gunslinger, this is Zara. Is everything looking good where you are?"

Gunslinger replied, "Ah, Zara, what's going on. I saw and spoke to you just a few seconds ago!"

Zara said, "I'm five minutes away on the bridge! How could I be down there too? Wait, maybe it's my cyborg twin Zara Cyborg! Chase her down and subdue her at once. Yell at her, 'Cyborg Zara Off.' Then get her up here for an interrogation."

The Gunslinger ran as fast as he could toward where he saw her last. He didn't notice the hatch slightly ajar as he ran by it. Suddenly, he felt the electric pain as a ray-gun load hit him directly in the neck. He stiffened up doing a swan dive to the floor sliding five feet. Still conscious the Gunslinger rolled over from face down bringing his slingshot around with a load of his keys ready to fire at Zara Cyborg. At the last second, she aimed the ray gun at him. With the turn of his arm and a flick of his wrist, he fired the load of keys. Zara Cyborg with her finger on the trigger screamed as the keys hit her wrist causing her to fire the ray gun scorching the wall to her left. She held on to the gun, however, because she was a cyborg and cyborgs have self-locking joints in times of crisis. She recovered instantly and steadied her aim at the Gunslinger, saying, "Drop your gun now, or I will turn you into soup."

The Gunslinger dropped his sling-shot as he experienced the novel feelings associated with someone getting the drop on him.

Zara Cyborg said, "Through the door over there."

As the Gunslinger complied by walking through the door, he yelled, "Cyborg Zara Off."

He heard the crumbling floor contact, and when he peered around the corner, Zara Cyborg lay flat on her back. He called Zara who told him to simply remove the contents of her head through the rear hatch under her hair and bring all of it to her.

The Gunslinger reached down and touched her face noticing that she still breathed. He felt for a pulse from her wrist and found one. He wondered if removing the electronic contents of her head would stop her vital functions and decided to carry her to the bridge. He would not be the one to instigate the decaying of this beautiful cyborg's human flesh. She seemed too much like a real woman – a human woman. In the heat of battle, he had killed many men, but this differed significantly and deep down inside he cared about life. Logically, it would take about the same amount of time as he hoisted Zara Cyborg onto his shoulder and carried her to the bridge.

He reached the bridge and said, "Here she is. I wanted to make sure that removing the contents of her head did not render her useless for the future. That is, kill the human cells in her."

Zara said, "She would have been okay, but perhaps this is better. 'Cyborg Zara On.'"

Zara Cyborg sprung to life, "What happened?" She looked at the Gunslinger. "Oh, you shut me off." She looked around finding Ray. "Oh, Ray, I'm sorry. They used a long-range blue-tooth connection to access my logic circuits and controlled me the minute I became coordinator of the planet Earth project."

Her head took a violent jerk, and she said with a deep male voice, "OK, we have your location now. All ships are on the way, and you will undergo a rain of firepower like you've never experienced before. We knew that we would have you once you made it back here to Zarnia. The only surprise to us came when you very resourcefully escaped."

Zara, during this diatribe, had reached in a closet for a full head covering helmet and placed it on Zara Cyborg's head. This ended the remote connection from the Dragoons and protected Zara Cyborg from further tampering. She then said to the Gunslinger, "Nice work. Keep looking. Make sure we have no more surprises like this one. Next time simply shoot to kill anyone in the hallways or a travellator." Into the intercom, she said, "There is now a curfew. Stay in your rooms. If you are seen in the hallways or in a travellator without permission, you will be shot dead on site. There will be no exceptions!"

To Ray, she said, "OK, let's use the DiCom to call General Franco and see if he can patch us through to the other ships on their way back. We need to coordinate with them and make sure none of their cyborgs are being used against them."

They did get the DiCom to communicate with all the Zarnian ships. Everyone would be there within one week. Ray said, "How can we stall for a week?"

"Easy," said Parathas. "We can go forward in time one week and change our location. I need about a half hour."

Ray said, "Get it done. One week from now we can contact the other ships and coordinate for an attack on the Dragoon ships."

Before Parathas could deploy the time machine, a missile rocked the Sun Chaser. Their position had, in fact, been pinpointed and they would be attacked from whatever Dragoon ships could reach their location with weapons. A damage report could not be performed fast enough. Parathas had to accomplish a time shift as soon as possible regardless of the consequences.

As they watched, on radar and from the bridge window, missiles raining down on them from every direction, Parathas flipped the switch.

After firing all their missiles, the Dragoons, looking on through their ship's window, saw a wall of missiles blocking their view of the Sun Chaser. Then the total detonation deafened them sending a cloud of smoke and debris into the air and over the top of the Dragoon ships.

When the debris and smoke cleared, nothing remained of the Sun Chaser. A cheer went up, and the Dragoon wine started flowing. Dragoons, almost human, had three of every body part that a Zarnian had two of. So, they celebrated by dancing on three legs and feet, holding hand in hand in hand, and singing through a mouth of three lips. The men watched the women lustily, through three eyes, gawking at their three breasts, and listening to their shouts with three ears.

What the Dragoons didn't know was that all in the Sun Chaser were safe in the same spot but one week in the future. The ship sat in a deep crater at the bottom of a canyon. The missiles they had avoided could not be avoided by the canyon. The canyon suffered.

Ray said, "That was a narrow escape! What damage did we get from that hit just before the time jump?"

"No problem," reported the structural crew.

Ray said, "OK, let's get out of here. And I hope I'm up to the challenges ahead!" Sun Chaser hovered straight up out of the crater, out of the canyon, and high enough to turn the canyon into a mere blemish to their view. Then it shot at a 45-degree angle into space and disappeared into a cloaking posture.

Zara Cyborg sat in the corner still wearing her helmet and staying out of the way and out of the action. "Ray, I remember everything. You were wonderful. I have complete confidence that you can pilot this ship successfully. You shouldn't worry. On the other hand, teaming up with more of our ships, certainly, is good insurance."

Zara replied, "Yes, I agree on both counts."

Using one DiCom, they established a real-time conference with four other ships, now located within the atmosphere of Zarnia.

Using the other DiCom, they spoke with General Franco.

Franco told them that the four Dragoon ships were moving on his command center. The sound of battle came through the DiCom channel.

Ray said, "Franco, we are on our way. Just hold on."

Franco replied, "Don't worry, we are keeping them busy."

In the meantime, Zara worked out a coordinated attack plan with the other ships. Shortly, they would have the Dragoons surrounded.

Benumb thought about that and came up with an interesting idea. *Why not set Stinger 1 to use one of the Dragoon's small craft's gravitation field for its propulsion? At a close enough range, even the small craft's weak magnetic attraction would be enough to direct Stinger 1 and its missiles. They would follow that thing like a heat-seeking missile.* He tried it, and it worked. He didn't know what they used for propulsion, but

Stinger 1 was catching them. Stinger 1 got closer and closer. Then another of the Dragoon small crafts began to approach Stinger 1. Benumb simply looped tightly from the first and came around to fire on the second. The second Dragoon missile passed Stinger 1 by inches and continued past Stinger 1 to hit the first Dragoon ship. Then Benumb's missiles hit the second Dragoon ship. While the explosions blossomed brightly, providing a diversion for all to focus on, Benumb landed on a large Dragoon vessel and latched on with Stinger 1's magnetic landing feet.

He stayed less than a minute or two while Walkout jumped out of Stinger 1 and onto the large Dragoon ship. Walkout, equipped with a breathing apparatus, his camouflage kit, a meter that could broadcast telemetry data back to Sun Chaser and a deep- space walkie-talkie, began a furious search for a way to get into the ship.

While Benumb flew off from the Dragoon Mother Ship 1 (DMS1) Walkout discovered and made his way down a grove in DMS1's outer skin. He could not be seen as he followed a depression in the ship's outer skin. Eventually, he found a pressure lock that would open a hatch to the outside. Since no one expected the ship to be entered this way, there were no security facilities, and he simply had access to all the controls.

He let himself in and waited for a couple to walk by and turn a corner in the hallway. Seeing the hallway clear in both directions, he then walked a short distance to a plain wall with a speaker on it. He deployed the telemetry meter and took all his clothes off except a pair of Speedo-type shorts and painted himself the color of the wall. The job was so good that it appeared that he disappeared. He put all his materials in a bag which he had already colored to fit in with the wall color and placed that bag at his feet. Essentially, he did disappear.

He smiled when Dragoons walked by and didn't notice him even though his smile showed on the wall. Walkout estimated that it took about one minute to paint his disguise before he began using vodka to speed things up. The time shrank when he began using vodka to increase his performance. Besides being faster, he believed the quality was much better. The seemingly living smiling wall became more jovial, as well. One couple heard the wall's chuckle and together turned toward the broad smiling wall. They stiffened, shivered, turned away, dumped the contents of their wine glasses, and hurried away. The man said, "This stuff is too strong for us!"

One time a pair of Dragoons stopped under the speaker he had stationed himself under so they could hear the commands better.

The male Dragoon said, "There he is telling us to prepare for a battle. Promises, promises. I just want to go home or kill all these smelly Zarnian animals."

The female Dragoon said, "I smell one now, but that is impossible."

The male said, "I smell one too. But where could that Zarnian animal be? Up in the ceiling maybe. No that can't be. It's solid up there. Maybe you're one, a double agent." He smiled at the other.

The female quipped, "If I were one, I'd have a lot fewer appendages, and you would not exist by now. If there is one here, he or she is invisible."

Then the captain of the ship, over the intercom said, "A Zarnian landing craft has landed on the ship after being shot down and disabled. The coward, instead of just dying, has made his way into the ship and is now thought to be on board. Be aware, and look around every corner."

The female said, "I knew I smelled one. Let's get help."

More Dragoons came looking, but in the end, they just couldn't see the stowaway. Walkout verified the functionality of the telemetry meter with Baklawa. Then he painted the level detection/walkie-talkie device to be invisible on the wall next to the speaker.

Once Walkout completed this installation, he made his way out again to the waiting Benumb, boarded the Stinger1 and did the same thing on the second ship that was close by. Benumb and Walkout were on the way to the third and fourth ship when their good fortune exhausted itself. The second Dragoon ship had fired a missile at Stinger1. The missile hit Stinger1 vaporizing it with Benumb and Walkout.

Baklawa detected the hit and explosion of Stinger1 and reported it to Ray.

Baklawa said, "Stinger1 is gone. They just blew it up with both aboard."

Ray said, "Oh no. Shit! It can't have been worth it."

Baklawa said, "It doesn't seem like it, to me either. But their lives have not been sacrificed in vain. The telemeters are returning every turn being made by both ships, as well as every other communication on board the Dragoon ships. Even when they are cloaked, we can follow them now."

Ray said to Zara, "You better talk to Katy and then the rest of the crew."

Ray opened two new windows on his computer and began following every twist and turn the two fully cloaked Dragoon ships performed.

Ray, over the intercom, said, "Okay, the two Dragoon ships that are close to us know we are near. The other two will be on the way. We have lost Stinger1 to hostile fire. Before, going down, Benumb and Walkout accomplished an extremely important task for us. We must not let them down. We are about to go offensively against these two closest Dragoon ships. By now, you know what your part of this battle will be. If you don't know, contact Zara immediately."

Ray said to Baklawa on the bridge, "Baklawa, give me a location for the first Dragoon Ship and every twist and turn it makes. This will be from "delicate" to damn-near "impossible."

Baklawa put the current location into the automation computer which would give Ray the exact location on Sun Chaser. Like a video game, the window on the captain's computer showed both Sun Chaser and the Dragoon ships that they received telemetry data for.

Ray watched carefully as the computer, in dogfight mode, moved the steering wheel and performed a loop. As he expected, he could see nothing, but the automation reacted quickly to the movements of the Dragoon ship based on the telemetry data. He had deployed all the cloaking methods at his disposal and had every reason to believe that Dragoon1 could not see him but might be able to track him using some advanced form of radar.

Just then a message came over the device that Walkout had installed on the Dragoon ships in the area. "OK, I've got him in my sites. If you do a circle around me, he'll be following you, and I'll blow him out of the atmosphere within one second. Ray, startled that the Dragoon captain would communicate battle situations over the Dragoon ship's intercom system realized why. Sun Chaser's automation did not, "hear," another ship's intercom!

Ray instinctively pulled up to avoid a missile hit that may have been fired by Dragoon2. Best of all, though, is that he had the exact location to each of the Dragoon1 and Dragoon2 ships. So, he kept going away for a few miles and then doubled back sending missiles to Dragoon1 and Dragoon2. Both missiles were designed to follow the same position location system that Ray used. However, both missed, and that made no sense at all.

Now everybody knew where everybody else was and the other two Dragoon ships must be on the way. So, Ray knew he had to get both quickly, or it would suddenly be four large ships against one. He manually flew all sorts of crazy avoidance maneuvers. They could see missiles passing by sometimes within a half mile. It would only be a matter of time before one of them hit the Sun Chaser.

Over Ray's computer came the sobbing voice of Katy Bulger. "sniff. Click on the red button on your computer screen NOW." Ray obeyed since he had no other ideas at all. Katy continued, "Zara and I put together a protocol to terminate these two (sniff) Dragoon ships. I automated it, and it has started. Hang on!"

Ray had no idea that the Sun Chaser could maneuver so violently. He, let go of the flight wheel while he and the rest of the crew performed a circus tumbling act sometimes crashing into each other or chairs and desks. During this whole time missile firings could be felt. Suddenly, the ship braked to a dead stop, paused for one second, and then continued the violent maneuvers and missile firings.

Then, they entered a slow variable series of turns and speed changes and Katy again texted him, "Ray, mission accomplished Dragoon1 and Dragoon2 have been destroyed. The protocol used both Sprint2 and Sprint3 and Sun Chaser. We could go over the battle protocol that Zara and I concocted, but there is no time. Dragoon3 and Dragoon4 are on the way to this location and fast! With these two, however, we do not have the devices on board their ships that Benumb and Walkout gave their lives to install. The standard default battle automation may work, but I suspect you'd better get ready to survive on your own for some amount of time. Zara and I are looking at the situation and I will report back as soon as I can.

But they did not have to survive on their own. Four of Zarnia's ships had reached their location. Now the odds became seven-to-two, and the battle ended within minutes. The two remaining Dragoon ships vaporized under the combined attack of five Sun Chaser class ships and the two landing crafts of Sun Chaser.

Zara Cyborg got up and slowly walked over to Ray saying, "I knew you would succeed. Our decision to include you in our plans has been totally validated. I'm glad I played a significant role in your acquisition into our crew! My role, however, is now done, and I will self-power off in the aft rooms of the ship. You can find me there if you have the need for my services again. Before I power off, I will attach myself to the automatic cyborg nourishment facilities. If the ship is kept powered up and supplied, my human parts will be maintained.

"I know I'm only a cyborg, but my systems are so advanced that I feel what humans feel. I love you very much, but obviously, cannot compare to my host sister Zara, for she is a real human through and through. I love her very much, also, and wish her all the happiness that she deserves. You two are made for each other. I know, because I am the test case that proves the point."

By then Zara had joined them and heard most of the conversation. She said, "Ray and I both owe you so much. You found him for all Zarnia, and you took the risk away from me when you journeyed to Starlight. You learned my intentions, policies, and desires, representing me accurately to the rest of mankind. You will always be my sister. Once all of the hostilities are over, and the wobble issue is resolved. the three of us will get back together and decide how our lives together will continue."

Ray said, "Zara Cyborg, I still love you. But now that love has changed significantly. I need time to decide what that means to you, me, and Zara. So, you rest until we come for you, hopefully, soon."

Ray, Zara, and Zara Cyborg group hugged for a minute then broke apart. Ray and Zara watched as Zara Cyborg walked away and disappeared from their view.

Chapter 29 – Meet the Wobbler

The Sun Chaser, Stinger2, and Stinger3 landed near Chibouk. The city had not been freed from the Dragoons. They didn't seem to know the outcome of the recent battle. The Dragoons didn't know that they had lost. So, the crew of the Sun Chaser had to begin a police operation as well as figure out the axis wobble issue the Dragoons had left them with.

They began by visiting the ousted armed forces leader at his hidden fortress in the mountains. Zara knew of his location and took Ray there in Stinger2. They were challenged when they landed.

One guard said, "Who are you? Do you have any ID?"

Zara said, "I'm Zara of the Starlight project. I know General Franco from before the project. Send him a picture of me, and he will verify my identity, and I'm sure he will want to see me."

The guard replied after sending the picture, "Franco wants to see you and the rest of your party. To be careful, you will be escorted by a few of his bodyguards."

Zara replied, "That is not a problem with any of us. We have really good news for Franco and can't wait to see him."

Ray and Zara were led through a fortified maze of solid adamant, the hardest substance known to Zarnians. After completing the maze led by three guards and followed by three guards, they reached an adamant constructed door with a combination lock of six characters. Each of the six guards had one character in the combination which they didn't ever share. One by one they entered their character which never showed. Finally, after the last character was entered the door slowly opened.

Three guards went in followed by Zara and Ray, and three guards followed. The door closed behind them locking tightly. They passed three more guards before finally reaching Franco.

Franco said, "Welcome to my home where I am a prisoner of my own people in the attempt to prolong my life until we can again be free of the oppressing Dragoons."

Zara said, "Franco, this is my friend Ray Berger, formerly of Starlight, who helped us all by learning to manage Sun Chaser in battle. We are free of the Dragoons. Sun Chaser and crew and the returned Zarnian ships have managed to destroy all the Dragoon ships. We put together a team of people, and we were victorious. The air war is over, and we don't expect that Zarnia has been receiving any more people from Dragoon, right?"

Franco interrupted, "Unfortunately for them, their planet has crashed into its own sun. This happened almost two years ago when all their ships were off chasing you! There can be no other survivors except those who were brought here before we started fighting back. Okay, so now, we must either incarcerate the other Dragoons on this planet or make them Zarnian citizens. In my opinion, we should put a very high priority on helping them become productive members of our society. I have two reasons. One, it is the humanitarian thing to do. Two, they are biologically much different from us, so their species should be preserved. Biological diversity could mean the long-term strategy for survival of intelligent life in this universe."

Ray said, "That's a great idea. If you give them an option after telling them about the rest of the Dragoons, they will pick the only safe way to go on living. If we just make an announcement, then some of the Zarnian people might take matters into their own hands! We must interrogate all of them so that we might locate the Dragoons who know how the wobble was put on this planet."

Zara said, "What if we announce that we are offering a three-year trip to Key West in Starlight. We need to pick up our research people at Starlight and get their results, so we will be going back there anyway."

Franco told them that he would announce it this way, "Dear inhabitants of Zarnia, the Dragoon leadership has decided that since their planet has been gone almost two years, with most of the population, they would like the remaining Dragoons to live in peace with us on Zarnia. We encourage all Zarnian people to help the Dragoons settle here. We are now trying to determine how to resolve the wobble in our planet's rotation. If anyone can help with that effort, please contact us immediately. Even the craziest idea may be of help. Our very survival, on this planet, may be at stake. Whoever is instrumental in developing a solution will be awarded an all-expense paid three-year vacation in Key West, Florida on the planet Starlight. One year will be spent in Key West or anywhere else on planet Starlight. One year to get there, and one year to return, will be on our new ship named the "Zarnia-Starlight Shuttle.

"The shuttle will include fine dining continuously. You set your schedule, and we will serve you. On board the ship, will be a salt-water pool, a fresh-water pool, ice skating, fencing, roller skating, water slides, and a hundred other attractions. Every attraction will provide free training to help you maximize your experience and become more physically fit in the process."

When Zara and Ray heard the announcement, they laughed at the obvious sell job for the Zarnia-Starlight Shuttle. But, after all, a free society would be blossoming here, and on the other side of the shuttle, someone would be doing the same thing in the other direction. It would be capitalism at its best.

People, immediately, started lining up at the processing headquarters in Dragoon City. Most ideas for stopping the wobble were absurd. For example,

Suggestion1, "Play some very loud music with a well-defined beat that follows exactly the wobble during planet rotation. Then tell everyone to move their hips forcefully in the opposite direction of the wobble. This will impede the wobble and eventually stop it completely."

Suggestion 2, "Use giant rockets in just the right place on the planet. Fire these rockets at just the right time and direction to slow down and stop the wobble."

Suggestion 3, "Drink vodka until the wobble, in your own mind, goes away. Then maintain that level of vodka consumption until the planet disintegrates and the wobble is no longer an issue."

Suggestion 4, "If everyone jumps up and down in synchronization with the wobble, the wobble will dampen and eventually go away entirely."

This went on and on and on. Ray and Zara kept a log of these so that someday they could publish a book with the suggestions. In the meantime, they made signs which they asked the owner of the Wobble Pot to hang in various places in his establishment.

Hundreds of Dragoons turned themselves in so that they could obtain the proper credentials establishing themselves as Zarnian citizens.

One day a small woman showed up wearing big spectacles, hearing aids, and braces on her legs. She limped into the headquarters slowly and persistently carrying over her shoulder two worn leather cases. Once at the head of the line she put one of the leather cases on the table and announced, "I am the wife of the world-renowned Dragoon physicist, Hemadico Logurton. Hemadico told me to bring these to whomever is in charge after he dies. He said that the cause of the extensive wobble is described in detail in the documents in the case I am carrying. I will leave these with you and pick up my papers if that is in line with your thinking, as well. There is nothing else on this subject at Hemadico's and my apartment. Please, read these documents carefully and implement a solution immediately. Hemadico said that there is not much time before the constantly-increasing wobble breaks the planet into pieces."

The little handicapped old woman collected her papers, put them in the second old and worn leather case, and left slowly and deliberately without the first leather burden she walked in with.

A team of physicists looked at every suggestion to make sure that if value existed, they would not rule the solution out just because of the surface explanation. When they examined the Hemadico Logurton case, they positively went berserk. This would be the first suggestion that might have some real value. They set about reading and understanding it immediately. Every physicist had a copy which he or she had been told to read in its entirety and be ready to discuss the next day.

When that day came, each physicist walked in with puzzled looks. They began the discussion by letting each person talk about the solution uninterrupted. Then they would have an open discussion.

Portbury Bromanil said, "I read the whole thing ten times. I mapped it out each of the ten times. I keep getting the equation that tells me the angle of the wobble equals the axis tilt times the distance to our sun in light years. My conclusion is that there is nothing here but a joke in these pages. There is no serious physics supplied in these documents."

Bromanil Solve said, "I get that the periodic speed of the wobble equals the average distance to our three moons times the product of pie times the ratio of D1 to D2, where D1 is a long oval diameter, and D2 is the short oval diameter. I agree with Portbury."

Blain Cravens said, "I have no idea how to interpret the part about the weight of all of the people in each hemisphere divided by the Moon 1 – Moon 2, etc. …What a mess? I agree with Bromanil and Portbury."

Blankenship Darnelly said, "Why the hell would the gravity of Starlight be proportional to the angle of our moon where $c = 25$ / distance to the reflection of a tree 100 yards from the observer? I have the same opinion as my esteemed colleagues."

Blarney Stone said, "There is definitely no correlation between the mass of Starlight and the mass of Zarnia depending on how fast the wobble period is. I've reached the same conclusion as the others."

Ray said, "There has to be something here. Why would anyone just bring nonsense to us?

Anyone in their right mind would realize that we will not award anything based on nonsense."

Zara said, "Let's get this old woman back here for an interrogation. I'll go pick her up at the address she gave us. In the meantime, would there be any value in showing this to Baklawa, our resident puzzle solver and data processor?"

Blarney said, "Well, he won't understand the physics, but neither do we. Maybe the person who understands less than we do will see something that is hidden from us."

The physicists took a break for snacks while Ray and Zara went together, in Stinger2, after the wife of Hemadico Logurton and Baklawa.

"This is crazy," said Zara. "How did we find these physicists. Is our dilemma that these guys are simply clowns trying to delay us until the planet blows apart? Or is this old lady the wife of Hemadico an impostor or idiot. But, then, why would the physicists want to ensure their own demise. For that matter, why would *anyone* want to delay the solution when delaying would mean they die along with the rest of us. It just doesn't make good logic."

Ray said, "Everything you say makes sense to me. Essentially, to paraphrase, nothing makes any sense about this. That much I get from your vocal conversation. But, I can understand your thoughts about boarding Sun Chaser and touring the universe together before this planet blows apart."

Zara said, "You know, we seem to be tuned into each other in a big way. We can have a conversation without speaking. All I must do is listen to your thoughts, and I can understand and reply. We both enjoy the challenges of space and even the excitement of combat." Then without speaking, she thought, *Each of us, on our own, has an awesome mind, but together we are the universal definition of awesome.*

Ray looked intensely into her eyes as she looked intensely into his and thought, *I agree.*

They picked up Baklawa first and then showed up unannounced at Mrs. Logurton's residence. Initially, on the way back to the conference, Ray, Zara, Mrs. Logurton and Baklawa had a conversation about everything known about the wobble. Baklawa had everything that went on so far. Then he just sat and read his copy of Hemadico Logurton's papers.

Back at the conference, Baklawa began addressing the whole meeting. "Mrs. Logurton, what is your name?"

She replied, "Salado."

Baklawa said, "Salado, was your husband afraid of something or someone?"

Salado said, "Yes, he thought that with the information he had, he would be assumed to be a threat to the Dragoon's plans. If the solution got out, what leverage would the Dragoons have over the people of Zarnia?"

Baklawa said, "So, did he take any precautions to convince the Dragoons that the solution would not be uncovered?"

Salado said, "Yes, in fact, he rewrote all of his papers and destroyed the originals."

Baklawa asked, "Did he tell you about any other documents besides the ones bound together in this leather case?"

Salado said, "Nothing else was with the documents. I printed the pages, from his computer, that I put, in that case, to make sure I gave you the latest copy."

Baklawa said, "We probably should have the computer to look at the files on the hard drive. Maybe he used some kind of encryption."

Salado said, "My husband did all of his work without a computer. He would write everything down and have me type it into the computer. What you see in those pages is exactly what I typed, for him. After he had died, I had no more use for the computer. I gave it to a young man whom I watched take out the hard drive and hand it to me. He took it without the hard drive. That was the condition I required to give it to him. He was elated to get it for school. The hard drive I destroyed."

Baklawa said, "OK, let's assume that he did not use any encryption, other than the obvious. The papers are in English a language in Starlight. Why did he write his papers in English?"

Salado said, "Zarnia did not have an exclusive on visiting Starlight. Many planets in the universe have visited there. My husband led a Dragoon expedition to Starlight in 1961 for discouraging the use of atomic weapons. The two countries that had atomic weapons, the USSR and the United States, locked themselves in a war of words and strategies involving placing Inter-Continental Ballistic Missiles pointed at each other all over the world. My husband learned English and Russian on the way over to Starlight from 1960 to 1961. He liked English the best, so English became the first layer of encryption."

Baklawa said, "I see. I did notice something when I read the documents. Every so often I noticed an error. There are some words with "ei" instead of an "ie." Sometimes an uppercase letter was in lower case. Sometimes a word was repeated. Sometimes an exclamation point replaced a question mark or the other way around. Did he make all of those mistakes?"

Salado said, "I asked him about those errors, and he told me to enter everything just the way he handed it to me."

Baklawa said, "Ah! He did his own kind of encryption. There are eight of us here. Everyone take 10 pages. There are more, but I'll do more. I want you to simply read from the originals and write to two separate documents based on the occurrence of an error or not. Does that make sense? Then we will have two documents which the physicists can read looking for wobble answers."

After about an hour they were done. Baklawa put the pages together into two documents, made 5 copies, and handed them to the physicists. As soon as they started reading, smiles appeared on all their faces.

Portbury Bromanil got the whole group of physicists together to discuss what they were reading. There was a lot of head shaking and enthusiasm going on while they discussed what they read. Finally, after about an hour, Portbury addressed the whole group of eight.

Portbury said, "The key was to read only the non-error pages. Then it all made sense. There is a mountain to the east of here, called Mount Ntiepaptle, that has a natural cave running all through it. Somewhere in that mountain is a huge nuclear device which generates power for a gigantic gravity drive array. Each system consists of an array like what you've been using to power your ships. The document describes, quantitatively, everything about that gravity drive array and its calibration. It also documents how to slowly reverse the actions in play now until the wobble is eliminated to less than what it was before the Dragoons set it up."

Ray said, "Baklawa, you are a genius! Portbury, does anything explain how to find the gravity drive array in the mountain? Will that be a problem?"

Portbury said, "No, nothing describes how to find it."

Ray said, "Zara, what do you think. I think we should go immediately in Stinger2."

Zara replied, "I agree."

They all climbed into Stinger2, including Salado and within an hour were circling the huge mountain, which had no visible means of entry. Ray guided the ship in a spiral all the way to the top of the mountain and then back to the bottom. None of them saw anything to indicate a way in.

Zara and Ray noted that this mountain seemed to be non-standard in many ways. First, the mountain looked volcanic in the shape of an inverted ice-cream cone, except there was no hole in the top where lava had at one time oozed out. Second, if it had been volcanic at some time in the past, it would be wholly unnatural for it to have caves and caverns in it. Third, it was the only mountain on Zarnia that looked anything like it did. Fourth, it just looked misplaced.

Ray radioed Parathas Languor, "Parathas, we are at Ntiepaptle Mountain. Can you join us for a trip into the past? We need you to execute the travel."

Parathas said, "Sure, I'll be there in an hour with my time machine. Keep a lookout and call me back if you don't see me in an hour."

Then Ray said, "I'll bet the entry and exit are underground. I didn't think about that until now. But, Parathas will be here shortly, and we can watch the installation in the past from a little over two years ago."

Then Ray called the Gunslinger, asking him to get over there.

Ray said while he talked to the Gunslinger, "Collegiately, we might have trouble once we enter this cave and I know of no one who can handle small arms combat better than you. Can you get over here? Bring your tactical sling shots. Silence may be important."

The Gunslinger replied, "No problem, boss. I'll be there within a half hour or so."

Everybody arrived or already sat in the ship waiting. Parathas used Stinger2's metal skin to limit the time-travel items. The whole ship and all its occupants would be going. Parathas set the past time and date to be two years, one month, and a day to make sure they had arrived before the work on the mountain started. The main thing was to make sure they could find out where the exit and entry to the caves in the mountain were. Parathas pressed the travel now button and off they went.

Salado was looking out the window at the part of the mountain that could be seen from her vantage point. As soon as the time travel completed, Salado screamed.

"What is it?" asked Ray.

"It's gone," replied Salado.

Sure enough, when Ray looked out Salado's window, the mountain of interest was gone.

They all got out of Stinger2 to look around. It took fifteen minutes for Salado to manage everything and safely get out of the ship. Then they all gawked at the area where this mountain should have been but was not.

Zara said, "When, in the mysteries of time, did this mountain get here?"

Ray said, "Did the Dragoons build it here? If they did, I guess we must wait around for a while. We meant to get here before the installation of the array of gravitational engines, and we succeeded in a way we did not expect. It should be here before the Sun Chaser returns from its ill-fated trip to Starlight. That's in less than twenty-four hours."

Everyone slept on the Stinger2 cramped into seats and a few bunks. It came as no surprise to anyone that Ray and Zara ended up in the same seat. Their excuse was that they would be up all night discussing everything that had come to pass. In fact, that's all they did as they looked into each other's eyes and talked most of the night. When daylight streamed into the ship, they awakened facing each other.

Everyone on board looked out whatever window they could. No mountain appeared. No surprise at all based on yesterday's revelation. So, they all went outside to drink their morning coffee and vodka; and think.

Zara and Ray arrived outside, each with an Expresso Martini[4]; and holding hands. Everyone took note of this but did not show any surprise. Why not was the overriding feeling. Life is short. Why shouldn't a couple show that they are a bit sweet on each other, even if they are no longer teenagers?

Ray let go of Zara's hand and said, "Something is either very wrong, or something significant is about to happen."

He didn't get the "happen" out when everyone's eyes were treated to a cone shaped object moving in a clear blue sky without the

_____

[4] 1.5 oz. Kahlua, 1 oz. Vodka, 1 oz. Espresso

associated roar from rocket engines. The cone rotated 90 degrees so that the large circular side pointed down. Curiously, it did not have smooth sides but seemed to have erosion marks all around it as if it were an old eroded mountain. As the gravity drive engine reduced the speed quietly, it became obvious that this was the mountain they had expected to find there. So, their mountain is really a ship from another planet. In a cloud of dust, it settled on the ground, and within seconds a door slid open, and a man stepped out.

Nothing about this man seemed out of place like you would expect alien life to be. Based on all the science fiction books and movies, aliens are ugly and murdering life forms. This man, who just stepped out of a flying mountain, was just an ordinary person exiting his three-thousand-foot-high mountain of a space vehicle. The door slid shut behind him leaving no visible seams. He looked their way. but they were a good mile or two east, and he probably couldn't see them at all.

Now the discussion went virile.

Ray said, "What in a black hole is that? How many Dragoons are protecting that thing?"

Zara said, "Is it armed or did they depend on their four ships that we destroyed? How do we get in?"

Salado said, "How do we find what we need to destroy it? Can we destroy the whole ugly thing?"

The Gunslinger said, "We have to surprise that bold, weird one and let him take us in under duress. If we all carry weapons with me in front, we'll do fine. We can shoot our way to the right place and destroy the gravity drive array. No problem."

Baklawa said, "But they will be defeated in two years. Maybe we can negotiate with them and save lives on both sides."

Parathas said, "Collegiately, let's try to minimize loss of life on both sides. Maybe we can talk them down. Let's go back in time to real live time now and attempt to communicate with them. If that doesn't work, we can come back. Haste makes waste."

Ray said, "I agree with Parathas."

Zara said, "Me too! Let's go back."

So, everyone labored back into the Striker2 and Parathas set the travel time to, "Real Current."

When they arrived, the mountain or ship, depending on your point of view, seemed inert. There was no way of knowing what kind of activity might be going on inside, but the thing just looked abandoned.

The Gunslinger volunteered to go and knock on the door when all other means of communication seemed to fail. The Gunslinger walked to within one-hundred yards of what everyone agreed might be the mountain's door. He pulled his slingshot from his belt, picked up a stone and placed it into the slingshot's ordinance holder which he gripped tightly in his right hand as he stretched the heavy elastic toward his eye to aim. When the slingshot rubber bands, stretched from the "Y" part of the slingshot in his left hand the full length of his arm, he let go of the stone in the ordinance holder.

The stone struck the door, and nothing happened.

The Gunslinger repeatedly shot, until he struck the door six times.

At the Stinger2, everyone saw the Gunslinger swing his pistol back and over his head like he was about to throw a football pass in a Starlight football contest. The metaphorical pass was blocked by the ship's door. At that instant, the door opened, and a man with a pistol stepped out and started shooting, firing at will.

Suddenly, a blinding flash left all witnesses retinal memory temporarily blinded. When the flash settled down to nothing, the Gunslinger had evaporated never to be seen again.

Zara said, "They must all die!"

Ray said, "Is everyone in the ship?"

"Yes," said everyone on the ship! Ray looked around and counted. Everyone was there except for the Gunslinger who had just been returned to his basic elements of creation.

Ray threw the Stinger2 into max takeoff speed, and they accelerated out of range within seconds. Rockets from the mountain fell short a safe distance away. Ray said, "OK, let's go back and get the Sun Chaser with its huge rockets and laser guns." They flew the Stinger2 right into the Sun Chaser and within seconds were in the air on their way to Ntiepaptle Mountain with malice intended. All systems were loaded and ready for Ray to use them.

Do any of you Physicists know what happens if we simply destroy that whole mountain with that fowl wobble device inside of it?

"No risk," was the reply from all five physicists. "The wobble without a wobbler will slow down fast but gradual enough to limit any planetary damage. We completed those calculations anticipating the need to just blow that mountain into cosmic dust."

Ray said, "Are you sure?"

"Well," came the reply, "Let's put it this way. If we fiddle around any longer the risk of the wobble destroying the planet is worse than vaporizing those dwellers of the evil realm!"

Ray waited no longer. He fired every missile and laser weapon at the mountain as they approached close to ten times the speed of sound. Any faster may have caused atmospheric friction. They flashed by the mountain just before it erupted in a conflagration of explosions. Not one piece could ever be found over pin point size. A pile of dust several feet high blew away slowly over the landscape and into the sky causing one of the prettiest sunsets ever seen on Zarnia.

Ray set the ship to hover, and the physicists watched their wobbling instruments log the wobble degeneration take place. As they had suggested, the wobble degradation was slow enough to allow the planet to recover gracefully without incident.

Once the lack of wobble had been detected and broadcast all over radio, TV, and loudspeakers, people danced in the streets. Freedom and safety were restored on Zarnia. The celebrations lasted for a week.

Chapter 30 – Searching

The people of Zarnia rejoiced with their freedom, and it was no secret that the two people most responsible for their freedom and their properly-functioning planet were Zara and Ray. The Zarnians were so thankful that they gave them the Sun Chaser for life. The romantic view of the pair had them traveling all over the universe in pursuit of knowledge and wherever they could help people in every corner of the universe. Ray and Zara, while tentatively accepting the Sun Chaser, did not totally embrace this idea. Heck, they weren't married. They didn't know if they wanted to spend their lives together. There was something undone between them. They hadn't been intimate. Right now, they were more like high school sweethearts from the late 1950s.

Zara and Ray became more and more fond of each other as time went by. However, they continued to avoid commitment. They both wanted to know more about how Zara Cyborg fit into both of their lives.

Cyborgs were real people in many ways. They were the integration of human flesh and advanced artificial learning and intelligence system. They even had some brain cells integrated with their hardware. Over time, it was generally accepted in the scientific community that the line between cyborgs and human beings would diminish. Someday it would be possible that real people could be produced, as adults of any age, from infants to seniors. Even before that eventuality, the significance of machine parts disappeared when a relationship occurred between a whole human and a cyborg as had happened between Ray and Zara Cyborg. Zara had her own sibling relationship with Zara Cyborg. Neither one could forget her. They had to talk to her.

Zara said, "How did you feel when you were intimate with Zara Cyborg. Did she totally satisfy you?"

Ray replied, "Well, at first, I felt like I was cheating on my girlfriend, but that went away quickly. We shared everything in the short time we knew each other, the running of the ship, the combat, our time in Key West together, the terrorist threat, sleeping together, and love making. About lovemaking, Zara Cyborg unleashed a passion in me that I have never experienced before. I'm not sure how or what she did, but the pleasure of the experience with her will never leave me. After working on the ship together and sleeping together, she and I became one, and I loved her so much, and she loved me so much. It was perfect, and she was perfect, until I found out that perfect is not necessarily perfect in this new technological universe!"

Zara said, "What do you think of me. You realize that we are sharing everything the same way you did with her, except the intimate contact. By the way, did you know that one of the biggest differences between Zara Cyborg and I is that she has no capability for reproduction? Also, she is programmed to respond in certain ways initially. Then, as time goes by, she has the capability to learn from her experiences. Intimate training is something I did not cover with her, so most of her responses with you are the initial default programming. I fear that our male programmers probably got a bit overzealous when they worked on that part of her." Zara smiled seductively!

Ray said, "What do I think of you? Well, now that you ask me, I must say that you are to me as Zara Cyborg was to me. I feel just as strongly about you as I do for her. I have the same intimate tension inside of me, but now I feel like I should wait until I finalize my relationship with Zara Cyborg before settling those desires. Also, we have never talked about your love life."

Zara said, "Well, I have none!" She smiled broadly and struck an alluring pose briefly flashing him. "If you want to satisfy that intimate tension, I am right here! There is something about you that brings out the wild side of me!"

She looked intently into his eyes noticing the desire he communicated back to her which she mirrored back to him. "I guess you like what you see. I'm not just a scientist and seeker of cosmic adventure."

Ray said, "I do like what I see. That is obvious, isn't it? However, I still think I owe it to Zara Cyborg to wait for a status on her. Even though I am a man, I was raised as a monogamous lover! I can't shake it yet, as unnatural as it may seem!"

Zara said, "Look, she is a machine no matter how you analyze your relationship with her! I'm here, and I'm real, and we are definitely locked in with each other."

Ray admitted, "Everything you say is correct, as far as I know, and above everything else, I could never go back to the way Zara Cyborg and I were before I realized that she is a cyborg. Let's go back to the ship and think on this a bit more."

Zara said, "OK, I agree. Let's go back to the ship and talk this over in private a bit." She gently grabbed his hand.

Zara Cyborg had not been forgotten, but a new intergalactic adventurous pair began a life together with the entire universe theirs to explore! No sooner did they get back to ship that the call came in on the DiCom from Roger Battier in

Stuart, Florida, USA. "Ray or Zara, what is your status. We have what may be a major problem here. Did you find any information on the pink-and-black-striped bikini symbol over a German swastika, I told you about?"

Ray and Zara rushed to the DiCom. Ray said, "Roger, what's up?"

Roger replied, "Well, this is really weird. The entire southern part of Florida witnessed what can only be described as an extra-terrestrial event of major proportions. Those F-14 Tomcat-sized UFOs began arriving in the sky early in the morning, just after sunrise, at about one per minute. There are thousands hovering at 30,000 feet. We've had no communications from them. So, we can only guess at their motivation.

"We have defensive assets in the air, but since there are no signs of aggression on their part and since we seem vastly outnumbered, we are taking no action. I fear that if they want to take over here, they can with little risk to themselves.

"I'm watching a TV station with a camera at Malory Square. The numbers of these ships seem to be increasing more and more with little indication of ending.

"Oh brother, this is really bizarre. I fear something significant is about to happen. The thousands of UFOs are positioning themselves closer and closer to each other like a hive of furious bees swarming in search of their lost hive. The individual UFOs are now linking together into one solid sphere maybe five miles in diameter.

"We have an audio-visual link to a photographer, in the Key West Shipwreck Museum. He is videoing the entire construction of this huge UFO. He is pointing his camera below now showing people, running in various directions, obviously insane with fear, and obviously without a rational way to react. Some folks are simply frozen staring at the thing. They are being run down by the mobile panicking mob. Injuries abound as the pavement turns bloody red near trampled people. Those who are still standing and moving are lining up at Key West bars. Ships are leaving the harbor as quickly as possible with collisions the rule. We are looking at some roads now. Nothing is moving with collisions clogging every road we can see through the photographer's camera.

"That super-sized UFO has taken no aggressive action yet but has caused many casualties just being there. I'm getting information now that our defense forces are preparing to fire upon the thing. I don't think that is a good idea. Either they are here in peace, or they are far too powerful to challenge. It is hard to imagine them coming in peace when they have a swastika emblem and German propaganda from WWII!

"Do you have any ideas? When can you get here?"

Ray said, "I have no ideas, but would advise that you simply wait until the intentions of this alien force are known. Then, you are probably well advised to surrender and attempt to stall. Our planet is secure now so we can head your way immediately with two other ships. But, it takes a year to get there.

"Since your communications are still running, maybe you can organize an effort for all nations on Earth to train their ICBMs on the thing's location, in case you have no other choice but to fight back."

"Zara, get the rest of our ships on a conference via this DiCom channel. Maybe we have someone, an ally perhaps that can respond more quickly than we can."

Soon there were five Zarnian mother ships on the conference getting the details of what seemed to be an attack on Earth, one of their newest allies.

Ray said, "OK, ponder hard, but please wait until I get back. I have something to do. It should take about five minutes."

Ray raced to the part of the ship that Zara Cyborg sat in shut down status. He opened the door to discover several other cyborgs all in shut down status. Then he turned a corner and came eye to eye with Zara Cyborg. She seemed dead but continued to breathe as did all the other cyborgs. He gave her the command, "Cyborg Zara power on." Zara Cyborg blinked her eyes a couple of times, recognized Ray, stood up tall on her toes, put her arms around his neck, and kissed him passionately. She had been so fast, and she had felt so good, that he almost forgot everything that was happening on the bridge.

Ray pulled away gently, saying, "Wait. We have a crisis, and I need your help, right now! Can you start the rest of these cyborgs and put them on the jobs they are trained for?"

Zara Cyborg said, "I'm sorry. Before I shut myself down, I programmed the passionate kiss to be my first response if you turned me on. And you sure did! Wow! But, I understand. I'll get everyone going. You know that intravenous drip keeps my human tissue alive, but I crave a steak and potatoes meal. I'm sure you are aware that we cyborgs have incredible digestive systems!"

Ray said, "Yes, I am aware. You can put away more than the normal female portion of wine as well! But, it's time to get down to business. I must get back on the bridge. Oh, here is a list of the people to contact. They need to get to the ship immediately. All the contact information is on the list. When everything is accomplished, come to the bridge wearing your lead hat."

Ray ran to the bridge getting next to Zara to tell her that the cyborgs would be helping with their upcoming travel.

Roger saw Ray return and said, "OK, we are holding off for now waiting for some kind of communication. We will chill out the public and wait a year for you to get here if nothing goes bad. We will unify all our countries to train their weaponry at that sphere, in case we are given no alternative."

No one else could get to Earth quicker that the Sun Chaser. So, Ray and the two Zaras provisioned the ship for a three-year-round trip to Earth.

Chapter 31 – An Unlikely Ally

Albrecht Stiefvater leads a happy and constructive life on planet Zoleron. Now, almost one-hundred years old, he maintained a very healthy physical conditioning. The health industry on Zoleron had developed methods of maximizing the longevity of its inhabitants. Some of these methods were very controversial.

Today, Albrecht, leads Zoleron's fleet of small space ships, as they assembled themselves together to form a huge sphere over southern Florida. Albrecht had a seventy-year-old score to settle that he soon would be able to fulfill. He wore a tattoo picturing a pink and black bikini-clad woman sitting on top of a German swastika with the inscription, "Herrenvolk."

Over the intercom, Albrecht said, "OK, we've delayed here long enough. Start our siege as planned, beginning with Key West."

Meanwhile, on Mallory Square, the vagrant watched as the tiny UFOs formed a gigantic sphere high above him and his Key West homeless home. He said to his, no-room roommate, "ah no who dey r n I can talk to dem! Ah, gat ta due smting bafre ats too late. A b bck. Wtch my stff."

He walked away carrying only a shoulder bag. Several blocks later he walked into a bar called, "Bill's Swill and Chill." He walked inside stepping up to the bar. "Hey, Billy, ah'll hab one a dem vardka mrtaninis, plaise."

Billy handed him a vodka martini, "That will be 4.65 cash!"

The Vagrant handed him a five-dollar bill. Billy handed him 35 cents and a small black button device. The Vagrant smiled, walked to the men's room, and entered the handicapped stall. He left the stall door ajar, stepped in front of the wall mirror, and pushed the button on the small black device. The whole wall mirror rotated 180 degrees leaving him in a room with no windows or doors or any other way in or out. He put the button in his pocket, turned around, pulled a laptop from his bag, placed it on the desk against the far wall, and ran a cable from the laptop to an electronic device nearby. Then he placed his vodka martini on the desk, opened the laptop, sat down in the desk chair, and began typing.

The Vagrant typed a text message, "Jacob, are you there?"

Jacob replied with a text message, "Yes, Vern. What's up? I haven't heard from you in a very long time."

Vern replied, "Well, the need to communicate did not present itself until now. As you should know, I'm on our favorite populated planet, Earth. When I look up at the sky, I see that the Nazi nation from planet Zoleron is forming a huge globe over southern Florida, USA. Do you know what they are up to?"

Jacob typed, "No, I do not. They have been preparing something big since about 1955 when the Nazi leaders took over the entire planet. They changed the planet's name to Zoleron, and since then they have built the technology to rival any of our more advanced planets."

Vern typed, "How can I contact the leaders of Zoleron?"

Jacob typed, "They talk to no one. I have tried repeatedly. All I get is silence! They have a history of taking over other less technologically endowed planets. You can assume that their intentions are aggressive. I don't know why they haven't started a full-fledged offensive action yet! There is no one close enough to help repel such an offensive other than the Zarnian people who are a year away!"

Vern typed, "Who do I need to speak to on Earth to find out what they know and help them if possible?"

Jacob replied, "Colonel Roger Battier at 772-546-1832."

Vern said, "OK, thanks. If anything passes by you, that can help me out with this problem, please send me an emergency message via the usual carrier pigeons. Later!"

Vern called Roger and introduced himself. "Colonel Battier, my name is Vern Talleyrand, from the Inter-Galactic Organization of Planets. For the past twenty years, I've had the pleasure of spending my days in Key West, Florida. It's a long story, but my reason for being here is to keep track of extra-terrestrial activity on Earth. I'm doing it from Key West. I can see from here the Death Star that has recently formed at a high altitude over Key West. I'm calling this collection of smaller ships a Death Star because I assume people assembling it will eventually become aggressive.[5] I understand that you are the go-to man for Earth's alien activity. We need to get together to discuss our options before hostilities commence. How and where can we physically meet."

Roger replied, "I've never heard of the Galactic Organization of Planets before. However, there are a lot of things I've learned in the last year or so. I must speak to you immediately. Please, come to my location in Stuart, Florida because we have a non-mobile communication device at this location. From here we can contact all our allied ships that belong to the planet Zarnia. Have you ever met Ray Berger?"

---

[5] See Appendix E – Death Star Architecture

Vern said, "As a matter of fact, I have. Just tell him that the vagrant is teaming up with you, ASAP! His reaction will be interesting."

Roger said, "OK, I will. Do you need transportation here? I can send a jeep that will take you to our jet port in Key West, and you can catch a flight to Stuart from there."

Vern replied, "Never mind. I've got my own small jet vehicle that I can take to Stuart." Vern checked out of, "Bill's Swill and Chill." Then he hurried back to his no-room roommate and brought him along. Their next stop took them to the Key West airport where Vern kept his jet-powered helicopter. He and his organization spent an enormous amount of money keeping his two-person helicopter and he and his no-room roommate's identity secret.

Vern's no-room roommate's name was Barnacle, and together they maintain their Earth observation point as the lowest common denominator for humanity - homeless. The feeling is the best way to observe without being seriously considered in the category of spy, is to be disguised as someone non-threatening. Even being suspected of being a spy is hazardous. So, Vern and Barnacle looked like a couple of old harmless and homeless vagrants.

Vern and Barnacle flew to Stuart. Once there, both Vern and Barnacle met with Roger who used the DiCom to contact Ray and Zara.

Roger said, "I've got a couple of volunteers who think they can help out. I don't know either of them. Maybe you do. One says he has met you before. Take a good look at him and tell me if he is an imposter or not."

Ray replied, "Yes, I know him simply as the vagrant. The other guy, I never met. What can they do for us?"

Roger said, "Vern, the vagrant, says he is a member of the Galactic Organization of Planets. Let him explain beyond that, so we both know. Vern you've got the floor!"

Vern said, "First, Barnacle and I are Senior Galactic Knights who have proven ourselves in a minimum of one-hundred battles at various planets in various solar systems in the universe. We have technological expertise in all areas of the universe and have some special powers ourselves. For example, with some minor modifications, this fifth-dimension communication device, DiCom, can be used to transport people from one place to another as easily as it transports verbal and video data. Give us a few hours, and we will show you how. We may need a few common parts that you should find on board your ship and a local electronics store for us.

Chapter 32 – Siege

Sarah, just 20 years and 1 day old, walked into the Buccaneer Beauty Boutique on Truman Avenue in Key West. She had received a gift certificate from her mom for her twentieth birthday. After handing the gift certificate to the receptionist, she went to a chair in front of a wall-to-wall mirror. The hairdresser walked up behind her and asked for an explanation of what Sarah needed for her hair.

Sarah looked in the mirror seeing herself and the hairdresser behind her so she could look at the hairdresser while explaining what had to be done to her hair. Behind the hairdresser, hung shelves lined with hairdressing products. "Just trim it a bit and use your own judgment about what else to do. And, sometimes my head seems to be non-symmetric. Can you use my haircut to disguise that problem? Are my roots starting to gray? If so, can you color my hair?"

The hairdresser smiled and said, "OK, I understand. Be right back."

Sarah saw the hairdresser turn around to go back to the supply shelves. Sarah blinked, and suddenly she saw in the mirrors' reflection a group of men in strange clothing behind her. The hairdresser and shelves of supplies had vanished. She focused forward to find the mirror, now a window, revealing another very confused woman looking back at her. Then it went black.

The hairdresser picked up a bottle of hair coloring and turned around to go back to Sarah. Sarah no longer sat on the chair. The hairdresser looked around in a panic. Where did she go? No one had seen anything!

The receptionist said, "I didn't see her leave. I'll check the restroom."

No one could find Sarah anywhere in the establishment, so they just figured she snuck out somehow and continued with their work day.

On Eaton Street at the Wooden Nickle Bar, Ben staggered into the men's room. He had left a group of friends who pumped him full of beer. Instead of mugs, they ordered pitchers for him to drink from. That is the kind of thing you do for a friend's stag party. However, pitchers of beer must come out sooner or later. Thus, the reason for Ben's trip to the men's room.

Right after Ben left for the men's room to drain the last couple of pitchers, Naughty Nicki showed up. She would be the entertainment for the night. Ben's friends had paid dearly for Naughty Nicki to perform a lap dance for Ben. After she had found out the current location of Ben, she opted for the Woman's room to relieve herself before her undulating performance.

Ben finished his urinal work and washed his hands. He glanced into the mirror to check out his hair, a flourishing black wavy arrangement which had two strands out of order. He fixed them both. Suddenly, in the mirror, Naughty Nicki's image replaced his as she adjusted her ample cleavage in her skimpy French Maid's costume. Just as suddenly he found himself standing next to her as they both looked out at a morphed image of the men's and women's room. Then everything went dark.

Out in the bar, the party began to lose momentum as two of the star performers never returned. Eventually, after checking the whole bar including the restrooms and calling both Ben and Nicki's cell phones, Ben's friends gave up and went home. Some figured that Ben received a private lap dance that evening and did not divulge a thing to Ben's fiancé.

The next day the Key West police received hundreds of missing person's calls. The day after that there were hundreds more. Then the missing person's reports began to move toward Miami from Key West hopping from Florida Key to Florida Key. Once in Miami, the reports continued in an orderly fashion north. Statisticians determined that 10% of the population disappeared before the disappearances in each area discontinued.

Panic and lawlessness resulted. Of the remaining population, 5% died at the hands of panicking mobs. The economy collapsed with people committing suicide at an alarming rate.

Christians interpreted the events as rapture or the sudden vanishing of Christians into thin air. Everyone else, left behind, should see a world gone mad. However, as we all know, madness is in the eye of the beholder. Surely, though, the world was becoming madder. A variety of disasters would begin to occur. The disappearances would begin a seven-year period called the Tribulation. A prophecy claimed that "During this panic, a man will bring order out of this chaos. However, he is evil, and the brave Tribulation Forces will resist his power."

Since the correlation between disappearing people and Christians seemed to be very low, this theory did not catch on.

As the disappearances spread the extraterrestrial Death Star began to move around the Earth like a robotic vacuum cleaner. After a week, everyone knew that the extraterrestrial aliens hovering over Earth had begun to harvest the people of Earth.

No attempts to communicate with the "Death Star" worked.

Chapter 33 – Two Zarnian Ships

Ray with his crew of Zara, Zara Cyborg, Baklawa Goldendale, Gelzek, General Franco, Katy Bulger, 100 Cyborgs, Parathas Languor, Victoriana Butanoate, Blain Cravens and others set out toward Earth as fast as possible. Two Zarnian ships, the Sun Chaser and the Moon Follower, with a total of eight heavily-armed landing crafts, shared the talented crew. They knew, however, that they would be too late. Devastation on Earth would be complete within a year, and they could not make it in less than a year. They had to figure out something unique and creative to save planet Earth from this horrifying alien force.

Before the Sun Chaser left Zarnia, the whole crew spent a day on the ship in preparation. Everyone, depending on their sleep habits, went to their assigned cabins. The cyborgs and humans shared a large room with hammocks for sleeping. The hammocks hung on three different levels, two, four, and six feet above the floor. Each person or cyborg had a gravity belt which they shut off enabling them to move up and down weightlessly. This way each could effortlessly guide him or herself into an unoccupied hammock and then turn the gravity belt back on. The hammock room provided sleeping quarters for everyone and kept the ship's space requirements to a minimum. Lockers around the hammock room kept everyone's individual possessions.

Some distinguished individuals had private cabins no bigger than eight by ten feet with a height of eight feet unless a couple shared a cabin and used a ten by twelve-foot cabin.

Katy Bulger qualified as a distinguished individual for two reasons. One, her automation computer apps had helped immeasurably to defeat the Dragoons. Two, she had lost her beloved husband Benumb in that same battle. Katy left her current automation project at 2:00 a.m. She walked to her cabin, entered, and plopped down on the double bed that she had shared with Benumb. She lay awake for some time remembering Benumb. She remembered that Benumb owned the rare property of immortality. She wondered when he would return. However, a Dragoon ship had vaporized him, and he never did return from that. She supposed that the immortal property had limits and cried herself to sleep.

Dreams often follow conscious thoughts that precede sleep. So, on this night before leaving for Earth, Katy dreamed of Benumb. In her dream, she watched Benumb's landing craft vaporize in slow motion until every bit of matter became so small it disappeared. Benumb's body vaporized separately completing a most disturbing nightmare. Katy cried in her sleep. She longed to cuddle with him but knew she never would again.

Then her nightmare took a turn, and she saw tiny clouds form in different rooms on the Sun Chaser. The tiny clouds moved down hallways and travellators toward her room. When two of these clouds collided with each other, they merged becoming denser. As this process continued, human organs formed from some of the clouds and continued moving in a macabre dancing march toward her cabin. Eventually, a likeness to Benumb's face vaguely became visible in one of the vapor clouds. From his face, formed Benumb's head which quickly attached to his newly formed neck. Then came his shoulders, torso, hips, legs, and feet. When she awoke, Benumb lay next to her smiling, "Finally, my immortal self is here beside you. The process takes time, sometimes. I've told everyone I can float. Sometimes, my body particles float until they link up and I materialize as I have just done."

No more sleep occurred in Katy and Benumb's cabin that night as Katy told Benumb what had happened in his absence for him to reunite with everyone.

The next morning a celebration to welcome Benumb back to life overshadowed the seriousness of their departure. The bad news from Earth darkened everyone's disposition.

Once underway, Ray contacted Colonel Roger Battier over the DiCom. Roger said, "Vern can describe for the Sun Chaser's engineers the changes which must be made to one of The Sun Chaser's DiComs so that humans and cyborgs can be dematerialized and travel via the fifth dimension to Earth and this location. Luckily you have two DiComs. You can listen on one and make the changes to the other. If anything goes wrong, you will still have the one DiCom to communicate with us."

Vern and Ray, aided by talented engineers, completed the changes to the backup DiCom which once had been used as a backup for the DiCom on Earth used by Ray's parents. Ray said, "OK, do we really want to use this. If so, I'll use a cyborg for testing."

Vern said, "Yes, we must use it. If we can get all of you with your many talents to this location, we can plan and then execute the plan to free Earth. Yesterday, we tried to blow the "Death Star" out of the atmosphere using nuclear missiles. It didn't work, and now we have fallout to deal with. That damn Death Star might be impenetrable."

Ray said, "You are all calling it a Death Star. Do you have any evidence that people are being killed after they are grabbed by that thing?"

Vern said, "We do not know anything about what happens to the folks that have disappeared! We do not know how the aliens grab and transport people to the Death Star. We really don't know if they ever end up *on* the Death Star. Maybe, they don't transport them but vaporize people on location. We need more information and need it quickly. Ray, who can pilot the Sun Chaser if you transport here?"

Ray said, "General Franco, can do it. Zara Cyborg has trained him as she did me and he has passed the simulation tests. Captain Damara made it off the Sun Chaser alive when the Dragoons fled, so he is the captain of the other ship, Moon Follower. Zara Cyborg, herself, is a capable captain!

"OK, let's transport Gelzek now. He has volunteered."

First, they transported a hot cup of coffee. On Sun Chaser, the entire crew watched the cup of coffee become increasingly transparent until it disappeared. Everyone at the DiCom on Earth watched as a vapor image of a cup appeared and become increasingly denser until it turned solid. Vern consumed the hot steaming cup of coffee. This test convinced everyone that Gelzek might safely transport.

Gelzek stood in front of the DiCom, as Vern started the transport. Gelzek's image slowly dimmed and disappeared as he vaporized like the cup of coffee. An hour went by with nothing showing up on the receiving DiCom in Stuart, Florida.

Vern said, "Ah, maybe we did something wrong here. We've got nothing! Let's go over all of the steps again, without disturbing anything in case it's really working. But, I'm becoming skeptical."

Vern, Ray, and all the engineers went over the whole change, step by step, that they had made to both DiComs. Nothing seemed to be missed. Now, two hours had gone by and Gelzek, if viable, still floated around in the fifth dimension somewhere!

Then, at the Stuart DiCom, a computer part began to form. One step at a time all Gelzek's hardware parts formed, first as a hologram and then very solid, in a disconnected array where they would be if he were standing in the DiCom with many pieces missing.

It looked like an airport x-ray of a traveler with a computer in his head, artificial joints, and a few other metal pieces. Then bones started to form over the metal parts. Next, came the human flesh, circulatory system, muscle, flesh, organs, and skin. Finally, Gelzek walked out of the machine smiling!

Gelzek dumped his memory of the transport to a printer near the DiCom. The printer slowly began to print the words of Gelzek's memory:

The DiCom produced an array of soft and flexible arms. The arms reached out around my back and slowly pulled me into the opening of a dark tunnel. It seemed as if someone unseen was pulling me into a big hug. Then my eyes separated from my head so that I could move them independently of the rest of my body and view my body as it separated into groups of molecules. Finally, the eyes stopped functioning when, I suppose, their individual molecules separated for transport. I felt and saw nothing else until my eyes reassembled and looked around while the rest of my body reassembled. Per the time stamps in the log, this took almost two hours! Then I watched as the room became visible in front of the Earth DiCom in Stuart, Florida. Everyone with mouths and eyes wide opened looked at me. Now I am here looking at the Earth's DiCom to look back at all of you. I ran my self-diagnostics, and all my systems are as good as before the transportation. None of my human tissue has been permanently disturbed.

So, in the same way, all the principle team members transported successfully. They immediately met to discuss what they could do. They figured they couldn't devise an effective strategy until they knew how the grabbing of individuals worked and what had happened to those who disappeared.

Since the disappearing process, limited to 10% of a given area, had moved to the Stuart, Florida area, they sent Zara Cyborg and Gelzek to visit bar after bar until one of them should encounter the grabbing instrument and then disappear. Everything they encountered was being recorded and saved to build a video that constantly streamed using mental telepathy to both Zara and Ray.

The two cyborgs separated and methodically visited every public place in Stuart. When, at a public place, they ordered small treats and walked every inch of the establishments they visited.

Finally, Gelzek broadcast to Ray and Zara the following record of his experience.

While washing my hands, I glanced into the mirror to check my hair and admire my good looks. Also, I wanted to make sure lunch had not partially trapped itself between my teeth. Suddenly, I found myself looking at a woman, in another room, instead of my image. Since Zara Cyborg and I went to our respective restrooms at the same time, she proved to be the woman I viewed in the mirror-turned-window. The mirror, apparently, doubles as an open window. Without choosing to do so, I flew straight through this opened window. However, instead of ending up in the ladies' room, I came to rest in a different small room with a computer that displayed a camp full of people working at tables. I had little time to determine what they worked on. I did see that guards whipped them occasionally.

I saw the computer growing dimmer and dimmer until I began to see the camp materialize in front of me. I'm at the camp now, and I hope that Ray has received my mental telepathy transmission. Zara Cyborg is with me. Please, rescue us.

Roger Battier said, "I'm going to contact our communication services to send out an emergency bulletin to reach as many people as possible. 'Immediately, cover all mirrors without looking at your reflection.'"

Ray said, "Wait. That is a great idea, but let's get as many people as possible to that work camp with a strategy of rebelling and taking over the camp. Then maybe we can take over the whole place that the camp is located on."

Vern said, "Guess what. We have traced the location in the universe of the work camp. It's located on the planet Zoleron, and our two ships will be close to that location tomorrow. I think we now have the skeleton of a plan that will turn this thing around!"

So, Ray, Katy, Benumb, Collegiately, and Baklawa visited the restrooms at local taverns until all of them transported to the work camp. Zara stayed at the DiCom location in Stuart. Roger arranged for one-hundred Navy Seals to make the same trip from the mirrors to the work camp. All the Seals, most of them unarmed, dressed so that they did not attract suspicion. Some had objects that didn't have, for their primary purpose, defense or offense. For example, one Navy Seal wore a work belt with a hammer, screwdriver, pliers, and other tools.

Once the information went out about mirrors, everyone started to avoid them. The warning stated that all mirrors might be hazardous and that, now, no one knew the extent of the risk when looking at your reflection in a mirror. Some thought that only mirrors in public places could be used by the aliens.

Women put makeup on each other instead of risking the use of mirrors. Men shaved without a mirror. Some people covered the backup and rear-view mirrors on their cars. The number of people in each location that disappeared decreased from 10% to 1%. That decrease or newscasts on Earth, let the Death Star crew know that their acquisition of people would be a great deal tougher.

Chapter 34 – Death Star

Albrecht Stiefvater received the report about the decrease in the acquisition of people on Earth. He frowned deeply, pacing back and forth repeatedly at his office in the middle of the Death Star. His face grew redder as time went on. He screamed out, "Okay, I wanted to avoid this, but now they've gone too far. Send the storm troopers down with the portable transporters. Have them grab people and transport them keeping the acquisition rate around 10%! After reaching 10% move to a new area. Vaporize anyone who resists. Transmit over all social media the message that they have three choices: transport, die, or bring someone to take another one's place. That last one should be fun. I never cease to amaze myself!"

The next morning, people heading into their morning commute in Ft. Pierce, Florida found themselves in bumper-to-bumper traffic behind road blocks. Audrey and Frank Adkins sat in their 2006 Chevy averaging five miles per hour on Route 1 while commuting to their real estate business. Eventually, they stopped completely behind traffic that no longer moved at all. Frank climbed onto the hood of his car to see if he could figure out what stopped everyone. Not far in front of their location, he could see a large camper van traveling in the wrong direction parked in front of the cars at the head of the line.

Police stopped cars and led the occupants into that camper van. After a short time, one of the camper van occupants would leave, drive the detainee's car away and eventually return on foot to reenter the camper van. The other detainees never left the camper van.

Audrey and Frank Adkins quietly walked away from their car and that camper van. After about one mile, they called 911 to report what they had seen. 911 put them in direct contact with Roger Battier.

In Stuart, Florida, Roger said, "Zara, the news is not good. Apparently, people are now being accosted in the streets and forcibly transported using DiCom technology. What do you hear from our people that have been transported to the Death Star's planet?"

Zara replied, "They are in a camp in the city Bunia on the planet Zoleron. Military forces occupy most of the land and buildings in Bunia. Ray tells me that he has watched the people from Earth being led from the work camp to a food processing plant in the center of the work camp.

"Trucks loaded with crates leave the food processing plants and deliver to grocery stores in Bunia and the rest of the towns and cities all over Zoleron. This whole planet is loaded with cannibals, and our people on Earth are the cattle! We must stop this immediately!

"However, the Zoleron military is everywhere. Their defenses look impenetrable."

Roger said, "There is a weakness somewhere. We must find it. You know, something that has made no sense to me is the way that Death Star formed from thousands of small ships. Why? How could it even work? Did they do that for the shock and awe effect? We must get someone inside to look at the construction."

Zara said, "What about Vern and Barnacle, the Senior Galactic Knights. What does that mean anyway? What can they do?"

Roger said, "They are just outside. I'll get them."

Roger left and came back with the two knights.

Roger said, "Zara and I wondered what Senior Galactic Knights can do."

Vern said, "We are modern-day Wizards who defend the rights of honest and morally-sound members of the universe. In many cases, we must make the determination of who is most honest and moral. Those are our favorite people, and we help them a great deal. We have advanced concealed weapons for which we cannot share the details. We have advanced knowledge in all technical areas and are required to maintain technical superiority in all areas. Physically, we have the reflexes, stamina, and strength of three top athletes. Much of our physical power comes from the fact that we have vodocons enabling us to benefit from a small dosage of vodka. Why do you ask?"

Zara said, "We need someone to get onboard the Death Star and figure out how to take it down. Can you do that?"

Vern said, "Barnacle, what do you think?"

Barnacle replied, "As you know, Vern, we have been researching the events that have taken a peaceful planet, now known as Zoleron, to a technologically advanced aggressor. We have found that in the final days of World War II, a Nazi weapons expert, with a reputation as Dr. Death, escaped with the help of the Zoleron people who brought him to their planet. Once there, he caused unrest in the way Hitler had done many years earlier in Germany. Eventually, he rose to power creating an army and a weapon's technology beyond most planets."

Vern said, "So, we need to get on board the Death Star, undercover, as Zoleron military people. That can be done best by finding a two-person Zoleron crew and replacing them. Where did they operate today with their forcible transporter trips to Zoleron?"

Roger said, "They will probably be in North Sebastian tomorrow morning since they operated in South Sebastian yesterday."

Vern said, "OK, I'll bet they'll be in the middle of the St. Sebastian River Bridge. That way they can trap people in either direction when they have nowhere to go and still fit a lot of empty cars on the bridge."

So, the next morning Vern and Barnacle showed up before dawn with grocery carts full of gear acting as if they had just come from a homeless shelter. The Zolerons set down their landing craft between the North and Southbound lane of the St. Sebastian River Bridge with their version of a DiCom onboard. The two Galactic Knights acted surprised and walked over to the Zolerons to ask them about their purpose for being there or if they needed help, especially that early. The Zolerons, not being at all suspicious, which they should have been, did not respect the capabilities of a couple of vagrants.

Vern and Barnacle had kept up their vodka regimen, so they were more than ready for action.

Barnacle said, "You two must be celebrities flying in like that. May we take your picture?" The Zolerons said, "yes," without hesitation. Now, Vern and Barnacle had facial pictures of the two Zolerons. Then Barnacle pushed a lever that released the second button on his camera.

Barnacle pushed that second camera button down causing a much different effect than photography.

The two Zolerons puffed up into a cloud of acrid smoke leaving all their clothing behind and nothing else. This camera concealed a weapon that evaporated flesh instantly! The two Galactic Knights grabbed the clothing, entered the small landing craft, closed the door, and began to change into the Zoleron clothing.

"Good grief," said Vern, "This stuff stinks!"

Barnacle said, "Yes, but what do you expect when we vaporized everything touching this cloth?"

Using the picture as a guide, they made up their faces to match the two Zolerons they had just eliminated. Now, they looked like Zolerons and smelled a bit like them as well. They openly showed disgust for each other. They hid their clothing and with a great deal of subtlety altered the Zoleron DiCom, putting it out of service. Then they had a good reason for leaving early.

They flew the landing craft easily because most landing crafts were similar. Vern flew close to Ray's Parent's house early so that Roger and Zara would know that their plan had, so far, gone well. Then they proceeded in a large arched path approaching the death star.

Over the intercom came,
"Γητι βλυτζι φαργον γοτσαη."

Vern said, "What language is that close to?"

Barnacle replied, "It sounds like planet Zircon language. If so, they might be asking, 'What you do?' Or something like that. Wait, I'll set my watch for a translation. Oh, 'Are you idiots lost?' Plug your earphone mike into your watch and let it translate for you. I'll wire the watch into the intercom input and output."

Barnacle finished the wiring so that now they could talk and hear the Death Star in English while everything would be translated to or from the Zircon language they thought might be close to the Zoleron language. By now, with no response, the Death Star folks screamed at them, "Tell us something, or we'll have to blow you out of the universe!"

Vern replied, "They ambushed us. We are all right, but our transporter is not functional. We must return immediately. What port do we land in?"

Intercom said, "Just pick the first opened one."

The Death Star loomed in their direct flight path now. Vern guided the small vehicle around the surface looking for a place to dock. Then he realized that the entire Death Star surface consisted of landing crafts wedged next to each other like the pieces of a three-dimensional jigsaw puzzle in which all the pieces are identical. Vern saw an empty one up ahead. While he tried to figure out how to hover, a voice over the intercom said, "Let Go." Vern let go, and a force took over the landing craft bringing them in and automatically docking them. The landing craft door slid open revealing a vast structure made up of landing crafts. Slowly, a panel slid out from under the door completing their part of the overlapping hallway floor.

Vern and Barnacle walked out, turned right, and proceeded down the hallway, which extended on either side of them consisting of landing craft extension platforms. Neither of them had seen this unique construction before in all their combined days. They snuck out and began investigating the ship, not knowing what they were looking for but confident they would recognize it when they found it.

Vern and Barnacle realized that they must find their way to the core of the Death Star to talk to the leaders, assassinate them, somehow detain them, or simply keep them busy. They had to figure out how to destroy this ship and end this threat to Earth. They just didn't know how yet.

The death star walkways presented an extremely complex arrangement. A series of concentric spheres pieced together with thousands of small space ships kept at a constant rotational spin caused centrifugal force and generated artificial gravity. As they got closer to the center, their stolen ID cards had to be used to allow access to the more secure areas. Eventually, they came to a door they could not open with their cards. So, they faked a conversation and a phone call for the security cameras and the men and women who happened to walk by them!

Vern said, "Okay, it is time." Every structure in the universe has a broom closet, right? The ship had plenty of broom closets, and they found one to hide in. Each Galactic Knight reached into his pocket for something. As it came out of his pocket, the item proved to be transparent or invisible. Each swallowed, with difficulty, these invisible items. Soon their exposed skin became invisible all the way through their bodies. The camera/weapon had to be left behind because they would not be within the invisibility effect.

Both Galactic Knights began removing their clothing. As they did, they, also, proved to be completely invisible. Their clothing lay in a pile behind them as they proceeded through the next door behind a man whose ID card gave him access. They glanced behind them to discover a couple of puzzled security guards picking up pieces of the clothing they had stolen and worn just minutes ago.

Vern said, "How much invisibility time do you figure you have?"

Barnacle replied, "About two hours, I think. Leaving the clothing behind gave me an extra hour. I wish we could see each other, so I know your position in case we are involved in hostilities.

Vern said, "Pure torture, neither of us would be able to stop laughing, and we are not muted!"

In the meantime, Roger dispatched the Earth's hastily-crafted spaceship modeled after Sun Chaser. The gravity-driven engines, the cloaking systems, the automation, and many other facilities could not be engineered in the short time required to have something effective to fight the Death Star.

However, the ship's maneuverability, weapons systems, and resistance to missiles were first class compared to the average Earth jet, helicopter, and other war planes.

Roger felt that this ship would be better than nothing in an attack on the Death Star.

So, Vern and Barnacle attacked from the inside of the Death Star. Starlight Hope, jets, ballistic missiles, aircraft carriers, and artillery gunships got ready to attack from the outside of the Death Star. No one knew when this would be, but thought that they would recognize the right time when it happened!

Chapter 35 – Zoleron

Ray, Katy, Benumb, Zara Cyborg, Gelzek, and Baklawa had all made it to Zoleron. One-hundred Navy Seals had also made it and were scattered about the holding area the Zolerons guarded. A password, "shibboleth," had been agreed upon so that the Navy Seals could be easily identified by Ray's team of Zarnians.

As each of them had materialized from the output DiCom, they had been checked for weapons. Only a few of the Seals had tried to bring weapons. The guards relieved them of those weapons, even the tool belt. So, each of them carried only his wits, wisdom, courage, and persistence into a crowd of humans being led to a food-processing plant whose human produce would provide food for the Zolerons.

Everyone looked over the security arrangements. A large field provided a place for the doomed to be held while they waited for their entry into the food-processing plant. A six-foot fence topped with barbed wire surrounded them. They counted ten guards with weapons of unknown power, type, and penetration.

Each guard stood in a ten-foot-high tower around the perimeter of the field. A ladder from outside of the barbed-wire fence led to the top of each tower. The towers had no cover since the Zolerons probably figured the prisoners would have no weapons to use against them and before hand-to-hand combat began, the guard would shoot an aggressive prisoner!

Ray's crew all felt that these fortifications had been hastily erected when Earth did not deter the Death Star effectively and the Zolerons decided, at the last minute, they could farm planet Earth! However, they all felt that the containment facilities would be too much to overcome without some very brave efforts and a great deal of luck.

This containment facility held a few-hundred people looking for a way out before they could be processed into Earth steaks for the Zoleron people! Baklawa, the puzzle solver, considered the "cattle" containment facilities in detail. He considered the people that could help in an escape attempt. Then he conversed with groups of Navy Seals as inconspicuously as he could. They must overthrow these bloodthirsty savages and live to tell their grandchildren about it, grandchildren who would not get the chance to exist if he and the others could not overthrow their cannibalistic captors.

Ray and Zara Cyborg felt that one high priority would be to destroy the DiCom so that no one else could be brought to this dastardly location.

Baklawa directed the Navy Seals to position themselves in small groups near each of the guard towers so they could simultaneously perform a sort of circus act.

Benumb started the action near the DiCom as he faked an accidental trip and fall into a group of three guards who stood on the ground near the DiCom. He fell knocking all three to the ground and successfully disarming them during the scuffle that followed. Next Benumb, reinforced by Navy Seals, used the Zoleron guards' own weapons to destroy the DiCom and put the guards into Zoleron hell. The guards in towers never had a chance to fire on Benumb because of the tight coordination between him and the Seals.

Simultaneously, with Benumb's action, ten Navy Seal teams each at a tower began their circus act, so the guards were distracted by Benumb's activities. On the prisoner side of the fence, two Navy Seals from each team bent over and grabbed each other's hands left to left and right to right. This crisscrossed their arms into a sturdy platform for the third Navy Seal's foot. Each team's third Navy Seal planted one foot into the interlocked hands of the other two. The two thrust up using all their back, leg, and arm muscles to raise their hands as high in the air as they could as fast as they could while the third Navy Seal, who had planted his foot on that pair of interlocked hands, straightened his leg with as much force as possible. This vaulted the third Seal high in the air.

The effort provided a coordinated spectacle of ten Navy Seals soaring high enough to land on the guards' towers. Seals are trained to be strong and skillful in hand to hand combat. Eight of the ten managed to tangle themselves up with their respective guard. The other two died trying as the guard saw them in time to fire his weapon and blast the unfortunate Navy Seal into burned pieces.

Of the other eight, seven wrestled the guard's weapon from him and used it to blow the guard into plant food. One Navy Seal succumbed to the fire from one of the two guards that had not been eliminated.

So, now only three guards separated the condemned from temporary freedom. Those three were taken immediately when the next wave of Seals vaulted seconds after the first wave. Immediately after that, the crowd pushed on the fence in groups until the fence gave way in several spots.

Ray, Zara Cyborg, Gelzek, and Baklawa began the assault on the food processing plant using a couple of the demised guard's weapons. The surprise and luck afforded them an easy victory as they set free a hundred people from the crushers. Unfortunately, they did not save everyone. Some died screaming and cursing that they had almost been saved and died in a mess of their own blood and tissue. The unnaturally twisted expressions on their faces would haunt the survivors the rest of their lives.

Chapter 36 – Coordination

Zara and Roger Battier communicated effectively with the two ships now on their way to Zoleron. Both believed that the Zolerons had no idea that the distance from Zarnia to Zoleron was so short that the Zarnian ships could be there within a couple of days. Neither Roger nor Zara had successfully communicated with Vern and Barnacle whom, they hoped, had found some way to beat the Death Star from within. Neither had been able to communicate with Ray or Zara Cyborg on the planet Zoleron. Both, also, knew that to be successful at beating the Zolerons, the Zarnian and Earth forces had to be well-coordinated. Everyone had to be moving against the Zolerons at the same time or close. There had to be some coordination especially on Zoleron where the Zoleron army reportedly existed in massive numbers with sophisticated weaponry. If the captives, waiting for processing, managed to free themselves, they could be recaptured quickly as soon as the Zoleron army had been alerted.

At the same time, the Death Star had to be taken out of the equation so that once things went bad for the Zolerons on their planet, they could not signal the Death Star to begin firing at cities on Earth.

So, Zara tried to communicate with Ray via ESP. It did not work. Possibly, Zara thought, there is a distance limitation on ESP. If there hadn't been, she rationalized, everyone would have known about intelligent life on other planets from the beginning of time. Anyway she looked at it, the problem presented a mystery that she didn't have time to solve. So, she acted quickly and decisively.

Zara said, "Roger, you must DiCom me to the Sun Chaser. From there I should be able to contact Ray. If Ray's team and the Navy Seals can somehow get free of their captors at the food processing plant, then they will need to be supported by our ships to make sure they are not recaptured by the vast numbers of military staff on that planet. We need to pick them up, if possible. Besides, if we wait for the Zolerons to be chasing down their escaped food supply, we can surprise them with their backs to us, possibly too occupied to see our eight landing crafts descending upon them."

Roger said, "I guess that makes sense. Let's get you there now. My only concern is that we cannot communicate with Vern and Barnacle."

So, Zara teleported via the DiCom link to the Sun Chaser. Once there, she began to immediately ESP to Ray simultaneously listening to a DiCom conversation with Roger.

Just then a call came into Roger's cell phone from Vern. Roger put the call on the DiCom so Zara could participate in the conversation.

Vern said, "Roger, we are in the main control room on the Death Star. In front of us is a fossil of a man attempting to control everything and everyone. His confusion will be one of our main assets. Besides his advanced age, he seems irrational, wearing a WWII Nazi Germany uniform. He, personally, flies the Death Star while giving orders to the Zoleron people on the Death Star and their planet. He is looking and listening to an array of television monitors showing activities all over Zoleron, the Death Star, and Earth. When something happens, that needs a decision he makes it. He cannot see where the Zarnian ships are yet. He cannot see you or us. Those are pieces of information lacking to him. He cannot see us even though we are standing right in front of him because we have put ourselves into invisibility mode. Our invisibility mode will end in less than an hour. We probably should take him out before that. Around him are three bodyguards who will mysteriously become deathly ill as soon as I finish talking to you.

The guards and Dr. Death can hear us talking to you because, although we are invisible, we are not muted. I keep moving, and they keep looking and hearing a confusing language,

English, that they cannot understand. This adds to the confusion working in our favor.

Do you hear anything from Ray on Zoleron? We watched, on one of the crazy man's monitors, when the Navy Seals took out the guards and people started tearing down the fence and fleeing. The alarms are deafening, and the army has begun to leave their barracks and will soon recapture the escapees. Mister Crazy started jumping up and down and shouting orders in a mixture of Zoleron and German! He looks like he is foaming at the mouth. He has given the orders to fire on Earth as soon as targets become available as the Death Star begins to move around the country."

Zara said, "No contact with our folks on Zoleron yet, but I'm back on the Sun Chaser so I can ESP to Ray and coordinate his plans and ours. Let me go. Roger can talk to you from here and pass on the information to me over the DiCom. I'll talk to you via Roger."

Ray answered within minutes, "We have sprung loose from our captors, but the Zoleron army has been alerted, and they are right behind us. How soon can you get here with force? We need your help, right now."

Zara said, "OK, what is your exact location?"

Ray said, "Per my information, we are at East 1045025, West 108694 on Zoleron."

Zara entered those coordinates and those of Sun Chaser in the ship's onboard computer. She read the resulting distance calculation and said, "We will be there in one hour. You must spread out as far and wide as you can, so they can't pick you up quickly and will be totally occupied. We will have all our ships loaded with ordinance. All the landing craft will be deployed and spread out looking for survivors and taking out any Zoleron forces we can locate."

Vern said, "Ok, hurry to their aid. We'll take care of the Death Star."

"Roger," said Vern, "Turn loose our new spaceship, Starlight Hope. Wait to dispatch our other forces. We will attempt to get out before the end. Be ready to hear from one or both of us!"

"Roger," said Roger.

Vern and Barnacle had nothing with them except their training and wits. They had had to leave everything behind to become invisible. Dr. Death, confused by English coming out of nowhere, witnessed two of his three guards collapse to the floor as their heads were snapped back with a loud crack.

Then it became Dr. Death's turn. The third guard tried to protect him as Dr. Death screamed, "Get over here. Get them off me." The guard began grabbing and punching invisible attackers as he pulled a knife and begin stabbing at the unseen aggressors.

Starlight Hope could be felt attacking the Death Star. Since the Death Star was made up of many smaller ships, it would be tough to take out the whole thing quickly. The individual small ships were separating from the Death Star and fighting Starlight Hope on their own. Starlight Hope repelled most hits and shot the Zoleron Ships into fireballs. All in all, it seemed to be a tie at this point.

Vern, after being stabbed once in the arm and once in the back, yanked Dr. Death around to block the next knife thrust. Dr. Death caught the blade between his rib cage in his solar plexus, piercing his heart. His struggle ended in a pile on the floor with blood soaking the insignia of a voluptuous, black-and-pink-striped bikini-clad woman sitting on a swastika. The last guard went easily when he cried over Dr. Death, a corpse, that should have been found three-quarters of a century before with the burnt remains of Nazi Germany.

Now they had control over the Death Star but suffered badly from their wounds. Barnacle managed to secure the door to the control room using an inside latch. Vern began looking at the Death Star's controls. By now, he had realized that he could understand the Zoleron language because of its similarity to the Zircon language he had studied on the way to becoming a Galactic Knight. He noted that one lever set the Death Star in hover mode. He, also, saw the typical levers and steering wheel used to fly a ship. One unique lever's description seemed to translate into "Immediate Forced Separation."

Vern called Roger, "Roger, get every combat aircraft in the air immediately. When the Death Star comes apart engage each craft that comes from it except the one in the middle. I'll be flying that and heading for a landing at the Key West airport. It might be a crash landing. Barnacle and I are badly hurt. Please, be prepared to patch us up."

Within minutes, F-14 Tomcats and other fighter jets filled the sky and began circling the Death Star, working in concert with Starlight Hope. The setting sun highlighted the action with yellow and orange clouds over a beautiful blue sky. Vern pulled the forced separation lever saying to Barnacle, "I hope this does what I think it will do!"

People all around Florida watched as the battle continued. Suddenly the remaining outer layer of Zoleron fighter craft began to peel off separating from the Death Star. As they did, it became obvious that most of these small crafts had either no pilots or pilots not prepared to fly them. Most Zolerons on the Death Star had not been prepared for the forced separation. Gravity, however, is always prepared and these fighters began to splash into the ocean, some exploding on contact. Some crashed in the swamp, fields of sugar plants, orange groves, highways, or Lake Okeechobee. Some, whose pilots did start flying them, started to exit the area climbing to higher and higher altitudes. Behind each one, an Earth-originating Fighter Jet followed until a well-aimed rocket sent another Zoleron fighter to the Earth and sea below.

The second layer of Zoleron fighters peeled off from the Death Star. This layer having witnessed the first layer's disaster was better prepared, but eventually suffered the same fate exploding in the air and falling to the Earth below.

Sunrise Hope began to knock them out with amazing quickness. This is the way it continued, one layer at a time. Eventually, the uncovered center core of the Death Star headed toward Key West Airport, negotiated a hard landing, and the Galactic Knights, known around Key West as vagrants, emerged naked except for the blood-soaked tablecloth coverings they hastily grabbed on the way out.

The vagrants recovered and now roam around Key West as honored citizens, waiting for their next mission, or their next vodka martini!

Chapter 37 – Zarnia vs. Zoleron

Roger let Zara know immediately that the Death Star had become a Dead Star. Both Zarnian ships began to celebrate while moving at top speed to rescue the spreading circle of escapees on Zoleron. Ray had instructed everyone to pass the word that everyone should distance themselves as far apart from each other as possible, thus giving the Zolerons a steadily widening and thinning target.

The first wave of Zarnian weaponized landing craft arrived at the perimeter of the action on Zoleron. The pilots witnessed Zoleron jet craft firing at groups and individuals trying to escape. The small targets insured that many misses would be mixed with the hits. Some people kept running only to be fired upon again. Some people's bodies exploded in a combination of cremation and dispersion onto a foreign planet.

The eight Zarnian landing craft all arrived in less than the projected hour. Zoleron pilots, focused on the fleeing masses below, did not see rockets approaching them. They just felt a wave of heat followed by a personal void.

Katy and Benumb ran together. A Zoleron jet flew right at them and fired an automatic weapon at them. Benumb pushed Katy to the ground and covered her. He received a dozen rounds before a Zarnian landing craft shot down the Zoleron jet that had fired upon them. Benumb died instantly, and Katy struggled to get out from under his body. After she had squirmed out and eventually survived, Katy decided to stay on Zoleron until Benumb's body organized all its pieces as it had done before and joined Katy again. Eventually, they made it back to their beloved home in Zarnia.

Ray and Zara Cyborg stayed together because of their previous closeness. No one wants to die alone. They saw the Zoleron jet approaching them at a very high speed but saw no place to dive for cover. Zara Cyborg said, "He is coming right at us. May I give you a kiss goodbye?"

Ray ignored the jet and grabbed Zara Cyborg kissing her with the passion of reunited lovers after a long absence. She tightened her embrace around him as much as she could and kissed him back. With eyes closed and embracing each other, they waited for the end. A tremendous explosion erupted nearby. When they realized, the end had not included them, they broke apart and turned toward the sound of the explosion, just in time to see a Zarnian landing craft swish by overhead and head to its next target. He rolled the craft 360 degrees to say, "You're welcome." They waved frantically to say, "Thank you."

Between the eight Zarnian landing crafts, the two ships, the Navy Seals, and a general uprising in Zoleron, the nation of death on Zoleron surrendered to the people of Zarnia and Earth.

Post Script

On Earth, the celebrations broke records set after WWII. Food, liquor, music, and conceptions ruled the days of this general celebration. Key West rocked. Everyone expected their loved ones who had disappeared to be rescued. Some would continue to celebrate. Others would eventually begin to mourn.

Victoriana Butanoate would never be seen again. Everyone else on Ray's team on Zoleron had been spared. The people from Earth and Ray's team transported via landing craft to the Zarnian ships. Using the DiComs all transported to the location of their choice.

The planet of Zoleron became a colony of Zarnia until a democracy formed with the help of Earth and Zarnia. Now, the people of Zoleron and Zarnia are good neighbors, and both are vacation destinations for the billionaires on Earth.

Ray and Zara Cyborg rationally decided that, although they had been very close, Ray could never see her the way he did when he didn't know she was a cyborg. The drama when they both thought their end had come happened only because they both had to say goodbye to someone. When Ray and Zara got back together, they knew they were right for each other. Zara Cyborg and Gelzek became romantically involved.

Ray, Zara Cyborg, Zara, and Gelzek transported to Ray's parent's house in Stuart, Florida. From there, they all drove together in two vintage-restored 1972 Volkswagen Campers all around Florida until they reached Key West, Florida. Ray and Zara used one, and Gelzek and Zara Cyborg used the other one. They camped the whole way during winter in Florida and were welcomed at all establishments for free. The four would celebrate in Key West until the Sun Chaser and crew joined them in Key West. When asked about the reason for touring in an ancient Volkswagen camper they replied, "The Volkswagen camper proved to be one of the best things that came out of Dr. Death's WWII Germany!"

Ray and Zara married in a civil ceremony at Malory Square during a fabulous Sunset.

Ray and Zara had a magnificent honeymoon evening in which they did not sleep at all. They were much too busy making love all night, as newlyweds, in their new home on Key West. The Sun Chaser, which would soon be parked at the Key West airport did not enter their conscious minds for one second. It would become a focal point again someday, but not their wedding evening.

They took a break from their intimacy and left the house hand-in-hand to walk to the end of the White-Street Pier. There, as if it had been manufactured for them, they witnessed together, a sunrise in which orange clouds appeared in the shape of a lion standing on his hind legs trying to touch the top of the universe. Cutting into the orange clouds was the profile of a four-mast sailing ship with sails full of wind. On the periphery of this scene were some bright visible stars and a crescent moon. Briefly, they forgot all about their past trials while they mentally took a picture of this wonderful sight they now witnessed.

Zara said, "Ray, I love you!"

Ray said, "Zara, I love you!"

When the Sun Chaser arrived in Key West, Ray and Zara took possession. The ship, after all, had become theirs for life. They ran a charter business that took people from planet to planet all over various solar systems in the universe.

Gelzek and Zara Cyborg would wait to marry on the planet Zarnia where cyborg weddings had been declared legal. Legislation in the United States to legalize cyborg weddings proceeded much too slowly.

Vodocon replacements for the human appendix became a very popular operation paid for by all medical insurances, including Medicare.

Picture plaques for each person who died in this chronical are mounted in the Hall of Fame room on board Sun Chaser and Moon Follower.

Μαψ ψουρ ϖοδοχον κεεπ ψ ου στρονγ, σαφε, ανδ ηαππψ!

Δρινκ ρεσπονσιβλψ

The End

Appendix A - Sun Chaser Technical

The inter-galactic Sun Chaser measures about a 150-yard diameter on the short side and 250 on the long side. Inside a community of travelers with incredible technological and political credentials from their planet Zarnia. Their list of credentials looked like they had all come from Universities that covered the disciplines of the combined schools of Princeton University, Harvard University, Massachusetts Institute of Technology, University of Cambridge, University of Oxford, Columbia University, California Institute of Technology, Yale University, and Stanford University. All the highly-educated passengers had twin major disciplines for their planet and Earth.

The Sun Chaser, a gigantic water tight oval shaped intergalactic space ship, about three football fields in size, travels through space at the speed of light. The ship, a remarkable mechanical organism, the epitome of engineering warfare, had been constructed from the strongest and lightest material known, by the builders. The material, adamant, had been tested against all known weapon systems. Only a direct high-speed megaton explosion could puncture the thickness of adamant used in Sun Chaser.

The Sun Chaser's engines used gravity-focusing technology. Gravity-focusing worked by using gravity shields to block the effects of gravity in the direction the pilot wanted the ship to move away from and gravity amplifiers to amplify the effects of gravity in the direction the pilot wanted the ship to move toward. Power to operate these power consuming shields and amplifiers came from the ships four nuclear power supplies.

The speed attained by these gravity-focusing engines is almost the speed of light, in space, where there is no atmosphere to cause speed limiting friction. Friction and speed produce heat, so Sun Chaser utilizes temperature sampling devices that send temperature data to a computer that limits the engine's speed based on the highest temperature measured on the surface of the ship. In a vacuum, the speed of light becomes possible. In the Earth's atmosphere, at an altitude of one-thousand feet friction and heat would vastly limit the maximum speed possible.

Sun Chaser employed several different cloaking methods. The transparency cloaking method presented an invisible ship to the observer regardless of his or her point of view. Transparency cloaking worked for most combat situations. What you couldn't see you couldn't shoot unless some other clue gave away the ship's location. For example, if meteors blow up from collisions against an invisible ship, fighter pilots have a pretty good clue that something is there and using invisible cloaking. No defense can be totally reliable.

The multiplier cloaking method lets the image viewed by an observer appear as multiples. One ship could appear, for example, as a fleet of four hundred! The multiplier is a bluff on steroids.

Enterprising pilots could employ artists to create their unique shields. One creative cloaking method showed the ship exploding and then going gradually to transparency! The ship looked like it exploded into small fragments and ceased being a threat until a missile came out of nowhere! The Zarnian people were very strategic and tactically intelligent. They believed that one good cloaking was worth two great combat maneuvers.

Appendix B – Subconscious Theory

1. Our subconscious mind monitors our conscious mind constantly.
2. The subconscious mind retains this data and puts it out on the subconscious network for other subconscious minds to receive.
3. The subconscious passes nothing to the conscious unless an individual is concentrating with a great deal of effort on a problem or task.
4. If information about your high priority task come over the subconscious network, then that information is passed to your conscious to help you with a resolution.
5. If your high priority task cannot be satisfied by the information held in your subconscious mind, a request is sent over the sub-conscious network.
6. The subconscious network does not take sides. If your high priority task can be resolved by a subconscious mind you conflict with, the information will still be made available to you.
7. Information on the subconscious network is kept in a universal language

that the subconscious mind understands and translates before handing over to the conscious mind.

8. Most important is that information on the sub-conscious network cannot be traced back to an individual. The network does not identify a source sub-conscious mind or a destination sub-conscious mind.

Appendix C – Mental Telepathy

1. Mental telepathy is the ability to receive another person's thoughts without the normal reading or hearing.
2. Some individuals are mentally telepathic to certain other individuals and not others.
3. Physical barriers do not seem to interfere with mental telepathy.
4. Some effort is required before a mental telepathic conversation can occur.
5. Mental telepathy is in a universal language that the subconscious mind understands and translates before handing over to the conscious mind.
6. One very important aspect of mental telepathy is that it is directed from one or more persons' conscience minds to one or more persons' conscience minds.
7. This data can make it onto the subconscious network, but there is no easy way without studying the content to determine the individuals involved in the telepathic conversation.

Appendix D – Death Star Architecture

The Death Star had a unique architecture.
- The Death Star never lands or takes off as a complete Death Star Sphere.
- Each part of the Death Star is a standalone space ship that can travel unlimited miles on its own.
- Each of these relatively small standalone space ships is nuclear powered giving it almost unlimited range.
- Each individual piece of the Death Star is piloted by a Death Star crew member and is flown into place like constructing a three-dimensional jigsaw puzzle where each piece is a 50 yard by 50-yard ship.
- First, the smallest sphere is formed using 12 pentagons and 20 hexagon shaped ships forming a truncated icosahedron. That is the center of the Death Star.
- Next, another layer of ships is fit together using more of the two different ships hexagons and pentagons.

- The layers are added until ten layers are reached.
- Between the layers, each individual ship provides its share of structural components to keep everything together.
- Each of the pentagon or hexagon ships provide hallway components and specific functional components.
- An even number of layers forms a completely functional Death Star.

Appendix E – Zara and Key West

Captain Damara, the space traveler and the rest of his crew, had been soaring through space in Sun Chaser an Intergalactic spaceship headed toward what they called Starlight and what we call Earth. Now docked offshore from Key West, Florida, they waited for the advanced team to give the okay to begin via Key West their trek to the countries assigned to them.

The captain introduced Zara, "Attention everyone, Zara your political analyst and leader of the team has graciously put together information on the city of Key West, Florida, USA. Please, listen carefully. Zara has college majors in Foreign Languages, History, Political Science, and Physical Education. She addressed you yesterday explaining your mission on this planet. Now she would like to give you information on Key West and its various attractions so you can enjoy your time there."

Zara said over the ship's intercom system, "Hello everyone. We are a few days from landing in the area of Starlight. We have a very important mission to accomplish that may take us years. That's the serious business of our stay on Starlight. However, when you have downtime, you should know a bit about the city closest to our landing point. We have sent a probe out to Key

West that has landed and installed itself on a high tower in the Wrecker Museum. Using that facility which taps into all their Wi-Fi routers, I have been able to put the following informational research together. All of you have your far-reaching assignments but will be spending a significant amount of time in Key West.

"This data should supplement all of the studies you've made about Earth. If, however, you have questions, please use my blog.

"Key West is a jewel of historical and entertainment value, the last and the furthest west island; you can drive to in the chain of islands, known as the Florida Keys. The Keys located on south side of Florida in the United States of America on the planet, Starlight or Earth as the locals call it. The south and north running U.S. Route 1 starts at the Southern mile marker 0 in Key West and proceeds east from island to island until it reaches Miami. Then it proceeds north staying on the east coast of Florida and then up the whole east coast of the United States, finally ending in Fort Kent Maine at the Northern mile marker 0. The total length of Route 1 is 2,369.

"In the Florida Keys, what is now U.S Route 1, in part was built near the railroad tracks in the Florida Keys until the devastating hurricane on Labor Day 1935 that destroyed parts of the Florida Keys. Rather than rebuild the railroad, the

U.S. Route 1 took over as the main thoroughfare in the Florida Keys. Since then a constant flow of traffic moves east and west along the Florida Keys using U.S. Route 1. The road is one of the most scenic places in the world.

"Key West abounds in entertainment in the form of restaurants and bars featuring gourmet food and live music.

"The author Ernest Hemingway and his wife fell in love with Key West while waiting for the late arrival of their new Ford car. They stayed, as Trev-Mor Ford Agency's guests at the Trev-Mor Hotel built in 1919 located at 314 Simonton Street. Eventually, Hemingway built a house on White Head Street which is still one of Key Wests most visited tourist attractions.

"Hemingway lived in Key West from 1928 until 1940 when he moved to Cuba. Hemingway produced a great deal of his best work in Key West, including short stories 'The Snows of Kilimanjaro' and 'The Short Happy Life of Francis Macomber,' his novel 'To Have and Have Not,' and 'Green Hills of Africa.'

"In Key West, you can visit the home he lived in from 1931 to 1939 when he began his move to Cuba. While there you'll see the descendants of Hemingway's six-toed cats, photos of his life, the room where he did much of his writing and a historical note of his life.

"Hemingway who also wrote the "Old Man and The Sea," was himself an avid fisherman who spent a great deal of his resourced deep-sea fishing around Key West, which is still one of the best places for deep sea fishing.

"The Key West Shipwreck Museum contains items from the period when over one ship a week wrecked on Florida reefs. Reefs were watched from towers or patrolled by boats. After the discovery of a wreck, wreckers would spring into action. They saved who they could and salvaged whatever goods they could. Profits, at auctions in Key West, went to the wreckers based on the salvage value and the difficulty of the salvage operation. Sometimes they made over 50% of the items salvaged. The occupation gradually ended when the completed railroad and navigational aids improved.

"The Truman White House is another incredible place to visit in Key West. Truman had to take over the presidency during the last months of World War II when Franklin D. Roosevelt died in office. Truman became a two-term president and one of the best presidents in American history. Truman had to make many difficult decisions including the dropping of atomic bombs on Nagasaki and Hiroshima Japan, to save allied forces' lives.

"Not far from the Truman White House is Fort Zachary State Park, another Key West Landmark-worthy of visiting. Fort Zachary boasts that it has Key West's best beach and has been the pick of many young couples to get married. Tours of the fort are available providing a look into the fort's rich history.

"One of the best places to watch the sunset is from Malory Square on the west side of Key West. An even better way to view the sunset is taking a sail boat ride while the sun is setting. The silhouettes of other sailing vessels against the setting sun provide dramatic photo opportunities.

"From the White Street Fishing Pier on the south side of Key West, you can, also, view incredible sunrises as the sun seems to rise out of the ocean water amidst orange colored clouds. Both dawn and dusk are beautiful times in Key West.

"A catamaran can be boarded in Key West to take you to the Grand Tortugas seventy miles west where you can tour Fort Jefferson, snorkel, and even camp out overnight. The boat ride itself is worth the time and cost.

"Cruise ships often dock at Malory Square.

"Cuba is 90 miles north and used to be a very popular destination before Castro lead a successful rebellion against the Cuban government.

"Key West has an Aquarium, beaches, shopping and museums. Many special events take place in Key West including motorcycle events, deep-sea fishing tournaments, fly fishing tournaments, the costume extravaganza called Key West Fantasy Fest, a body painting festival in which colorful layers of paint become clothing. A variety of T-Shirts are found in Key West. Many shops feature artistic items from creative signs to sculptures.

"You can rent sailboats, paddle boards, and kayaks to exercise your saltwater adventure needs!

"On Key West chicken hens and roosters roam free. These chickens are the ancestors of the chickens that used to fight while men bet on their favorite rooster to win. Coq fights are illegal now, and as a result, the chickens have been released to live free.

"Jimmy Buffett established himself as one of America's most popular artists while living in Key West.

"Key West itself had become an adult playground. The area around Duval Street is loaded with bars and eating establishments that provide fine food, and alcoholic beverages as well as live music almost all day long. People enjoy walking from place to place eating well-prepared meals and listening to as much live music as possible while drinking a variety of alcoholic beverages. If you are walking from place to place, much of the danger of drinking is mitigated. Key West has become a tropical paradise with its special living flavor and a non-stop happy hour or more accurately happy week."

www.ingramcontent.com/pod-product-compliance
Lightning Source LLC
Chambersburg PA
CBHW060809030726
47503CB00002B/415